"YOU'VE M
ALL YOU

Rebecca's voice was a chilling whisper.

"You're wrong. I haven't gotten what I wanted. Not always."

Rebecca caught her breath as Wes reached out to touch her hair, wrapping it around his hand. "Like the moon up there," he said in a strange voice, "some things forever seem just outside my reach."

"Don't, Wes, please..." she pleaded as she tried to pull away, but it was impossible.

"Do you want to know something? I've never forgotten the feel of your hair. Not in all these years. The scent, the texture, the way it hangs so thick and full down your back..."

The heat of a familiar flame blazed a path of warning through Rebecca's veins. "Let me go," she whispered.

Wes's eyes burned into hers as if he would read her mind. "Why did you run away, my love, without ever telling me... goodbye?"

ABOUT THE AUTHOR

Katherine Burton got the idea for her first Superromance about three years ago. Since then, she's been writing and revising with the help of her published friends. The Mississippi native knew she would be an author from the age of ten, but after she married her childhood sweetheart, she was temporarily sidetracked, for "in the South, husbands and babies still come first." Now a longtime resident of Louisiana, where she set *Sweet Summer Heat*, Katherine spends her time horseback riding and painting ceramics when she is not plotting new books.

Katherine Burton

SWEET SUMMER HEAT

Harlequin Books

TORONTO • NEW YORK • LONDON
AMSTERDAM • PARIS • SYDNEY • HAMBURG
STOCKHOLM • ATHENS • TOKYO • MILAN

Published January 1988

First printing November 1987

ISBN 0-373-70292-2

Printed in Canada

This book is dedicated with love to Jerry,
who gave me the courage;
to Amy and Jeff,
who gave me the time;
and to my friends at N.O.L.A.,
who taught me how to build
foundations under castles in the air.

PROLOGUE

IT WAS THREE O'CLOCK in the morning. Wes Garrett had been drinking since nightfall. The shot glass on the table beside him had been abandoned hours before. Now he drank straight from the bottle, filling his mouth and bracing himself against the involuntary shudder that racked him, in spite of his efforts, as the whiskey rolled like a fireball to score a blistering brand in the pit of his empty belly.

Wiping his lips with the back of his hand, he nestled the bottle in the vee of his legs and wondered for the dozenth time why he wasn't dog drunk. Heaven knew he ought to be. He glanced down at the half-drained bottle—one-hundred-proof Kentucky whiskey—guaranteed to dull his senses, drown his sorrows, and obliterate his mind of all coherent thought. But it wasn't working. Wes closed his eyes, and though his head swam more than a little, memories of Will Daniels's funeral the previous afternoon surfaced with surprising clarity. Though he had never been particularly fond of the man who had been grandfather to his now-deceased wife, he could still picture them lowering the old man to his grave, still hear the words he'd been waiting eight years to hear....

"She's coming back," J. P. "Son" Deaton had confided, squinting his eyes against the harsh rays of the Louisiana sun. "Seems like she would have tried to make it home for her own grandfather's funeral. But, seein' as how she didn't come back when your wife died, either—and her own sister, yet! Well..." Chomping down on the fat cigar, the squat banker had finished with only a shake of his head.

Wes opened his eyelids, forcing the scene from his mind. But he couldn't banish the corrosive bitterness that sizzled like an acid, rising up inside him. Dark brows digging sharply into his tanned features, he refocused his gaze on the only source of light in the room.

In a shadowy corner, a small fluorescent tube glowed above an artist's easel, and there rested the portrait of a beautiful blonde, her features bathed in the smoky, white light.

"I ought to burn the damn thing," Wes muttered under his breath. And, as if destruction could be achieved by a mere look alone, his black eyes blazed into the painted depths of the stormy gray ones, staring back at him from that face. *That face!* How many times had he painted that same face over... and over and over in the course of seven years?

Tossing back his head, Wes took another blistering swig from the bottle. He was a wildlife artist, he reminded himself, not a portraitist. But shortly after Mara died, the woman who'd been his wife for only a few short months, Wes had felt compelled to put her face on canvas, to capture her image in some concrete, tangible form. Something he could touch. Something he could see.

He had hoped that creating his impression of Mara would help him somehow to put things into perspective, to sort out the guilt and settle the confusion surrounding the strange circumstances that had prompted him to marry her in the first place.

But the painting hadn't succeeded in its therapeutic intent, nor had the image emerged as the form he'd originally envisioned. Perhaps, Wes thought, groping for a logical explanation, there was some truth to the remark a rather philosophical friend had made to him once. She had said that he painted "not with his head or his hands, but with the eyes of his soul." At the time, he'd only laughed. But now and then he'd had cause to wonder. For in his head, Wes recalled that Mara's eyes were soft and brown—excruciatingly fragile looking in her thin, pale face. But, from the shadows of his soul, he had conjured another pair of eyes—wide and cool, like frosty mirrors reflecting smoke. Eyes that haunted him... accused him. And now, ironically, through the mastery of his own hands, these were the eyes that stared back at him with a lifelike intensity transcending mere canvas and paint.

Wes drew a haggard breath and pulled his lanky frame from the squat confines of the low barrel chair, dragging his whiskey bottle with him. His limbs felt like lead, and staggering slightly, he cursed the uncharacteristic sluggishness of his feet, even as he moved to the corner where the portrait stood.

For a long time he stood there, frowning down at the image, his lips grimly set, features taut and pale with strain. A thousand memories whirled through his brain, and with them came the questions... and the guilt... and the blame. Who was to blame? Like the eyes in the portrait, the question haunted him. With his free hand, Wes reached out and touched the canvas.

At the moment of contact, an agonizing mixture of emotion took hold of his face. Pain. Frustration. Futility. Each registered in that fleeting second as his fingertips lingered on the welt of dry paint, so stiff and cold beneath the heat of his touch. But it wasn't the brittleness he felt when he touched that face, when gently, tentatively, he stroked the textured surface, his forefinger moving in one, long unbroken line from the highlighted swell of a faintly flushed cheek to the proud shaded tilt of the chin.

No, Wes conceded, his eyes growing cold as he let his hand fall to his side. The likeness here could never be mistaken for Mara's. But this woman—the one with a storm in her eyes and a flash of summer lightning in her hair—this was the one he could never stop himself from seeing every time he had ever looked at Mara.

"Damn," Wes swore softly. Raking his hand roughly through his hair, he wheeled around and stalked to the window. One broad shoulder propped against the casing, he stared out into the thick, black night.

He could have loved Mara, Wes thought in desperation. *Should* have loved her. God knows she needed someone to. And yet, for all her gentleness, for all her love and courage, Mara had never been more than a pale light in his path, not enough to illuminate the darkness in his heart. He hadn't meant to hurt her, that much at least was true. He'd only wanted to help her, to do what was right by her. Only later did he realize his motives for marrying Mara had all been twisted up in a selfish attempt to absolve himself of guilt. Hardly a noble gesture, Wes thought grimly, since his wrong had been committed against another.

In the window glass, his unshaven face reflected his fatigue, the effects of the liquor he'd consumed, and the knowledge that he would find no solace in the darkness.

Inevitably, he'd known he would see her again—that someday, one way or the other, she would be back. It should have been a helluva lot sooner as far as he was concerned, but that was all water under the bridge now. And maybe, just maybe, it was better this way. After all, he thought cynically, he'd had eight long years to figure out what sort of woman she really was. Self-centered. Uncaring. Unfeeling.

Disgusted with the thought of her now, Wes shoved himself away from the window. The abruptness of his gesture nearly cost him his balance, but relying on his natural agility, he recovered quickly, despite the dull spinning in his head.

Slumping back down in his chair, he took another staggering gulp from the bottle and grimaced at the taste. Once more his gaze strayed back to the woman in the portrait, but this time his face was hard, his jaw set, and his eyes narrowed to glittering black slits.

He would see her again, there was no doubt of that. But this time wouldn't be like the last. This time he would tell her what he'd never had the chance to say before—one single, heartfelt word, etched in blood from the bottom of his heart.

Wes closed his eyes and dredged his lungs for a decent breath. Once and for all, he promised himself. This time he'd tell her goodbye.

CHAPTER ONE

THE SPANISH-STYLE VILLA, originally built in the late 1920s for a reputed Sicilian bootlegger, stood ablaze with lights—a glittering jewel studding a hilltop in the peaks of Bel Air, California. The current owner was an award-winning director, turned outspoken political activist, and his parties were nothing less than headline events, where players of one game met and mingled with those of another.

Beneath the canopy of the open gallery, Rebecca Whitney stood apart from the waves of guests, who filtered in and out of the house as freely as the balmy night breezes ruffled the potted palms and rippled the surface of the azure-blue pool.

At five foot five, she wasn't a tall woman, although her slenderness suggested height; that and the way she held herself, shoulders erect but not stiff, the graceful curve of her throat and jaw exposed in the subtle, upward tilt of her chin.

Her gown was a blue-gray silk, and her hair, a startling natural shade of platinum blonde, was swept severely away from her face, without a single loose tendril to soften it. But then, she didn't need the effect. At twenty-six her skin was youthful and her classic features smooth. Only the look in her eyes was old.

Lifting her glass to her lips, Rebecca savored the taste and feel of the crisp champagne on her tongue. In the year since she had become a consultant to Senator Adam Dane, she had attended a few parties like this one. Not many, but a few.

Yet this one was different. This one, in fact, might well have been a little girl's dream come true, for as a child Rebecca had often imagined herself just as she was now: dressed in silks and sipping champagne in the dazzling world of society and privilege. And tonight she was attending this particular celebration—in honor of their host's acclaimed documentary on American civil rights—not as a tolerated outsider, the senator's note-taking employee, but as his recently announced fiancée.

But something felt wrong, Rebecca thought uneasily. The cool silver of her eyes darkened to a stormy gray for a flickering instant, cloudy with the turn of her thoughts. In her daydreams, she had always imagined that she would be satisfied and happy in an environment like this, proud of herself for the distance she had come and looking forward to her future. In reality she felt apprehensive and uncertain.

"More champagne, mademoiselle?" A tuxedoed waiter with a polished French accent paused to ask in passing, but Rebecca shook her head.

"No, thank you," she murmured and set her glass on the silver tray without retrieving a fresh one. She had a long trip ahead of her tomorrow and was dreading it enough already. Why complicate matters by risking a start with a sick headache from the night before?

The waiter gave her a cursory nod and moved on toward a small chain of guests, milling out through the wide stone archway. And seconds later, Rebecca caught sight of Adam.

He smiled when he saw her and stepped onto the sunken gallery. Rebecca watched him approach and thought again, just as she had the first time she'd met him, that he moved with a worldly assurance no younger man could afford.

Not that Adam Dane was old. At forty-eight, he was in the prime of health, trim and tanned, his features possessing that certain well-preserved look Southern Californians seemed to have patented. He was a man who knew not only where he was going, but precisely how to get there; the kind few woman could resist and no man could ignore.

"I've kept you waiting, darling. Forgive me." His smoothly cultured baritone voice fell caressingly on her ear as he caught her hands and drew her forward, brushing his lips against her cheek. "Even at parties, I'm afraid, business is business. But of course you understand."

"But of course," Rebecca echoed, her smile only faintly derisive. "No rest for the dreary. Or isn't that how the saying goes?"

Adam's brows, still dark despite the heavy streaks of gray threading his meticulously groomed hair, rose in bemused speculation. "Why, my dear, if I didn't know better, I would think you were in a snit. The word is 'weary' and you know it. Now, tell the truth." Ice-blue eyes looked directly into hers, amused, and yet slightly reproving. "Are you really angry with me? Or merely testing the powers of your charming wiles?"

His tone was light and teasing, but for all his apparent humor Rebecca sensed the underlying edge of seriousness in his voice. Adam Dane was a man of position, family wealth and tireless ambition. That he would not tolerate the conventional harness of married life with a wife at the rein was a position he had already made abundantly clear. Having grown set in his bachelor ways, he had no intentions of wasting his time checking in with "the little woman" at every turn. It was an attitude Rebecca had duly accepted, but not without occasional reservation.

Still she smiled, though carefully schooling the rest of her features to reflect none of her true feelings. Rebecca had learned long ago that emotions revealed on the planes of the face were easily turned against their maker. And she never intended to present herself to anyone as that vulnerable, that defenseless, ever again.

"No, I'm not angry with you," she answered, her own tone as light as his had been. "Just because you prefer the company of exiled chiefs of state and their jewel-laden wives is surely no grounds for a snit. A miff? Perhaps." She shrugged carelessly, and Adam chuckled his approval. "But certainly not now or ever a *snit*."

At that, Adam laughed aloud and lifted her hand to his lips. "Ah, Rebecca, darling, you are a genuine delight. So young and yet so admirably devoid of the ridiculous demands and expectations of youth."

"I'm not certain that's a compliment," she murmured dryly, to which he replied by taking her hand and tucking it into the curve of his arm.

"Coming from me, darling, I can assure you it isn't a compliment but a tribute. Now, come—it's getting late, and you haven't danced with me yet."

Despite their obvious age difference, Rebecca and Adam made a striking pair; he with his suave, swarthy looks, shown to advantage in his dark tux, and she, pale and willowy, standing nearly level with him in her strappy three-inch-high sandals.

As they moved through the elaborate, albeit appropriately decorated mansion, several well-wishers stopped to offer congratulations on their recent engagement. Some Rebecca knew. Others she merely recognized. And still others were friends or acquaintances of Adam's whom she had never met.

In the music room, a handful of couples swirled and swayed to the hauntingly nostalgic film score from *The Great Gatsby*, compliments of a twelve-piece orchestra.

"You look very lovely tonight. Have I told you that?" Adam asked, slipping one arm around her waist, his left hand rising to lightly support her right.

"Yes, I believe you did." She smiled and moved into his arms, following his easy, gliding steps without effort. Among other things, Adam was an excellent dancer. And, as Rebecca had already discovered, he went about it with the same urbane confidence his presence and manner suggested.

Without a doubt Rebecca realized that Adam Dane was the catch of a lifetime, everything she'd ever wanted...in a husband, in a man. And yet sometimes, when he kissed her, or held her as he did now, she found herself closing her eyes and pretending that he was taller, younger; that his hair was a reckless jet black and his eyes weren't pale ice blue, but dark and passionate. Sometimes, Rebecca found herself pretending that it really wasn't Adam who held her at all, but...

A shudder trembled through her and Rebecca stiffened, as if to physically halt the painful direction of her thoughts. Ancient memories that had no place in her life now.

Sensing her slight movement, Adam frowned and drew back to look at her. "Are you cold, dear? I thought it seemed rather warm in here myself."

"No...no, I'm fine," Rebecca insisted, avoiding his eyes for fear her own might reflect the guilty nagging of her conscience. "I'm just a little tired, I guess. And wishing I didn't have to strike out across country tomorrow."

"Ah, yes. Your little trip." The disapproval in Adam's voice was punctuated with a long-suffering sigh. "I don't have to tell you how I feel about that."

Despite his comment, Rebecca felt certain he would have reminded her of his opinion regardless, had the music not ended then, forcing them to comply with the customary round of applause.

The following number was a fox-trot. Or a rumba. Or a polka. Rebecca wasn't sure which, and had no interest in finding out. In fact, she was relieved when a short time later, just after midnight, Adam suggested they make their farewells.

It was a grueling ritual, requiring better than a half hour. And later Rebecca wondered, cynically perhaps, if even celebrities didn't grow tired of living life as though it were some eternally public perfecting-ground for the art of method acting. She wondered, too, why this odd impression of the "good life" had never presented itself to her before.

The subject of Rebecca's impending journey to Louisiana, the trip "back to her roots" as Adam had termed it, failed to surface again in conversation until they were settled in the limo and heading back to her apartment.

Seated across from her in the plush gray velour seat, Adam leaned forward, reached into his breast pocket and pulled out a flat silver case. Flipping the lid with a flick of his thumb, he removed a thin cigarillo, lit the tip with a small, gold lighter, then settled back, inhaling deeply, his eyes on her.

"You don't have to go, you know." He blew out a slow, steady stream of smoke, squinting his eyes as he watched her thoughtfully. "I could have one of the legal boys handle it."

Rebecca's eyes traveled to the window. Beyond the tinted glass, she vaguely noted the silent parade of headlight beacons and city lights flashing past them as they coursed the darkened streets of Los Angeles.

But her thoughts were far away from the city.

"No, Adam," she murmured. "I don't want you to do that." Her voice was oddly low, but steady with resolve. And yet, she didn't bother turning to him. It irritated her sometimes that Adam was so imperiously convinced there wasn't a problem or a person on earth he couldn't have "handled" one way or another. Usually it was with money. Sighing softly, Rebecca privately admitted what bothered her most was that he was so often right.

But in this case...

Continuing to stare out the window, she was only half aware of Adam's curious scrutiny. She was lost in her own thoughts, remembering the call she had received just under a week ago. That there had been no love lost between her and the grandfather who'd raised her hadn't lessened her shock at the news the old man had been stricken with a fatal stroke.

Even now, Rebecca wasn't certain she had accepted his death as reality. Maybe because she'd never considered the possibility before. From early childhood, she had harbored the secret but unshakable belief that Will Daniels was somehow immune to the infirmities of mortal man; a damnable soul who would live forever to spite both God and his fellow man, and especially his youngest granddaughter, if he could possibly find a way.

A sudden chill shook her, and Adam reached over to help Rebecca draw the wrap about her shoulders. His hand lingered for a moment, caressing, almost imperceptibly, the bare flesh of her upper arm through the silk.

"Rebecca, darling, I realize, of course, how concerned you are over this matter of settling your grandfather's estate," he began, his tone patronizing. "But surely you must see how you've let this thing agitate you, and override your common sense. A trait which I have so admired."

He let his hand glide downward to her wrist, and then, to the base of her fingers, where his thumb began a light, careful stroking of the great, emerald-cut diamond that she wore heavily on her left hand.

After a few moments he lifted his head, and Rebecca met the cool blue of his gaze with the frosty silver of her own. "This has nothing to do with common sense, Adam."

Her tone held a note of annoyance, owed mostly to her own apprehension and her desperate wish that she and Adam weren't at cross-purposes with each other. She admired and cared for him deeply, or at least as deeply as she dared. And despite the doubts and quarrels that plagued most serious relationships, the two of them had never indulged in emotional fireworks or verbal brimstones. Theirs was a relationship built on the solid earth of reality, compatibility and common goals.

A house constructed on sturdier ground, Rebecca told herself, than those haphazardly raised on the treacherously shifting sands—or fragile loam—of so-called love.

Sighing, she forced herself to smile. "Oh, Adam, let's not argue. And I know you're probably right—I am overreacting. But I want you to understand. It's not that I don't appreciate your offer to help. But this is something I just have to do on my own."

Adam's face reflected no change in his calm, impassive expression as he turned aside to extinguish his cigarillo. "Very well, then, we won't argue. I wouldn't want to send you away thinking I'm unreasonable now, would I?"

"No." Rebecca smiled, knowing that no one could ever accuse Adam Dane of being unreasonable. He was a practical man, who dealt in facts rather than emotions. And for Rebecca, that was, perhaps, his most appealing trait. He didn't offer, and therefore did not demand of her, emotional responses that she could never give. "I will miss you, though," she admitted honestly.

Adam's lips curved into a small, complacent smile. "On that, I'll insist. And you'll be away. . . ?"

"For no more than a few days, I hope. And besides," she added, relaxing slightly now that she sensed the subject resolving themselves. "You'll be as busy as ever, hardly realizing I'm not around. Your summer itinerary is all planned out, and Diane can handle the necessary press releases."

"Are you certain of that?" He lifted a brow in mock skepticism of the woman's ability, and Rebecca had to laugh.

Diane Herrington was Adam's administrative coordinator and general right-hand "man," supervising almost everyone from his smiling, hostesslike receptionists to the brilliant speech writers who put the very words in his mouth. It was Diane who had trained Rebecca, when she'd "come over" as a publicity consultant a year ago, on a P.R. referral from prior employment in special-guest relations at the Beverly-Wilshire Hotel.

And no doubt, Rebecca thought now, it would be Diane who would train someone else to take her place after she and Adam were married. Not that she particularly liked the idea of giving up her job, but as a senator's wife there would be other, more important duties demanding her time. Nearly all of them directly related to Adam's career.

For the duration of their drive, down San Diego Freeway to Rebecca's apartment near Santa Monica, the conversation turned to business. A short while later, the car rolled to a halt and the black-uniformed chauffeur slid out, hastening around to open the door for their exit.

"Would you like to come in?" Rebecca asked, once they had climbed the steps to her duplex, and she had unlocked the door.

Adam's brows rose in faint surprise but his smile remained, as always, unaffected. "Now, darling, you know I'd love nothing better than to spend the rest of the evening alone with you. But as you've reminded me, I've a busy day tomorrow, and you've a long trip ahead."

Rebecca smiled. It was another of their polite little rituals. She'd ask him in, and he'd imply the thought was tempting. Although in reality, she doubted if it ever was.

Unlike some of the younger men she had dated on occasion, Adam wasn't a groping sex monger, gauging his manly prowess by the number of notches carved in the door of his rented locker at the spa.

Instead, he was a mature adult with nothing to prove and other things on his mind. And so, whenever he left her with no more than a chaste kiss at the door, Rebecca was sometimes troubled, but most times . . . relieved.

"Take care of yourself," he said, slipping his arm around her waist and brushing his lips almost perfunctorily against hers.

She shrugged as he released her and took a step back. "Of course. And you'll do the same?"

"Unquestionably," he answered with a quirk of his brow. "Now, be a good girl and promise me you'll do whatever is necessary to resolve this..." He paused for emphasis. "This personal matter. And don't be too long about it, or I warn you. I just might fly down there and bring you back myself."

But Rebecca knew he wouldn't do that. Just as she had known he wouldn't stay the night, and that she would tell herself, as she always did, that it didn't really matter.

And yet, as she stood alone, watching the dark limousine pull away from the curb and disappear into the night, she almost wished, just this once, that Adam had stayed with her. Because tonight as never before, she needed someone to hold her. Someone to chase away the ghosts from a past that was quickly closing in on her, jeopardizing her future.

But there was no one. And as usual, Rebecca thought ruefully an hour later as she lay awake dreading the trip ahead of her, she had only herself to depend on. Only herself and the strength of her own resolve. Before she could commit to her future, she had to put the past behind her. And no matter how much it hurt, it was time.

AN ACHING KNOT churned in the pit of Rebecca's stomach as she approached the narrow cutoff in the road. It was just after sunset, the third day of her journey. And there were clouds moving in from the east off the Mississippi. But the fading light did little to obscure the sight of her destination.

How could she miss it?

Silver-gray eyes narrowed as she peered through the dust and road grime layering her windshield. In the distance, a wilted grove of mulberry and scrub oak hunkered down around the old farmhouse like a mutant bouquet, amid the seemingly endless fields of tall, green cotton.

Slender hands tightening on the steering wheel, Rebecca drew a deep breath and struggled to keep a frown of dread from marring the contour of her brow.

How long had it been? she asked herself. Seven years? Eight? Was it really only eight years since she'd run away from here—a lonely, frightened child of eighteen barely out of high school and desperate to make a new life for herself? So much had changed, and she was so different now. It didn't seem possible that the sight of this old place still had the power to turn her inside out.

It was only because of the memories, Rebecca thought, as she drove past a rickety toolshed and parked her car a few yards from the house. Memories. Dear God! Would they never stop tormenting her? How long did she have to keep paying for one mistake?

Caught in the web of her thoughts, she remained behind the wheel for a moment longer, staring out but seeing nothing. She didn't want to think. Didn't want to remember...old hurts, ancient longings. But impressions seemed to surround her, and against her bidding, the images came, rolling like a fog through the channels of her mind. Memories...

Summer and steam, heat and rain; a dark, abandoned barn with the scent of freshly mown hay filling the air... And one man, lean and dark, his warm, wet flesh pressed intimately against hers in the shadow of a lightning bolt...so long ago.

Rebecca closed her eyes and massaged her throbbing temples. No! She shook her head. She wouldn't think of him today. Not today. Not with all the other memories clattering around like sharp stones in her brain. That man no longer existed, as far as she was concerned. He was a memory, nothing more. And she no longer resembled the desperately naive, young girl he'd taken thoughtless advantage of. She was a woman now, and one who had never forgotten the lesson he had taught her. Surrender, she had learned its cost well...the hard way.

Opening her eyes, Rebecca chased away the ghosts of her past and reached for the door handle. As she slid from the Mercedes' plush leather seats, a heated gust of wind snatched a pale tendril of hair from the sedate coil bound at the nape of her neck. Brushing it impatiently aside, she headed around the car to fetch her suitcases from the trunk.

The threat of rain clung heavily to the sultry June air, weighting her steps with an uncharactertistic sluggishness. Humidity molded the ivory, pleat-front slacks to the curve of her slender hips, and a tiny rivulet of perspiration trickled between her breasts, dampening the matching silk blouse.

Strange, she thought. Eight years of her life had been spent in trying to shut out the memories of this place, and all she had really succeeded in forgetting was the relentless Louisiana heat that scorched the fields and simmered the lazy waters of the nearby Bayou Macon.

Moments later, Rebecca climbed the sagging steps to the porch of the farmhouse, then stooped to set her suitcases on the plank floor. Her hands trembled slightly as she pulled back the tattered screen and reached for the main door.

If you leave this house, I don't ever want you back here as long as I'm alive.

The words rang out unbidden in memory and echoed in her ears, assaulting her senses with an age-old bitterness that lingered like the musty scent inside the dark house—the smell of lost hopes and dreams gone sour. Rebecca stiffened, apprehension holding her immobile for a moment. *I have to do this,* she reminded herself. And then, with a breath of resolve, she squared her shoulders and stepped into the stronghold of her past.

Armed with her luggage, she made her way through the living room, her steps treading lightly over a worn braid rug. The house was so empty. . . so silent. It was still hard for her to believe that her grandfather was really gone. Somehow she half expected to find him here...waiting in judgment for her, as he had been on the day he'd hurled those brutal words.

Pain twisted deep inside her heart, but Rebecca's features remained unmoved. Never again would she allow emotional weakness to betray her. Never again would physical circumstance make her a burden to someone who didn't want her.

Outside, the thunder rolled and a vivid flare of lightning flashed through the bedroom window, illuminating her way as she set her suitcases on the floor beside the bed she'd once shared with her sister, Mara.

Reaching over, Rebecca lit the small ceramic lamp on the bedside table. The soft, yellow light was easy on the tiny room, kindly disguising the signs of age and deterioration. Pale shadows streamed across the patchwork comforter and the crocheted throw pillows that Mara had taken such care to fashion. Gingerly, almost reluctantly, Rebecca picked up one of the pillows and ran the flat of her hand over the intricate design. Her thoughts drifted back in time, and she could still hear Mara's soft voice, always so calm, so gentle, even when they were children....

"LOOK AT THIS ONE, Rebecca. Won't Mama be proud when she sees it? I'm going to save it and surprise her at Christmas."

They were sitting in the front room: Mara, Rebecca, and their grandfather. Seeing the pride beaming on her sister's small face, Rebecca smiled and was about to praise her handiwork when a rustling of newspaper and snort of bitter laughter drew their attention to the gray-haired man, frowning as always, beneath his bush of heavy brow.

"Christmas." He nearly spat the word. "Got a long wait if ya think ya gonna be seeing that ma of yours come this Christmas nor any other. When you gonna figure out that woman ain't never comin' back for you two?"

At the harshness of his words, Rebecca's gaze moved to Mara who was older by a year, but slighter, weaker and more vulnerable. Mara said nothing. Only her expression gave her away. How could Rebecca have missed the terrible, pain-stricken look that momentarily crossed her sister's delicate features, before she lowered her eyes and began to pluck absently at a loose strand of yarn in her lap.

Later, in their room that same night, Rebecca did her best to repeat every profane oath and swearword her ten-year-old mind could recall. "I hate him," she vowed through angry, scalding tears. "And he hates us, too. But I don't care! Do you hear? I'm gonna run away from here one day, and when I do I'm never, never coming back! I don't care if he sends the sheriff and a hundred deputies after me. I'll spit in their eyes and tell 'em all. He's cold and he's mean and down deep he ain't nothing but a hateful old basta—"

"Rebecca, don't talk like that!" Mara admonished in a whisper. "Papa doesn't mean to be that way. It's just that he doesn't understand. He doesn't know how to care about other people. Maybe that's why Mama left us here. Maybe she had wanted us to teach him."

A LUMP ROSE in Rebecca's throat, and she swallowed hard, shaking her head at the irony of her dead sister's words. Sweet, innocent Mara—how blind she had been. How blind they had all been to the hopes, the dreams and the needs of one another.

The wind was rising and a tree limb banged against the side of the house, flaying leaves and scraping branches across the bedroom window. Rebecca placed the pillow back on the bed and walked over to look outside.

It was dark now, and a pale glimmer of lightning sparked the distant horizon, running a chill up her spine. Lord, how she hated rain! But then, with a wry smile, she recalled that it hadn't always been that way. Funny, she thought, how time changes things. As a girl, she used to pray for summer rain, since its arrival meant that she wouldn't have to work in the fields.

Sighing, she leaned her shoulder against the window frame and closed her eyes. In her mind's eye, she could almost see the shimmering waves of heat rising off the sunbaked rows of cotton, shaded by tall blades of Johnsongrass that had to be hoed by hand because her grandfather didn't believe in any other way. Oh, how she had despised those dusty, blazing-hot days, working from sunup to sundown until she thought she would drop, until her hands were raw and her fair skin sunburned with blisters on top of blisters.

But Hurricane Bluff was a small town, and fortunately everyone believed in helping his neighbor, especially at harvest and hay-baling seasons when farmers would often band together, working each man's field in turn. It was during one such season that Rebecca met Wesley Garrett for the first time.

At twenty-five, he was seven years Rebecca's senior, the restless, devil-may-care son of a locally prosperous crop-dusting entrepreneur, and the heartthrob of every breathing female from Caddo to East

Carroll Parish. Mara thought he was "dreamy" and invariably went into a fluttering frenzy when, on occasion, he'd stop by their house for a drink of water or to wash his hands at the pump house.

Rebecca, however, found his presence oddly disturbing. She didn't like the way he looked at her sometimes, his dark eyes half mocking, half amazed, always watching her as if he knew she was struggling inwardly to show him how unaffected he left her. Determinedly, she had avoided him whenever she could, dismissing him from her thoughts...and her daydreams, the way his smooth, tanned skin glistened like polished wood in the midmorning sun, the way his hair seemed forever flying in wild disarray—in need of cutting and a combing.

Rebecca's eyes flew open as the rain began to spatter in fitful spurts upon the roof. The sound pulled her mind back to the present. Why did she have to think of him? she wondered dismally. Even now, the memories were painful, so filled with anguish and regret that sometimes she felt she would never be free of the past.

Her head ached and exhaustion was beginning to catch up with her. She turned away from the window abruptly and searched for something constructive to occupy her willful thoughts. Her gaze wandered to her suitcases, still packed and standing in a neat row between the bed and the dresser. Snatching up the smallest one, she flipped the latch and scooped up a stack of delicate undergarments, then started toward the dresser. Rebecca had expected to find the drawers empty, but when she slid the first one open something caught her eye.

The envelope was old, yellowed with age, and the faded ink made the address barely legible. But the name was clearly discernible, scrawled by Rebecca's own hand. Her heart stopped; she didn't need to open it to know what was inside. *Congratulations,* the card said. *Congratulations on your marriage, Mara. Be happy, Mara.* The card was addressed to her sister, but the name on the envelope read: Mrs. Wesley Garrett.

Rebecca slammed the drawer and stumbled back. Tears filled her eyes and pain gripped her chest so tightly that she could scarcely breathe. He had married *her*. How could he have done it? Wes had married Mara, and so soon after...

In a flash the memories engulfed her, a choking, drowning wave of pain that forced her to remember all she'd tried so hard to forget. If only she had known then, if only she had realized how swiftly a life could be changed. In a day...an hour, worlds could be destroyed and hearts torn asunder, like hers had been in that summer of her eighteenth year....

SPRING CAME LATE to Louisiana that year, and planting had been delayed due to the heavy amounts of rainfall. Rebecca was grateful for the few rare days of freedom she'd have before returning to the toils of the cotton fields and the garden.

On this particular morning, their grandfather had left just after dawn to purchase a new blade for his tractor disc in a neighboring town about forty miles away. Rebecca watched him leave, and when she was sure he had gone far enough that he wouldn't come back even if he'd forgotten something, she slipped out of bed and began to dress.

Mara was still asleep and Rebecca was careful not to wake her sister as she wiggled into a pair of snug, cutoff jeans and knotted the tails of a faded, plaid shirt inches above her flat midriff.

The air outside was warm and humid, and the sun peeked out intermittently from behind a thin gauze of cloud. Expecting the sky to clear as the day wore on, Rebecca headed for her favorite spot on the bayou. The walk was a long one, and she was more than an hour's distance from the house when the weather took a turn for the worse.

With a startling blast of thunder, huge raindrops came splattering down and sent Rebecca scrambling for cover. She was drenched to the bone by the time she reached the barn near the old Windspear place. Breathlessly, she bolted in through a narrow crack in the door, but in her haste, she failed to notice the green tractor parked at the rear, not quite out of sight.

It was warm and dark inside the hay-strewn shelter, but her teeth chattered as she sloughed the water from her bare arms and legs, then bent to wring the heavy mass of her hair.

"Well, what a pleasant surprise."

The sound of a man's voice, seductive and low, caused Rebecca to wheel around, eyes wide with shock. "I...I didn't know anyone else was..." Her words trailed off, as she peered frantically through the darkness, straining toward the direction of the voice. Then, from out of the shadows, she caught the flash of stark-white teeth, and recognition was instantaneous. James Wesley Garrett. Rebecca would have known him anywhere.

Like a lazy black leopard, he was carelessly sprawled, half sitting, half lying on the floor under the loft. His back was leaned against a loosened bale of hay, one leg propped up at the knee, the other stretched out full-length in front of him.

He was soaking wet from head to toe, dark hair spilled in random clumps over his forehead, giving him a wickedly impish look that set Rebecca's knees to trembling.

His chambray shirt was rolled up at the sleeves, unbuttoned and gaping with tails brushed casually aside, revealing his bare, bronze chest. A trickling of jet-black hair ran in a narrow line down his flat abdomen and disappeared into the wet, low-riding jeans already beginning to inch into the whiter flesh below his hipline.

Rebecca didn't know how long she must have stood there, staring ridiculously, as if she'd never set eyes on another breathing soul. Yet in that moment, when her anxious gray eyes collided with Wesley's glittering black ones, something made her ache all over. And suddenly she no longer saw him through the eyes of a child, but through those of a blossoming young woman, experiencing for the first time that confusing mixture of yearning and fear... of wanting, yet not knowing what. For the first time, Rebecca knew, she was seeing Wes Garrett as a man.

Ultimately it was the rain that brought her back to her wits. A cold drop of water, suspended from a leaky crack in the roof, plummeted from its height and struck her squarely on the tip of the nose.

"Oh!" She flinched and jumped back in a reflex action, that she later decided was terribly unbecoming. But Wes only laughed—a curiously unsettling sound—and a covey of fluttering butterflies took wing in Rebecca's stomach.

His movements were swift and silent as he rose and crossed the soft earth floor, coming to stand directly in front of her. "Didn't anybody tell you you're likely to get all wet walking in the rain?"

His eyes glittered as he studied her and his voice, a thick, hypnotic drawl, seemed to pass right through her, drawing her breath away. Rebecca shook her head, not trusting herself to speak.

"Then someone needs to teach you," he said, and she saw him reach down, gathering up the loose tail of his shirt.

His hands were large, powerful and tough skinned from hard work and exposure to extreme weather. But when he took hold of her chin, when he began to gently blot the rain from her face, his touch was as fragile as a child's first caress, and Rebecca's knees went limp.

She was mortified and yet lacked the will to pull herself away. Her eyes roamed the naked muscles of his chest, noting the sparse peppering of fine, ebony hair and the way the dim light danced on the rain-slick sheen of his skin. The sensation of his touch left her breathless and weak. And, Rebecca felt certain, had he not supported her chin in his palm, her legs would not have stood her trembling weight.

He was standing close... so close she could feel the heat of his body radiating into hers. If she leaned forward, she wondered, could she actually hear the beating of his heart above the driving sound of the rain?

The very thought of such intimacy sprang a blush to her cheeks, and her own heart raced with a painful cadence.

"'Fraid this shirt is already too wet to do much good." Drawing back slightly, Wes cocked his head to one side and grinned down at her. "But then, who's complaining?"

Rebecca swallowed hard and opened her mouth to reply, hoping to say something—anything—that might dispel this tense throbbing building inside her. But when her eyes met his, the words died in her throat.

Even in the half-light she could see the sultry glittering of his eyes as his gaze drifted over her, warm and smoky like a fog. His eyes seemed to reach out and touch her, lingering first on her parted, rain-moistened lips, before trailing downward to the supple swell of her breasts.

Were her clothes clinging indecently? Could he see through the thin, wet fabric of her blouse? What was he thinking, Rebecca wondered anxiously, when he looked at her that way?

A dull, smoldering flame crept up from her knees and spread throughout her limbs, burning with a new, intriguing sensation she had never felt before, and one that left her frightened, quivering and aching for something more.

"I've been waiting for you to grow up," Wes whispered, tightening his hold on her chin and rubbing his thumb gently, seductively back and forth across her bottom lip.

Dimly, Rebecca was aware of him drawing her closer, without haste or force, but with an easy, sensual, unnamed power that tingled through every vein and teased her nerve endings alive. She saw his hair, wet and glistening with rain that streamed in tiny rivulets down his face. The lightning flashed, quicksilver, and in that second she could see his eyes, too, indefinably black and filled with a dark, invading hunger.

All sense of reality vanished as she waited, still and unblinking, her breath becoming almost nonexistent in the thick, humid atmosphere that seemed to solidify the air around them.

When at last Wes bent his head to capture the soft flesh of her fevered mouth, his lips were wet and steaming and...oh, so unbelievably supple. There was no pressure in his kiss, no demand, and yet, so drugging, so intoxicatingly tentative was the feel of his mouth against hers that the very hesitancy of his touch became its own kind of agony.

Racked with emotions she didn't understand, Rebecca began to shake. Then suddenly she felt Wes pulling away from her, tearing his lips from hers as his hands dropped from her face and moved to her shoulders to steady her.

"My God! You're trembling." He held her at arm's length, his voice sounding ragged and confused.

In that initial second of sudden separation, Rebecca thought she must have stumbled, her knees too weak to support her, but Wes's hands held her firmly. Cold, damp hair clung to her flushed cheeks, and her sodden clothes made her shudder all the more as she stared up at him, her eyes dazed and pleading.

Understanding began to dawn on Wes's features, and his mouth crooked into a slow, sympathetic smile. "Well, I'll be damned," he swore softly. "You've never even been kissed before, have you?"

His voice was tender with wonder and disbelief, but Rebecca was unable to bear the wry amusement in his eyes. She hung her head, hiding her tears of embarrassment and the painful longing she was certain must have been apparent in her expression. How could she admit the truth, knowing he would only laugh? Or worse, think she was some kind of freak, because she was nearly eighteen and she had never even been out on a date. Her grandfather had never allowed it.

She swallowed hard and kept her eyes downcast. "No," she whispered at last, simply, miserably.

The pause that followed seemed to go on forever, and Rebecca wished for nothing less than to die that very moment. But in the next Wes groaned and pulled her to him, his lips grazing her temple. "Oh, Re," he breathed only a part of her name, and she was never sure if he'd spoken the rest, as shaken as she was by the feel of his strong arms around her.

He cupped the back of her head and buried her face into the protective hollow of his shoulder. "Don't be embarrassed," he whispered into her ear. "There's time, love. Plenty of time. And you'll have your chance to experience . . . things."

He held her gently against his chest, stroking her hair and threading his fingers through its damp length. Only then did Rebecca realize that he was shaking, too.

"You have to go now," he said, brushing his lips against her forehead. His breath was warm, and his voice muffled; oddly, it trembled as he spoke. "You understand, don't you, love? You shouldn't be here. I . . . I don't want to hurt you. Ah, Re . . . you're so beautiful, so sweet. I can't let myself hurt you."

But you are hurting me, Rebecca wanted to exclaim. She didn't want to go away from him. Not now. He had given her a special name and called her his "love," and no one in her life had ever said that word to her before.

"Please, Wes," she whispered, pressing her cheek against his chest and clinging to him almost desperately. "I want to stay. Please don't make me go."

She heard him groan as he slid his arms around her, murmuring her name over and over, his voice barely audible above the deafening drum of the rain on the tin roof. His mouth swept her face, kissing, tasting, sipping the moisture from her brows, her cheeks and the fragile curve of her jaw.

"Leave now, Rebecca," he pleaded once more. But he made no effort to pull away, and she was too weak to pay heed to his words.

In the openness of his shirt, she could feel the scorching heat of his flesh seared against her bare midriff, and without thinking, her arms encircled his lean waist, and she pressed closer, moving against him. She drove her hands beneath the tail of his shirt, scaling the taut, rippling muscles in his back. She heard him moan, and her own flesh quivered as she clung to him recklessly, relishing the feel and the scent and the taste of him while the drum of the rain and the lightning's ghostly flares made it all seem imagined, unreal.

His mouth moved to the tiny hollow behind her ear, his tongue probing with an intimacy that set her afire with an aching fever. His lips grazed slowly down the tender cord of her neck, creating tremulous shivers. Then he bent his head and eased his tongue across her collarbone and below, to the vulnerable swell of her breasts.

"Wes," Rebecca moaned, and caught her fingers in the dark web of his hair. Her head fell back and his mouth came up to take possession of hers again. But this time there was no hesitancy, no holding back. His lips claimed hers with a passion and a fury that, like the lightning, suddenly erupted with an electric, volatile force, staggering them both.

The thunder growled its low warning, but Rebecca was beyond caution. "Tell me to stop," she thought she heard him whisper. But later, she wasn't sure if the words had actually been his, or if they had come from somewhere inside her—perhaps she'd heard the suddenly alien voice of her own conscience.

With fluid, dreamlike movements Wes stooped and slipped his arm behind her knees. He swept her up effortlessly and carried her to lie beside him in that darkened hay-strewn corner under the loft. There, in the obscure light lit only by the intermittent sparks of the distant lightning, their bodies faded into mere silhouettes, shadows of substance, moving in time with a slow and languid sense of some mind-suspending dream.

"I want you," he murmured thickly, his eyes never leaving her face as his fingers worked to unbutton her blouse, and his large callused hands slipped inside the garment to draw it open, down past her waist, revealing her bare breasts. He caressed her shoulders, and then his hands came up to hold her face between his palms.

"Rebecca..." His eyes searched hers, and his voice held a strange, almost beseeching note.

"Teach me, Wes." Had she really spoken those words aloud, or had he read them in her eyes?

"God, forgive me." It was the last thing he said before his mouth crushed hers, and Rebecca was swept away on a whirlwind of sensation and all-consuming passion.

But their moment of surrender wasn't a dream. And all too soon Rebecca found herself back in the real world, left with only the sounds of their exhausted breathing and the soft, trickling of the subsiding rain.

For a long while, she continued to lie in his arms, listening to the slowing rhythm of his heartbeats and savoring those precious moments that were so swift in passing.

As the rays of sunlight began to seep through the cracks and boards, she sensed the distance settling between them, a kind of detachment—however unbidden—as destined to be as the retreat of the storm and the faraway sound of the thunder.

She didn't cry afterward. Was she supposed to? And in turn, Wes offered no contrivance of an apology. Had she expected that he would? Or, did the thought only occur to her because she had seen the instant look of regret in his eyes, and the grim sober lines etched in the taut strains of his face?

"Re...I...I don't know what to say. We shouldn't have..." Groaning, he turned away from her and raked his fingers savagely through his hair.

Rebecca's heart fell. So this was it, she thought, wretchedly, that thing her grandfather called lust, that secret covenant between a man and a woman—a thing that hurt like nothing else could. *I love you,* she wanted to say, but what good would the confession do her now? Instead she reached for her blouse and took refuge in the strange, but welcomed numbness that had crept into her limbs.

He tried to help her dress, but his hands were stiff and awkward then, not at all like before. He offered her his comb, and then, because she was still shaking, asked if she would take his shirt.

But Rebecca shook her head, refusing all but the comb. It was ironic, she thought, in a funny-sad sort of way, for them to be so clumsy and awkward with one another now, when only minutes before they had shared the ultimate human intimacy.

"I'll walk you home," he offered.

"No," she said, managing a faint smile. "It would be better if I went back alone."

Wes nodded his understanding and reached over to roughly smooth a strand of damp hair from her forehead.

"Are you all right?" he asked, long fingers fumbling ineffectively to tuck down her rumpled collar.

There was a strange, tormented note to the sound of his voice, and his eyes searched hers with a gentle sadness that broke her heart in two.

This was his goodbye, Rebecca thought, and because her throat knotted painfully, making it impossible for her to speak, she merely nodded and turned away.

They never uttered another word...didn't even kiss goodbye, but she had never forgotten the image of him standing there, a tall shadow, blotting out the light in the doorway of that old barn. For a long time she felt him watching her as she walked away in the warm, misting rain. But he didn't call after her, and she didn't look back, and after a while she promised herself that she never would.

THE DAMPNESS seeping in from the window caused Rebecca to shiver, and she turned away, wrapping her arms protectively around her shoulders. Even now, she could hardly stand the pain of recalling the terrible domino effect set in motion by her brief encounter with Wesley Garrett.

It had begun the moment she arrived back at the house that afternoon and found her grandfather waiting for her on the porch. He was standing at the top of the steps, a giant of a man, hard and ruthless, with flint-gray eyes that seldom wavered and a mouth that never smiled.

"Where you been, girl?" His tone was as uncompromising as the expression he wore. Shying away from the condemnation in his gaze, Rebecca glanced nervously at the ground.

"Nowhere special. Just walking." She shrugged slightly, trying to appear unconcerned, but her voice was unsteady, and her knees shook as she nudged at the dirt clod with her bare foot.

"Walkin', ya say? Think I don't know trash when I see it? Come draggin' up here with your clothes wrinkled—your face lit up like a drunk's. Still got hayseed matted in yer hair. Look at me when I'm talkin', girl. Been wallowin' with some field scum, ain't ya?"

His words hit her like a cold slap, and Rebecca proudly raised her head until she met his eyes with her own defiant gaze. He made their loving sound so ugly, so dirty and crude. But it wasn't like that! She wanted to scream. *It meant something! It meant something to me!* Scalding tears flooded her eyes, but she clenched her teeth and lifted her chin high.

"No, Papa. It wasn't what you think. You don't understand. I lov—"

"Don't you go sassin' me, miss." He took a threatening step toward her. "And don't go forgettin' who took you in when your own maw wouldn't have ya. No good that one. And, you...you're just like her. I knew it from the minute she dumped you here—you and your sister, so's she could go traipsing off after anything in pants!"

His mouth twisted, and he turned and spat a puddle of brown tobacco juice on the ground. His eyes narrowed, and when he looked at her again, Rebecca thought she had never seen such disgust, such open contempt on a man's face before.

"Who was it?" he demanded in a tone deadly cold. "Ain't havin' you shame this family by coming up with no bastard youngun nine months from now. If you're good enough to bed, you're good enough to wed..."

A LOUD CLAP OF THUNDER rattled the windows in the small house, and Rebecca pressed her hands over her ears, trying to block out the excruciating sound and the memories that echoed even more painfully.

She could still remember how she and her grandfather had argued late into the night, but she'd never breathed a syllable of Wesley Garrett's name, not even to Mara. The next morning, ignoring her sister's tearful pleadings and her grandfather's edict that she was never to return as long as he lived, Rebecca left Hurricane Bluff on a Greyhound bus bound for California. Afraid and desperate, she had no idea how she would live and support herself. But she was certain of one thing: not her grandfather nor anyone else would ever force her on Wesley Garrett. He would only come to despise and resent her for it, just as her grandfather had resented her being forced on him.

The rain was coming down harder now, and the wind roared with a vengeance that creaked and rattled every board and beam in the frame house. A faint rapping noise that seemed to come from the living room interrupted Rebecca's thoughts and drew her out of her reverie. It was the screen door, of course. She had forgotten all about latching it. With the wind banging it mercilessly against the side of the house, she recalled that the tattered thing hadn't looked like it could endure much more abuse. She hurried down the hall and seconds later yanked the door open, one hand already poised for the latch.

"Hello, Re." The familiar husky voice drifted in on a low groan of thunder, and Rebecca felt the earth shift under her feet.

CHAPTER TWO

"WES." She whispered his name, and the sound of it lingered on the sudden still of the wind. The lightning flashed, bathing his features in a blade of silver light and silhouetting his dark form against a darker sky.

In shock, Rebecca could only stand and watch as he moved toward her. Long, easy strides brought him into the stream of light fanning out from the doorway.

The years had hardened the lean, masculine lines of his face and deepened that familiar groove in the left side of his cheek. He seemed taller, broader, more imposing than she remembered. But, there was something else different about him, too. Something even more disturbing. Rebecca could feel it. A wariness. A faint aura of...of what? Anger? Contempt? It was there in the hard twist of his mouth and in the depths of those unholy black eyes.

"Aren't you going to ask me in?" His voice was low, taunting, and when she could find no words to reply, Wes didn't wait for her invitation. Ducking his head under the low doorway, he strode past her and into the room.

Still clinging to the open door, Rebecca fought for some semblance of control. Her hands were shaking and her knees felt limp and rubbery, ready to buckle at any moment. *How could he do it?* A barely coherent voice clamored through the dull ringing in her ears. How could he come breezing into her life again, tearing down the walls of her careful reserve, and making her appear as weak and ridiculous as that same love-starved little fool who was once foolish enough to throw herself into his arms?

"Are you going to stand there all night letting the rain blow in?"

His voice came from behind her, and the insolence in his tone made Rebecca square her shoulders. Her spine went rigid as shock gave way to pride, and somehow she found the presence of mind to turn and lean her back against the door, easing it shut.

"What are you doing here?" Defiance frosted her silver eyes as her gaze met and locked with Wesley's.

He was standing near the center of the room, one hand hitched carelessly on his lower hip, long legs encased in faded jeans and spread in a deceptively negligent stance. His eyes narrowed, just for an instant, as his gaze flickered over her, and lingered, Rebecca thought, for an undue second where the ivory silk molded the subtle swell of her breasts.

Impaled beneath the scrutiny of his gaze, she held her breath, willing her heart to cease its erratic pounding and praying its telltale flutter couldn't be seen through the flimsy fabric of her blouse.

"Obviously, I'm here to see you," he answered with a casual shrug. But Rebecca didn't miss the slight quirk of a dark brow, or the hint of mockery in the husky grain of his voice. He was fully aware of the unsettling effect he was having on her. Still, Rebecca was determined to maintain some shred of composure.

Tilting back her head, she did her best to regard him as coolly as she could. "Really? And to what do I owe this unexpected . . . pleasure?"

"Curiosity. Old-times' sake." His gaze drifted lazily to her sleek, blond hair, and a crooked smile touched his lips as he noted the severity of the style. "You've changed," he murmured, then added almost absently, "I always preferred your hair down."

His eyes traveled to hers, and for an instant his face betrayed a look of utter bewilderment, as if he couldn't believe he'd voiced his thoughts out loud.

Rebecca stared back at him, knowing she should pull her eyes away, but helpless to do so, just as she was helpless to dam the flood of memories that seemed to flow in rippling waves between them. Vividly she remembered the feel of Wes's hands in her hair, his lips on her face and her breasts while he whispered words to her she couldn't understand, his voice muffled, his breath moist against her skin.

The thought brought a wash of color to Rebecca's face, and she shook her head as if to clear it. Her gaze slid from Wes's, and in an effort to disguise her sudden shakiness, she lifted her hand to smooth an errant curl back into place, unaware that the gesture caused the light to glance off the diamond ring she wore.

"Time changes everything, Wes. Or haven't you noticed?"

Her movement caught his attention, and she saw his eyes widen, then narrow slightly as they focused on the huge, emerald-cut stone.

"Oh, I've noticed," he muttered flatly. "And how is good ol' Adam these days?"

"How did you know about . . . ?" The question in part was out of her mouth before she had time to hide her surprise.

"I read the papers, Rebecca," he stated, matter-of-factly. "And since your social life is hardly a secret these days, that's how Son Deaton was able to track you down. Not that anyone really expected you to show up for your grandfather's funeral. But the settling of the estate? Now, that's a different matter."

"Just what are you trying to say?" Rebecca demanded sharply.

Wes tipped back his head, a caustic smile edging the hard line of his mouth. "Only that I understand how pressed for time you must be. And you are anxious, aren't you, to take care of this nasty little business and get back to your other . . . affairs?"

He sounded bitter. Rebecca matched his tone. "Yes, well . . . everyone is entitled to at least one, right?"

Their eyes clashed, and even from across the room Rebecca could see the fire leaping into his. Why was he taunting her? And why did he make her feel so defenseless? Unconsciously, she folded her arms across her breasts.

"Why don't you just get to the point, Wes? I've had a long trip, and I'm willing to bet a good night's sleep that you didn't come out in weather like this just to say 'hello' for old-times' sake."

"Then you win," he answered, inclining his head condescendingly. "Actually, the word 'hello' hadn't even crossed my mind—until I saw you. And now, I guess you could say I've had a slight change of heart."

Rebecca stared at him, eyes wide and wary. "What are you talking about?"

"How long were you planning on staying in town? Three days? Four? Well, I wouldn't be in too big of a hurry if I were you. Truth is," he said, his eyes traveling lazily down the length of her body, "I'm considering making your visit a little longer and a lot more complicated than you anticipated."

If he was trying to disconcert her, Rebecca thought angrily, he was doing a very good job. But she wouldn't give him the satisfaction of knowing it. Spine rigid, she waited for him to conclude his leisurely study of her. When his gaze met hers again, she replied icily, "You have no power over me, Wes. Or over this land, either, for that matter. I've already talked to Son, and there's nothing you can do to stop me from getting this estate settled."

"Maybe." He shrugged, black lashes veiling the ruthless sheen in his eyes. "But I can delay you if I want to. That is if I decide it's worth my time."

Dropping his hand from his hip, Wes abandoned his lounging pose, and began striding toward her, menacingly slow.

"Senator Adam Dane." He drawled the name in a way that matched the lazy rhythm of his steps.

Caught off guard by his abrupt change of manner and conversation, Rebecca uncrossed her arms and clenched her fists at her sides.

"The Golden Boy from the Golden State," he continued, moving closer to her all the while. "And, what is it the press has taken to calling you these days? Ah, yes, 'The Alabaster Dove.' Catchy." His mouth curled into a brittle imitation of a smile. "Sort of fits, though, don't you think? Ms Public Relations. Cool, pale . . . above reproach?"

He lifted one brow in a dark, knowing look that prickled the hair on the nape of Rebecca's neck.

"What's the matter? Don't you think I'm good enough for someone like Adam?" she challenged.

"On the contrary," he retorted. "I think you two probably deserve each other. Of course, some might consider the good senator a little too old for you. But if the size of that rock is any indication of his incentive plan... well, what's twenty years one way or the other?"

He was standing directly in front of her then, eyes dark and boring down into her features with a searing intensity that seemed to fuse every bone in her body. She couldn't move, and there was no air to breathe. From out of the corner of her eye, she saw his arm come up and felt the subtle movement behind her head as he shifted his weight and braced himself with one powerful hand against the door.

He didn't touch her, but his body was only inches from hers, and Rebecca could feel the heat of his breath on her lips, see the outline of bronze flesh and muscle, straining against the whisper blue of his shirt. Was he going to kiss her? Would she let him if he tried? Her pulse thudded quickly in the hollow of her throat, and silently she damned herself—and him for her weakness.

"Do you love him?" His voice was low and carefully controlled, his head bent so close the shadow of his face fell over hers.

It was a question Rebecca hadn't anticipated, and for a second, she stared at him uncomprehendingly, aware only of his disturbing nearness and the flicker of a white-hot flame in the eyes that held her captive.

"What? What did you say?" she asked, almost abstractly.

"I asked if you are in love with Adam Dane?"

When at last his words sank into her exhausted, muddled brain, Rebecca didn't know whether to laugh or cry or to tear at him with questions of her own. *Did you love her?* she wanted to scream. *Were you in love with my sister when you seduced me, then married her five months later?*

Years of pain and bitterness roiled inside her with a force so fierce, Rebecca began to shake. Still, she was determined to prove to Wesley Garrett that he would not—could not—intimidate her, either mentally or physically.

Calling upon all her control, she matched his gaze, glare for unflinching glare. "Why did you come here, Wes? What do you really want from me?"

He didn't reply right away, and for long, tension-filled moments they faced each other in silent combat until, as if premeditated, his gaze slid to her half-parted lips and remained there. "What do you think I want?" he whispered huskily.

Rebecca's heart lunged against her ribs, and her head spun with conflicting emotions, thoughts that met each other coming and going. Against her will, she found her own gaze transfixed on the smooth, sensuous lines of Wesley's mouth. She saw the vein pulsating in his neck, the thin slit of chest with its splay of jet hair revealed in the open vee of his shirt. His thighs, not more than a hair's breadth from hers, burned like columns of fire against her unsteady legs. And . . . she hated him. God, how she hated him! Because he was there—no longer a memory, but flesh and blood. It would be so easy...so easy, she thought, just to lift her fingers to his cheek and give in...again.

Again.

The word brought Rebecca back to her senses and made her forget all but her fury at his insinuation.

Hands balled into tight fists, she dug her nails into her palms and gritted her teeth against the urge to claw out his arrogant, black heart. "Why you conceited..." She couldn't even finish the sentence. "Let me tell you something, Mr. Garrett. I don't care what *you* want, but *I* want you out! Out of this house before I call the police, or the sheriff, or the justice of the peace, or whoever has the authority in this town to...to throw you out."

Abruptly, Rebecca pushed herself away from the door, and just as abruptly Wes let his arm drop to his side.

"While you're at it, why not call your boyfriend, too," he said with a sneer. "Maybe he can send in the FBI."

"Oh, that's cute." Her eyes narrowed and her mouth twisted sarcastically. "But why don't you just save us all the trouble and show yourself out like a good little boy."

Sidestepping him, Rebecca had intended to stalk right past, but her steps had carried her only a short distance when he extended one lightning-fast hand and clamped it on her elbow.

"Not so fast," Wes grated out, swinging her around and pressing her back to the door. He was frowning now, and the look on his face was as harsh and unrelenting as the crushing hold he had on her arm. Rebecca's eyes widened in stunned confusion.

"Don't look so horrified," he said in a voice that was surprisingly calm. "I have no intentions of forcing my...my person on you, if that's what you're thinking. But, I do intend to get what I came after. It's been a long time, babe." He smiled cruelly when he spoke the endearment. "Now, I want a few explanations."

As if to underscore the imperativeness of his demand, his fingers tightened on the fragile bones at her elbow, but she lifted her chin and forced her gaze to level with his, refusing to give him the satisfaction of knowing he was hurting her.

"You're not only rude, Mr. Garrett. You're crazy, as well. I have no idea what you're talking about. And, even if I did, I don't owe you the time of day."

"Don't you?" he challenged, grasping her by the shoulders and giving her a hard shake. "Don't you think I deserve to know why you left here without a word? Why you didn't even bother to come back when Mara was dying, when she needed you and she was calling out for her only sister?"

"Leave me alone," Rebecca cried, struggling against the turbulent swell of emotions that threatened to crack her self-control. "I have nothing to say to you. Nothing! Now, get your hands off me!"

In an attempt to twist away from him, she shoved her palms hard against his chest, but his body was unyielding, and his fingers only dug deeper into her tender flesh until she had to bite her lip to keep from crying out. But her efforts were no match for Wes's commanding strength, and finally panting with rage and exertion, she was forced to abandon her struggles.

"Are you satisfied?" She glared up at him. "Now that we both know you can outwrestle a woman if you have to."

His lips tightened, and a muscle ticked in his jaw, but Wes continued to hold her, pinning her shoulders against the door. "I'll let you go when you tell me the truth, dammit. The truth! Do you hear me, Rebecca? She was your sister, for heaven's sake. She loved you, and you didn't even have the common decency to come home and see her buried."

His voice rose and he shook her again, this time hard and furiously until her head lolled and banged against the door.

"Stop it!" She gasped and tried once more to pull away from him. Her head was spinning and her vision blurred, but Rebecca could see the angry flare of his nostrils and the wild, blazing fury in his eyes.

The truth. He wanted the truth, and the very thought of it twisted her insides with a pain so deep, so filled with guilt and despair that for a moment she was afraid she might be sick. Perversely, she was almost of a mind to tell him then, to punish him, to hurt him—like he was hurting her. Yet what good would her story do any of them now, after all these years?

Through sheer force of will, Rebecca found the strength to calm herself. "The truth, Wes?" Her voice was strained, and oddly, she heard herself laugh. "You wouldn't believe me if I told you. And who are you anyway? Judge? Jury? A one-man vigilante force? What gives you the right to question me, to pry into my life? My life is none of your business... and neither was my sister's."

"Ah, but that's where you're wrong."

Something cold and dangerous flickered in the smoldering coals of his eyes, and one of his hands moved then, slowly, deliberately, gliding across her shoulder to her collarbone and finally to her neck. "Mara was very much my business. Or have you forgotten? She was my wife."

Wife. Like a blade of tempered steel the word sliced through her, tearing open old wounds. "No, I haven't forgotten," she whispered bitterly. "And how convenient for you that she died before she became too much of a burden. Was it a shotgun wedding, Wes? Or are you going to lie and try to tell me that you really gave a damn about Mara?"

His eyes widened; his face went deathly white. And then in a rush, the blood came surging back, darkening his features with a rage so black Rebecca wondered if she had only imagined his first stunned reaction.

"I should have known you would believe something like that. Did you think I married Mara because I had to? Because I was forced into it?"

This time it was he who laughed, but there was no pretense of humor in the guttural sound that seemed almost torn from him. "I never touched her. Does that surprise you? Your sister was the bravest, most gentle person I have ever known. I'd have cut out my heart before I'd have done anything to hurt her. And, unlike you, I can't simply pretend she never existed."

In pain and shock, Rebecca stared at him, her mind whirling in circles. What was he saying? Dear God! Was he actually admitting that he loved Mara? Was the torment she saw on his face, heard in his voice, because of her? Because he had loved . . .

"No!" Rebecca didn't realize she had uttered her denial aloud until he answered her.

"Yes, Rebecca. Selfish little Rebecca. You can't believe it, can you? You can't believe that everyone is not like you—cold and insensitive and caring for no one but themselves."

His hand had been resting lightly at the base of her throat, but as he spoke his fingers began to tighten ever so slightly. And slowly Rebecca became aware of the increasing pressure, the shallow sound of her own breathing.

"And do you know why?" Wes continued in a hard, cutting whisper. "Because you don't feel what other people feel. Love. Guilt. Pain. Those emotions are only words to you, aren't they, Rebecca? Because you haven't the slightest idea what it feels like to care, to hurt for somebody else, more than even yourself."

Rebecca's eyes narrowed as she looked into his. "And how would you know how I feel?" she demanded, her tone low and bitter. "You don't even know me . . . not anymore."

The anger in his face was still apparent, but for an instant his eyes shadowed with something deeper—pain?—at her words.

"Damn you," he swore, letting his hand slide from her throat as he caught her up by the waist and hauled her roughly against him. His lips were near enough that his breath seared the moisture from hers, and his eyes blazed with inner fire. "For eight years you've been nothing but a thorn in my side, a nagging question in the back of my mind. But you won't let me forget, will you? Even when you're miles away, those silver eyes keep haunting me, turning my blood to ice. You're always there. Always . . ."

His voice broke off, or Rebecca went beyond the point of hearing it. She knew only that she was in his arms, crushed against the familiar length of his body, her knees weak, and her heart pounding so hard and so painfully she was frightened by it.

With the savagery of a man possessed, Wes drove his hand into the tight coil of her hair, yanking and dragging his fingers through until the pins flew and the heavy folds tumbled down past her shoulders and over his forearms.

"Don't..." Rebecca moaned in feeble protest, but resolution disappeared when Wes tugged back her head and ground his lips into hers. His mouth was hard and bruising and filled with a kind of anger that seemed to drive him, in spite of himself, as if he longed to kiss her into oblivion—so that she would be exorcised eternally from his mind and body.

And in spite of herself, Rebecca responded to his vengeful embrace. Groaning, she strained against him, arms encircling his neck as she pulled him closer, returning his brutal kisses with the same rage of desperation, of passion and despair. His tongue probed deeply inside her mouth, and the taste of him seized her with a hot, maddening desire. His hands roamed her shoulders, her back, her hips, and the feel of his fevered touch blistered her skin at every point of contact. She arched against him, molding center to aching center, and he gave a ragged groan, every muscle in his body going taut and rigid.

"Re... you... still..."

She thought she heard him murmur something, as his lips slanted across her cheekbone to the tiny hollow below her ear. But his words were lost on her, muffled, incoherent sounds muted by the pulsating surge of her own unrelenting need. It was insane! She knew it, and yet she couldn't stop herself from wanting him. How far would she have gone, if she hadn't, in that second, sensed the subtle chill that passed between them?

Willing her eyelids to open, Rebecca glanced up to find Wesley scowling down at her, tension lines white at the corners of his mouth. Still clinging to his neck, she could feel the heavy thud of his heart against her breasts as gently, but dispassionately, he reached up and removed her arms.

"You still haven't learned when to say no, have you?"

"Oh," Rebecca gasped in shock and stumbled back. He couldn't have hurt her more if he had doubled up his fist and shattered her bones into bits with one powerful swing. Muffling a half sob, she threw her hands over her lips, which were throbbing and swollen from the force of his angry kisses.

Was that what he thought of her? That she was promiscuous? A "loose woman" incapable of controlling the instincts of her body?

Humiliation coursed through her, setting fire to her skin, yet she threw back her head and forced a bitter laugh from her throat. "And so the truth comes out." Her voice sounded high and strained. "Is this why you came here tonight, Wes? To test my powers of resistance? Tell me, did you decide before or after you saw me again, to find out if little Becky Whitney could still be had?"

"Rebecca..." His voice held an apologetic note, but she was too hurt, too angry to let it affect her.

She shoved away from the door, and he reached to take her arm, but she pulled away. "No. Don't touch me."

He saw the anguish on her face, and regret lanced through him. "Rebecca, listen to me. I didn't mean—"

"Of course you did, or you wouldn't have said it."

A dull pain began to throb in her head, and she ran a hand through the tangles in her hair, though she really wasn't concerned with the way she looked. Suddenly she was so exhausted, so terribly tired of... of everything. Haggardness showed in her face when she turned back to Wes, her eyes dark and lusterless.

"You said you came here seeking answers, Wes, but I believe you've achieved what you set out to do. You wanted to hurt me, and you've done that. So now, I think you'd better go." Her voice cracked, and she saw him flinch, but when he replied his tone was as hard as steel.

"All right, I'll go. But you're wrong if you think I just came here to hurt you. And wrong again if you believe you can appease me with a play for my sympathy. I'll be back, Rebecca. You can bank on it. And, I'll *keep* on coming back until you come through with some real answers."

In three angry strides, Wes cleared the distance to the door and wrenched it open. But there he paused and looked back over his shoulder. "Just one more thing." His voice was low, his mouth curved into a grim, one-sided smile. "Ever hear the old saying 'everything is relative'? Well, take it from me, lady. You don't know what hurtin' is."

THE FRAIL BLEACHED BLONDE in a faded pink satin bathrobe had been standing by the window in the foyer of the big house, peering out for what seemed like hours before she heard the sound of the Bronco spinning gravel in the circular drive.

The storm was over now, leaving behind only a drizzling mist, but slivers of retreating lightning occasionally marked the blue-black horizon. In the faint glimmer of one such streak, the woman saw Wesley Garrett emerge from the vehicle. Quickly, she secured the tie on her robe... and waited.

IT WAS A STUPID, idiotic thing to do! Wes Garrett thought, as his booted heels ground pea gravel into powder under his feet. He dug long impatient strides across the drive to the house. He should never have seen her. He was a fool for going over there. When was he going to learn to leave the past dead and buried?

He reached for the door that always had a tendency to swell and stick in stormy weather. When he turned the knob and nothing happened, he muttered a profane oath, then stepped back and kicked it open with wall-banging force.

Startled by his abrupt entrance, the blond woman jumped and threw her hands to her breast. "Merciful heaven! What is it? What's happened?" Alma Whitney clutched at her heart.

She had that kind of shrill voice, nearly always on the edge of hysteria that could cut right through a man's eardrums with the grate of a hay rake running on a cement row.

But for once, Wes hardly noticed that irritating quality in the woman's voice. Flashing black eyes merely flickered in her direction, as he strode past her without a falter in his stride.

"Wes? Tell me. Oh, please, what's the matter?" Alma wailed, scurrying behind him down the hall.

"The door was stuck. I got it open," he stated, not bothering to slow down or turn his steps around.

Alma cried, breathless as she fought to match his pace. "Oh, Wes, you know that's not what I meant, at all!"

At the door to the den, Wes swung the corner and stalked straight to the liquor cabinet, wishing like hell his head would stop pounding and that Alma would leave him alone. She followed him in with the relentlessness of a bloodhound, practically breathing down his neck.

"Did you see her?" she pleaded anxiously.

"Yes," he snapped and reached for the brandy.

"Well, then what did she say? How does she look? Is she all right?"

"Yes," he answered in response to all three questions. His hand closed around the slender throat of the brandy decanter. But then, thinking better of it, he set the thing aside, and stooped instead to grab the whiskey bottle from a lower shelf.

"And?"

"And what? For the love of peace, woman!" He slammed the bottle down hard on the sideboard. "What do you want from me? I saw her! She lives, she breathes, she..."

A brooding, dark scowl moved over his face, and Wes clamped his jaws together, biting back his words as if he feared himself what he might say.

"Wes, please," Alma begged. "Can't you just tell me about her. I've waited so long, and now I—"

"Good God—Alma, please! She's here. That's what you wanted. Now, what else is there to tell?"

Tossing down a full shot glass of whiskey, Wes closed his eyes and breathed in through his nose, a long, deep gulp of air, the prelude to a sigh. When he opened his eyes again, Alma Whitney, despite his hope to the contrary, was still there, filling his line of vision.

Desperate brown eyes, full of pain and pleading uncertainty, hung on to his as if he carried simple answers to complex problems in the same blasé fashion one carries a wallet in a hip pocket.

Sweet Lord, Wes thought, *why does she have to make me feel like I have to be more than I am? Stronger. Wiser. Unerringly in control.* He was beginning to think it was some kind of trait that ran in the family. Or at least, through two-thirds of it.

This last thought caught him unawares. And instantly something hard and cold and familiar tightened in his chest like a crushing vise.

He ran his hand through his thick, black hair and crammed one fist into his front pocket. "All right, Alma," he relented, his husky voice sounding tired, soul battered. "What exactly do you want to know?"

Her thin body began to shake visibly, but she shrugged with a rueful smile. "Is she well? Really happy, I mean? Like she looked in the picture we saw in that news magazine?"

Wes's face went flint-stone hard in the rush of a sudden and inexplicable rage. *Hell, yes!* he wanted to shout, recalling the photograph in question. A what's-new-with-whom shot of Adam Dane and his "aesthetically lovely" fiancée, as they exchanged smiles above a brief caption so bloated with bliss it almost stank.

In the end, however, he did shout. "She's fine, okay? Fit as a fiddle. Snug as a bug. Couldn't be better. And she looks..."

It was then that his voice cracked, shocking him, even, with the realization of how shaken just seeing her again had left him.

Wheeling around he sloshed another shot of whiskey into the glass, downing it quickly to fortify himself before he spoke again.

"She's beautiful, Alma." His voice steady now, he drew a deep breath and turned slowly to face her. "Poised. Polished. All grown up. I think you'd be proud of her." His mouth twisted with a strange smile.

Alma's eyes wavered with tears. "Did you...did you tell her about me?"

"No." He shook his head slowly. "You asked me not to, didn't you?"

Alma's face turned white with relief, and for a moment Wes thought she might actually faint away from the sheer force of it.

"Oh, thank God. Thank you, Wes," she breathed. "I will tell her, though. I swear it. I just need a little more time to...to figure out what I'm going to say."

Wes blinked and stared at her in a sort of awestruck disbelief. If it weren't that the sharp irony underlying her statement had been so unintentional, and was so totally missed by her, Wes thought he might have laughed out loud.

But Wes didn't laugh. Instead, he turned his back and poured himself another drink. "Eighteen years isn't long enough, I guess, to figure out how to tell your daughter you're really sorry your little vacation ended up lasting the better share of her life?''

A piteous sob, made even more so through Alma's feeble attempt to stifle it, escaped her lips and reached Wes somewhere near his conscience.

''Dammit, Alma, I...'' Frowning, he swung around reluctantly to face her again. ''I shouldn't have said that,'' he muttered gruffly, and an unspoken apology hovered in the darkened depths of his eyes.

''But it is the truth, isn't it?'' Her chin quivered, and her fingers began a nervous plucking at the molting ostrich-feather trim on the neck of her dilapidated robe. ''I should have called or written...all those years. Papa always said I didn't have the good sense God gave a goat. But every day I kept telling myself, 'Now, Alma, tomorrow you'll write and tell those babies how fine you're doin' and how much you miss 'em. And maybe even that you'll come home, one day real soon.' I wanted to show them all that I could make it on my own.''

Her eyes went distant, and she smiled as if the mere memory of that long-ago good intention brought her some minute sense of absolution.

Wes could barely suppress the biased reproach in his tone. ''But tomorrow never came, did it, Alma?''

At the sound of his voice her head jerked up, as though for a moment she had forgotten his presence altogether. But then she shrugged and looked down at her hands. Like a guilty child she began pinching and twisting the thin flesh on her knuckles.

''I never was any good at lettering,'' she offered in explanation. ''And back then, it seemed like time just kept on moving so fast. And then one day it was too late, and I couldn't come home. So much time had passed, and I was afraid of what they might think. Afraid they wouldn't love me anymore."

In all his life, Wes had never met anyone quite like Alma Whitney, so hungry for approval, dependent and clinging to the point of near strangulation. And he stared at her now with the same odd mixture of pity and disgust he'd felt the first time he'd ever laid eyes on her face.

It had been over seven years ago when he'd opened his door to find her, standing there on his front porch step, bag and baggage in hand, looking like a dime-store floozy...and an overpriced one at that.

God only knew what freak of fate or moral calamity had prompted her unheralded return to town, coincidentally, only weeks before Mara's death. Alma had gone to her father's house first, knowing nothing of Rebecca's absence, of Mara's marriage or her serious illness. But Will Daniels had turned her away.

And so, with no one to turn to and no other place to go, Alma had come to find Mara. And it was because of Mara that Wes had taken her in. For no matter what else she was, Alma *was* Mara's mother. And, somewhere in the back of his mind, the woman was yet one more link to Rebecca.

Sighing as if he carried the weight of the world on his shoulders, Wes crossed the room and sank down on the sofa. "Well, I guess there's no cause in shaking fists and pointing fingers now. What's done is done and can't be changed. Not at this late date, anyway."

"No...no, that's right." Alma eased over to where he sat, and stood, looking down at him, her bony hands clenched under her chin. "But there's the will, you know. Monday. Son Deaton said we'd take care of it then. And I know I should go and see her. Tell her who I am and, before she finds out through him, that Papa left the farm to us both. But I'm afraid, Wes," she whimpered. Prying her hands from their prayer-like pose, she clutched one hand to the satin folds at her breast, while the other found and tugged nervously at the ends of the narrow belt cinching her waist.

"What are you afraid of, Alma? She can't sell the farm without your consent. No more than you can take possession of it without hers."

"Oh! That's not it!" she wailed. "I want her to like me, can't you see? But I need *time* to try and make her like me. Two days is such a short while to make up for..." She bit her lip, cutting off her words, but her anxious eyes slid cautiously, tentatively to Wes.

Lifting his gaze over the rim of his glass, he regarded her steadily but said nothing.

What does she want from me now? he thought, taking in the too-thin hands toying nervously with the limp sash of a garment that looked like a castoff from an old Jean Harlow movie. Her hair was a straggly mess, her face old and wrinkled beyond her years.

Guilt. Regret. Self-recrimination. Emotions could do frightening things to a person. And he should know, Wes thought cynically. Hadn't he seen some of those same ravaging effects, whenever he took a hard look at himself in the mirror these days?

Killing the last of the liquor in his glass, Wes set it aside and rose to his feet, massaging the muscles in his neck. "It's late, Alma. Why don't you go on to bed? We can talk some more tomorrow."

"But, Wes, I wanted to ask you—"

"I said tomorrow!" Fresh out of patience, he shot her a sharp, potentially lethal, slit-eyed look.

With an audible gasp, Alma quickly gave in. "Yes...yes, that's a good idea. We'll talk in the morning," she said. "That's just what we'll do... tomorrow."

She scampered off in a flurry of nerves, the tail of her faded robe flagging like a sheet on a bean pole.

Wes watched her leave, and then, dragging his hand through the hair on his forehead, strode wearily to the fireplace.

There were still ashes left in the open stone hearth, and a half-charred log rested on the grates. Bracing his forearm on the mantel, he leaned down and stirred the ashes with a booted toe. Some of them were almost white, he noted—like the color of Rebecca's hair—and evoked her eyes when they were bright and passion glazed. He closed his eyes and tried to recall that look, holding the vision in his memory until another image emerged, blotting out the first one.

Now, he envisioned her with tangles in her hair, her lips puffed and bruised, her chin lifted proudly, despite the lingering imprint of his hand on her jaw, and the raw pain he'd seen in her eyes. He refocused on the room, but the memory remained. Why had he said those terrible things to her? What was it about her that drove him beyond reason and sanity? And what was it going to take to get her out of his blood?

Dropping his arm from the mantel, he crossed the room to the doorway and flicked off the light switch on the wall. In the hall he turned toward the staircase and headed for his bedroom. He couldn't count the number of nights he'd spent lying awake in his bed, staring at the ceiling...and wondering. Was her skin still as smooth? Her hair as fragrant? Her lips as soft and warm and yielding as they had been that day?

Now he knew.

Before, there had been times when he was so torn up with guilt and confusion that he thought he had imagined their first lovemaking. But tonight, when he'd touched her, when he'd felt that familiar, throbbing ache inside him—that almost insane need to uncover and rediscover every inch of her, he knew beyond a doubt that day in the barn had been real. Real.

And now, he also knew what he had to do.

It would take just once, he was certain of that. If he could have her one more time, prove to himself that she was just a woman. Only a woman like any other. Not some unattainable figment of his own imagination. Then it would all be over and he would be free. Free of her. Free of guilt. Free to banish from his thoughts and his conscience forever the memory of that rainy afternoon. And then, just maybe . . . maybe he could take control of his life again. Free to forget those haunting last words of a dying girl, who had loved him . . . anyway.

CHAPTER THREE

IN THE QUIETING of the whirlwind that surrounded the soundless closing of the door, Rebecca turned away and stumbled to the bedroom. Stiff and numb, she changed out of her clothes and slid between the welcome cool of the sheets. She prayed for sleep that wouldn't come and peace of mind that, too, eluded her for endless hours as she lay awake, staring with sightless eyes in the dark.

She shouldn't have come back. It was a colossal mistake. One more in an ongoing parade of many, many others. When Son Deaton had phoned her with the news of her grandfather's death, she should have told him then to simply sell the farm. Or burn it, for all she cared. But Son had made it sound imperative that she should come, and Rebecca had had her own reasons for doing as he'd asked.

Wes.

An acid wave of bitterness rose to her throat, and she swallowed hard, biting down on her lower lip, still tender from the angry onslaught of his kisses.

Eight years. Eight empty, lonely years, and not a day gone by without a thought of him. How often had she wondered if he ever thought of her? She'd had to find out. And now she knew just exactly how he thought of her.

To him she was a pushover. An easy mark. A woman who couldn't say no. Tonight he'd talked of pain and accused her of being callous. But what did he know of her secret anguish? Of the guilt and the grief she had suffered alone.

"You don't know what hurtin' is. You don't know..."

Rebecca squeezed her eyes tightly shut and tried to close her ears to the playback of his words. Sliding her hand beneath the covers, she flattened her palm in a protective gesture along the middle section of her abdomen.

Hurting? she thought, lips twisting in grim irony. Indeed, she knew precisely what it felt like to hurt. For one stolen moment, one precious breach in time when loving and being loved was all that mattered, Rebecca had paid for the risk she'd taken. Pain had been her wager. The payoff was her soul. Loving had cost her everything.

She was working, waiting tables in a small diner in Los Angeles, by the time she'd realized she was pregnant with Wesley's child. Pride wouldn't allow her to contact him directly. But as the months dragged on, drawing her strength along with them, Rebecca wrote frequently home to her sister. She never confessed her pregnancy to Mara, nor dared to mention Wesley's name in any way.

Still, she had harbored the secret hope that maybe he would ask about her, inquire of her to Mara, and she would in turn tell him where to look for her. Wes would come to find her. That had been her prayer—a wish never destined to be granted.

Rebecca drew a deep breath and turned on her side, fighting an unpleasant sickness in the pit of her stomach. It was the same feeling that always came when she recalled the last letter she had received from Mara. She was five and a half months into her pregnancy. Twenty-two weeks to the day since she'd left Hurricane Bluff.

With a rush of renewed anguish, Rebecca remembered how her hands had shaken when she'd noticed the envelope was postmarked from Hawaii. She'd torn into it anxiously, unfolded the neatly pressed page, but her mind had gone numb as she began to read, and hours later she was still standing, staring down in senseless shock at the small, rounded letters near the bottom of the page, where Mara had signed: "Lovingly, Mrs. Wesley Garrett."

Rolling over on her stomach, Rebecca buried her face in the crook of her elbow and tried not to think of the weeks that had followed. Long, grueling days and sleepless nights without end had passed in a warp of hopeless despair. Daring no thought for the future, she'd continued to work at her waitress job, going through the motions in a pretense of living.

But she had had the baby to think of then. Wesley's child. The child who would be her joy, her salvation. And nothing else mattered except making it through first one moment, and then one more.

And she'd almost made it. She and her baby. Almost...

Exhaustion finally claiming her, Rebecca drifted into a shallow state of restless sleep. But dreams, fragmented and orderless, floated to the surface and mingled with long-buried memories and dark, half-conscious thoughts.

Life goes on.

Consoling words from a starched-white, faceless stranger filtered through the foggy passages of her mind.

But how? The memory of her own drugged reply came from somewhere deep in her subconscious.

In the dream, doctors and nurses surrounded her, and yet she couldn't make any one of them understand. Her baby was gone and all she had left was the hollow shell of her body, and two empty arms to remind her that sometimes life does not go on. Sometimes it hardly begins again.

MORNING CAME with the smell of sunshine, the sound of a rooster crowing and some neighbor's dog yapping to the sputtering grind of a tractor, at work in a nearby field.

Rebecca awoke with a start and bolted to a sitting position in the bed. Pearls of perspiration beaded her brow and trickled downward, spiking the tips of her thick lashes with a salty, crystalline sting. She blinked and glanced about in confusion. The half belief that she was still dreaming lingered for a moment, until it gradually dawned on her where she was . . . and why.

Shedding the last vestiges of sleep, she threw off the thin muslin sheet and swung her legs over the edge of the bed. No, she wasn't dreaming, she thought ruefully. The sights and sounds around her were as real as the coarse wooden floor beneath the soles of her bare feet.

She was "home." And instantly a remembered truism hit her like a bad joke. *Home is where the heart is.* She almost laughed out loud. This town, this house had never been her home. She didn't belong here—not then, not now, not ever again. Sighing, she reached for her robe and headed for the bathroom.

Forty-five minutes and a lukewarm shower later, Rebecca stood before the mirror over the lavatory, dressed in a satiny blouse of pale taupe, and a slim-fitting skirt of natural-textured linen. Her pale, waist-length hair was still damp and shimmering from a quick shampoo. Hastily, she brushed it back, away from her face, and twisted it into a sleek French knot.

You've changed. Wes's words came back to her. *I always preferred your hair down.*

Irritated at the sudden trembling of her hands, she jammed the last pin into the tight coil and turned to stare with wide, sterling-hued eyes at her own outward reflection, the remote, marblelike image of the woman she had become.

How calm she looked! Rebecca marveled, lifting her hand to touch her cheek. So cleverly self-possessed in her artful disguise. Sometimes she hardly recognized this stranger in the mirror. This woman who had gone from waiting tables by day to putting herself through school by night.

It had taken her over two years, including summers, to earn her associate degree in secretarial administration. Oddly, however, her first real job had come as a result of being at the right place at the right time. A local newspaper columnist, who possessed an apparently unappeasable penchant for bad atmosphere and day-old coffee, had hired her straight out of the diner, not even a week after she had finished school. When he suffered a heart attack a year later and decided to give it all up, moving to Omaha to be near his grandchildren, Rebecca left her job as administrative assistant for a more prestigious spot in guest relations at the Beverly-Wilshire Hotel, where ultimately she met Adam.

Rebecca snapped the lid on the enamel box that held her hairpins and slipped it back into the pouch lining in her makeup bag.

Drawing a deep breath, she straightened her shoulders and glanced once more at herself in the mirror.

Yes. She had changed. Wes himself had seen to that. She was a realist now. A hard-core survivor, who had seen hell from the bottom looking up. She had pulled herself up by the bootstraps, clawing her way back on her own, because there had been no one else to do it, no one else who gave a damn. And if that made her cold and callous then so much the better, she decided.

Flipping off the bathroom light, she went back into the bedroom, made up the bed and slipped on her shoes. Let Wes Garrett believe what he chose, she thought, picking up her handbag. She owed him nothing, and nothing was exactly what she intended to give him. Regardless of last night's encounter, and her humiliating response to his kiss, he wouldn't succeed in breaking down her defenses another time. She wouldn't let him, Rebecca vowed. Not as long as she breathed.

And then, closing the door behind her as she left the room, she assured herself Wesley Garrett would never have the power or the opportunity to hurt her again.

IT WAS JUST AFTER NINE when Rebecca slowed to the stop sign at the crossroads on her way into town. Her appointment with Son Deaton, president of the local bank and executor of her grandfather's estate, was for ten o'clock Monday morning. Today was Friday, but

Rebecca saw no purpose in waiting until after the weekend. Son couldn't possibly be that busy.

Besides, she reasoned, with the exception of her mother—and God only knew where she was—Rebecca was Will Daniels's only heir. How long could it take to sign a few documents? And the quicker the paperwork was done, the sooner she could leave, lessening her chances of another confrontation with Wes.

Fingers tapping impatiently on the steering wheel, Rebecca waited for a flatbed truckload of hay to pass. Venturing a glance to her left, she recognized the cutoff that led to the cemetery where her sister and her grandfather were buried.

Her heart constricted. She had to go there. Sooner or later she knew she must. But now? She bit her lip, dread and indecision creasing her brow. The truck finally passed, and Rebecca shook her head. *I'll stop on the way back,* she promised herself. Then turning onto the highway, she made a sharp right and headed for town.

"WHEW!" Heaving the last of seven fifty-pound sacks of feed into the bed of the black-and-tan Bronco, the stout, carrot-topped teenager jumped down from the tailgate. "This be all for ya, Mr. Garrett?" Buckteeth shining, the boy wiped his hands down the front of his overalls and prepared to receive his customary tip.

Wes bent to slam the door on the tailgate. Features shaded under the brim of a well-worn Stetson, he glanced across the street to the graveled drive outside the bank. There were several cars parked out front. One was a silver Mercedes, its hood ornament winking in the dazzle of the morning sun.

He straightened slowly, muscles tensed, and for a moment forgot all about the boy standing beside him.

"Hey? Somethin' wrong, Mr. Garrett?" Following the direction of the older man's gaze the youngster spotted the expensive 380 SL parked in the lot across the street. But Wes's attention was centered elsewhere.

Black eyes guarded by the dark glasses molded to his face, he quickly scanned the area for any sign of Son Deaton's green-and-white pickup truck. There was none. Wes relaxed and realized, only then, that he'd been holding his breath. He let it out slowly in a long, sighlike stream.

Mistaking the signal, the boy sighed, too, and remarked with a trace of envy, "Nice set o' wheels, huh?"

"Yeah," Wes agreed, a bemused half smile crawling lazily across his lips. He wasn't thinking of Rebecca's car. His thoughts were on Son and the little talk they'd shared earlier that morning.

At first the bulbous, cigar-chomping bank president had been vehemently opposed to the idea of taking a week's vacation on the spur of the moment. But Wes had been patient in reminding him of how well the bass were hitting on Big Lake this time of year, of how dearly Mrs. Deaton would love a second honeymoon, and of course, how unfortunate it would be if someone—take himself, for instance—were to suddenly withdraw enough cash on deposit from the Deltaland Bank and Trust, which was running in the red, to have the president of the tiny bank crying "uncle" at the very least.

Wes hadn't been sure his bluff would work. After all, it wasn't as if he had millions stashed away. But in a farming community of less than five hundred people, cold cash was a scarce commodity. All the money most men had was tied up in crops and the machinery needed to cultivate them. And more often than not, the small farmer spent his life, season after season, borrowing and reborrowing against the land that never seemed to yield enough, piling up debts that soon outweighed the value of the land itself.

But Wes wasn't a farmer. His house and lands were paid for. Between the sizable sums his paintings had begun to bring in and the intermittent sale of a horse or two, he remained one of the few men in town who didn't owe his soul to the Deltaland Bank.

"Yeah, nice wheels," the boy, whose existence Wes had almost forgotten entirely, repeated a little louder. Poking his hands in his pockets, he rocked slowly back and forth on the balls of his heels, stalling for time, still hoping for a good tip. "Don't nobody I know around here drive a car like that, though. Must be somebody visitin'... or lost."

"Lost, huh?" Wes's eyes crinkled slightly at the corners, as he reached around to draw his wallet from a snug hip pocket. "No, I don't believe she's lost." He used the pronoun "she" as if he were speaking of the car instead of the woman who owned it.

"Visitin' then, I guess," the boy mumbled inanely, his real attention focused on the wallet in Wes's hand.

"Yeah, I guess." Wes pulled out a bill and planted it in the boy's eagerly waiting palm.

"Hey, thanks, Mr. Garrett!" The boy said, grinning. "Just holler now if ya need anythin' else."

Wes watched him lope away in his Tom Sawyer "gone fishing" overalls, and strangely, he thought again of ol' Son.

Stranger still, Wes had to admit, it had been Alma who had first given him the idea last night of talking to Son, with her rantings on about time and how she needed more of it to convince her daughter of...whatever. Probably the fact that she wasn't a bad person, he guessed.

But it just so happened that he, too, had reached the grave conclusion that if he wanted to get next to Rebecca, it was going to require a little more than a day or two of charming persistence. It had occurred to him that he hadn't been too charming with her last night.

It had occurred to him, also, that he could just have Son try and stall her for a while. But knowing she'd be anxious to settle her business as quickly as possible, Wes had decided a stall tactic wouldn't work.

Besides, he thought, Son Deaton wasn't good at holding up under pressure. And Wes was certain if Rebecca could get to him, she would apply plenty of it. As it was now, the executor of Rebecca's grandfather's estate, was, for the time being at least, tucked quietly away in a phoneless cabin, so far back in the boondocks it'd take a helicopter and a pack of prison-break bloodhounds to flush him out.

And the beauty of the whole scheme was, Wes thought, shifting his weight and poking his wallet back down in his faded jeans, that even if Rebecca managed to learn where Son Deaton was vacationing, she'd never find him in a million years.

How long?

Wes's smile began to disappear as his lips tightened and a dark, brooding frown settled steadily over his brow. How long? Yes. That was the question, all right. Now that he had gone to the trouble of keeping her in town, how long was it going to take to get Rebecca out of his system... and then out of his life for good?

Long enough, a voice shouted in the back of his head.

Tall frame leaning against the fender of the truck, Wes pulled off his hat and raked a rough, impatient hand through the now damp mass of jet hair. Resettling the Stetson slowly so that its brim sat low on his forehead, he ventured a glance back across the street.

He wondered how she was receiving the news. A taut muscle corded in the blade of his jaw. He reached for a cigarette, and then remembered. He didn't smoke anymore.

"FISHING!" Rebecca exclaimed in a voice so loud and furious she hardly recognized it as her own.

"I... I'm sorry, Miss Whitney," the young receptionist stammered, eyes wide and cheeks flushed. "I assure you, I had no idea of Mr. Deaton's plans to go on vacation. Normally he gives us advance notice, of course. But sometimes things come up, you know, and perhaps, your appointment simply slipped his..."

At the look on Rebecca's face, the woman's voice dwindled away on a feeble note. She coughed and glanced about in a futile search for help. When none could be found, her eyes slid back to Rebecca, whose stormy gaze had never left her face.

Nervously, the woman cleared her throat and clamped her hands together, resting them on top of her desk. "Miss Whitney," she began, projecting the utmost professionalism, "I understand you're in a bit of a dilemma here. But until my employer returns, I really don't know what else I can tell you."

"You can tell me where to find him," Rebecca stated flatly.

The woman looked aghast. "Oh, but I couldn't possibly. It's against our policy to—"

"Look, Miss..." Rebecca glanced quickly at the nameplate on the desk. "Look, Miss Butler. I've just driven nearly two thousand miles—at the request, I might add, of your employer. Now," she said as she drew a deep breath and made a concerted attempt to control her mounting anger, "if Mr. Deaton left only this morning, then it stands to reason he couldn't have possibly gone far. He can't have reached an airport by now. So if you would be kind enough to give me some idea of where he was headed, then I should have little trouble in locating him myself!"

Her voice had risen again, and the receptionist shifted uncomfortably in her chair.

"Well..." Miss Butler hesitated. "This isn't at all in keeping with our company policy. However, under the circumstances..." She paused for a moment, casting a sidelong glance at the teller's window, then leaned forward and began to speak very rapidly in hushed, urgent tones.

"All I know is that Mr. Deaton came into the office this morning around eight o'clock, as usual. At the time, I don't think he had any intention of going anywhere. But then, he got his phone call, and a little while later Mr. Garrett—one of our more prominent patrons—stopped by with the keys to his cabin on Big Lake. Well, then Wes...I mean Mr. Garrett...had no sooner left the bank, than Mr. Deaton came bustling through and announced he was taking a week off. Just like that! And the next thing we knew, he was...why, Miss Whitney, are you all right?"

Cold rage swept like a wind through her bones, and Rebecca felt the blood drain from her face. *Damn him!* she silently cursed, and gritted her teeth against the impulse to speak the name trembling in a fury on her lips.

"I can delay you if I want to." Wes's threat pounded with a vengeance in her ears. *But you won't!* she wanted to scream aloud.

"Miss Whitney! Are you sure you don't want to sit down or something? You look so pale. Joanne, get Miss Whitney a glass of water. Quick!"

The note of alarm in the receptionist's voice penetrated Rebecca's thoughts. "N...no, I'm fine, really. Thank you for your help, Miss Butler." She managed a wan smile, and a nod for the other bank employee who had promptly arrived with a paper cup in hand and a startled look on her face.

Minutes later, trudging through inches of sand and gravel, Rebecca headed for her car under a now blazing-hot sun. She would find Son Deaton, she vowed. Someone besides Wes had to know where that cabin was. All she had to do was ask around. Maybe she'd try getting information over at the dry goods store.

Lost in thought, Rebecca didn't notice the frisky, tow-headed boy playing zigzag, out and around the parked vehicles. From out of nowhere, he darted in front of her, near enough to upset her balance. She stumbled, but caught her step moments before the errant child was halted dead in his tracks.

"Bobby Joe!"

Snaring the boy by the back of the collar, an obviously pregnant brunette stooped to scold her wayward son. Wielding a finger near the tip of his pug nose, she ordered him to "get himself to the barbershop" along with his uncle and brother.

Warning taken, the boy dashed away, and the woman rose and straightened, pressing a hand to the small of her back.

"Sorry about Bobby Joe," she said, shoving back a lock of limp hair from her forehead. "Don't know what gets into him sometimes. But I guess boys will be—" Her sentence was left unfinished as the woman's eyes met Rebecca's for the first time. "Becky? Becky Whitney?" Recognition lit her face, and her mouth fell open in amazed disbelief. "Oh...I can't believe it!" With arms outstretched, the woman rushed forward, grasping hold of Rebecca's hands and squeezing them tightly.

Stunned for an instant, Rebecca was unable to place this woman who addressed her with an unfettered familiarity and by the nickname she'd always despised.

"Good heavens, you look fabulous!" The woman exclaimed. But it wasn't until she giggled, cheeks dimpling with an irrepressible grin, that Rebecca finally recognized the jaunty brunette. Vicky Hodge. Her childhood friend.

"Why, Vicky Lynn. How have you been?" she managed to ask politely, despite her impatience to get on with the business of locating Son.

"Oh, please, don't ask," Vicky wailed, and Rebecca almost wished she hadn't when she saw the woman heave a heavy breath, gearing up, no doubt, for a long-winded disclosure.

"Today has been one of those days." Sighing, Vicky placed a hand on the generous swell of her middle. "Ted is out of town. My washer broke down. This heat makes my ankles swell up like elephant legs.

And—'' she slanted a glance toward the barbershop ''—my two darling sons are conducting an experiment: what makes Mommy pull her hair out by the roots?''

She rolled her eyes and made a horrendous face. Rebecca couldn't help but laugh. An incorrigible clown in her primary school days, a notorious gossip as a teenager, Vicky Lynn was the type of person one could always rely on to toss off a joke or talk a blue streak, blurting out everything she ever knew. And Vicky always made it her business to know just about everything...

Of course! Rebecca's pulse quickened as she suddenly turned to view her old friend in a vastly more interesting light. Wes used to pal around with Vicky's husband, Ted. Chances were she knew of the cabin on the lake, and directions shouldn't be too difficult to pry... not from Vicky Lynn.

With a sudden boost in morale, Rebecca stole a glance up the street, then turned her attention back to Vicky.

''Well, I see the café is still the same ol' eyesore.'' A hint of a smile settled smugly on her lips. ''Why don't we go over and get something cold to drink? Then you can fill me in on all the latest happenings.''

''Great!'' Vicky agreed, and without hesitation, she launched into a spiel of incessant chatter, pausing only when they reached the door of the tiny drugstore-grill.

Aside from a portable snowcone stand, Buck's Cafe was the only eatery in town. It stood on the corner across from the general store—a rustic, frame structure with multipaned windows to the left of a single entry door. Inside, its floors were wooden, clean but unvarnished and marred with ancient paths of wear.

On weekends the place was packed, but for now they had it to themselves; a cool, dark hideaway, perfect for a private discussion.

"Let's sit over here." Vicky motioned. Rebecca nodded and followed behind her, weaving through a maze of tables draped in checkered cloths, to the green vinyl booths near the back of the room.

"Ugh." With a grunt and a grin, Vicky struggled into the booth across from Rebecca. "I keep forgetting I'm not so good at wedging into tight places these days."

Rebecca smiled but her gaze slid away, eyes growing dark in recollection of similar feelings. The aches and the awkwardness she remembered from her own pregnancy, but it was the expression on Vicky's face that tugged at her heartstrings. Had she worn this same look once? That special flush of pride that came with knowing a new life was growing inside? A tiny new person, untouched, unspoiled. Oh, the things she had planned for her baby. So much love...so much—

"Afternoon, ladies. What'll it be?"

The appearance of the waitress shook Rebecca from the hounding jaws of the past. She smiled faintly, gave her order of a diet soda and, while Vicky ordered, fiddled with the moist napkin under her water glass and tried to rechannel her thoughts to her purpose for being here. For a moment, it hadn't seemed altogether clear.

When at last the waitress left them, Vicky folded her elbows on the table and leaned forward. "My God, I can't get over the size of that diamond!" she whispered in awe. "Adam Dane, right? *Senator* Adam Dane. Where on earth did you meet him?"

On an odd reflex action she was hardly aware of, Rebecca snatched back her hand and curled it into her lap. "Through my job actually," she replied, shrugging to cover the peculiar uneasiness she had begun to feel lately whenever she discussed Adam and herself in the context of their personal relationship. "I'm sure you don't want to hear boring details, so let's just say he was impressed with some public relations material I helped coordinate for him through his office and the hotel where I worked."

"And so now you work for him," Vicky jumped in.

Rebecca nodded.

"But that's not all," Vicky insisted. "And if you don't tell me something meatier than that, then I'll just have to reconstruct the events myself! Let's see..." She touched her forehead and feigned a frown of deep concentration. "It was love at first sight and he swept you off your feet, proposing by candlelight with champagne and roses and violins playing in the background. Right?"

"Right," Rebecca murmured placidly. In truth, Adam had proposed to her in his usual, highly civilized and unemotional fashion over the telephone, long-distance, between Washington, D.C., and Los Angeles.

The waitress returned and Vicky wasted no time in diving into her chef's salad.

Rebecca sat back and studied her old friend for a moment, fingertips treading lightly over the rim of her glass. Thoughtfully, she wondered how to broach the subject of locating Son without stirring up a tidal wave of curiosity. She didn't want to explain herself, or her problems to Vicky Lynn.

Sipping her tasteless drink, Rebecca eyed the woman cautiously over the edge of the glass and waited for the right moment to take the initiative in their conversation. Her patience paid off. The moment came. Rebecca set her glass aside just as Vicky filled her mouth with a large tomato wedge.

"Tell me," Rebecca began, glancing down to guard her eyes as she assumed a tone of idle curiosity. "You wouldn't happen to know anything about a cabin near Big Lake, would you? I hear it might belong to the Garrett family. I was wondering what sort of place it was?"

Fork halting in midair, Vicky looked up, arching her brows inquisitively. "The Garrett family?" She swallowed hard. "Why, they moved away years ago. Except for Wes, of course, and he left, too, for a while."

Rebecca drew in an exasperated breath. Maybe this wasn't going to be as easy as she thought. "But the cabin?" she prodded, trying to nudge Vicky Lynn back to the subject. "Do you know if Wes kept the fishing cabin?"

"Beats me." The brunette shrugged, failing to take the hint. "You know what, though? I always thought it was strange the way he left like that." Her eyes narrowed thoughtfully, and Rebecca realized a straight answer from this woman was out of the question. Vicky was in the mood to talk, and she'd just have to listen. Maybe if she sifted through the conversational debris as they went, she'd manage to learn something yet.

"So, Wes left Hurricane Bluff, you say?" Rebecca swirled the crushed ice in her glass, trying to ignore the nervous jitters in her stomach. Wes Garrett was the last person she wanted to discuss.

Vicky nodded. "Yes, and suddenly, too. Don't think anybody ever knew where he went or what he did. But one day—been about five years ago, now, I guess, he just reappeared. He's fixed up the old Windspear place. You know the one, don't you? That old plantation house near the bayou?"

Know the place? Rebecca nearly choked. Dear God! Of course, she knew the place. How could she forget the once-great manor, concealed by undergrowth, with briars and creeping vines that covered the veranda and clung to the tall pillars midway to the second floor? For as long as she could remember, the house had stood in vacant shambles. But to her, it was a castle. Windspear had been her enchanted land. Her secret mansion, keeper of dreams. She had been headed there one day, a thousand years ago, when a sudden storm had forced her to seek shelter in a barn on the mansion's grounds instead.

The jitters in her stomach hardened into a bitter knot. Wes didn't deserve Windspear. In her heart, Windspear had always belonged only to her.

"Why would he want it?" Rebecca hadn't realized she'd uttered the question aloud, until Vicky answered.

"I don't know." She reached casually for her water glass. "But you wouldn't recognize the place now. All the renovations he's done! Must have cost him a fortune. He's built new stables and he raises quarter horses for breeding stock now. But Ted says that's just a sideline."

She leaned forward, her eyes sparkling in fascination. "You know, they say he's beginning to make a real name for himself with those wildlife paintings of his. Remember when he went off to that art school?

Think it was up north somewhere.'' She frowned slightly and forked a slice of radish. ''Course we weren't much bigger than minutes, then, Wes being older and all. But I swear to you, I almost keeled over when Anita Deaton told me what those paintings were selling for down in New Orleans.''

''So, he's doing well for himself now?'' Rebecca didn't know why the words came out of her mouth, when in fact, she could have cared less.

''Well, I guess so,'' Vicky said, looking as if that fact went without saying. But then, she quickly added, ''Why, Ted says he's probably about the richest man in town. But I guess, that's not saying much when you compare him to someone like Adam Dane.''

She spoke the name in a tone approaching reverent awe, and Rebecca smiled benignly. ''Adam was born into money.''

Now, why had she said that? Had her confrontation with Wes last night left her so paranoid that she suddenly felt she had to start making excuses for Adam's wealth and position in order to justify her engagement to him?

''Well,'' Vicky lifted a shoulder nonchalantly and let her gaze slide away, only a trace of speculation lighting her eyes before she commented again. ''The Garretts always did have a knack for turning a dollar, you know. But Wes?—wild and reckless as he was? I don't think anybody ever expected him to amount to much. Never seemed to care about anything or anyone until Mara di—''

Vicky caught herself and flushed a guilty red. ''Oh, Rebecca...I'm sorry. Does it upset you? To talk about her I mean? I wouldn't want to...''

"It was a long time ago," Rebecca said slowly, her own face betraying nothing of the cold, sick sensation that gripped her insides at the mention of her sister's name. Again she lifted the glass to her lips. Stiff and dry, they seemed no more a part of her than the voice that softly urged, "Go on, Vicky. Finish what you were about to say."

At first, Vicky looked uncertain but gradually an unusual pensiveness eased across her plump features. With slow, precise gestures, she put down her fork and brought her napkin to her lips.

A dull warning sounded somewhere in the back of Rebecca's mind. She didn't want to hear this. Somehow she knew. Still she seemed unable to make herself move, to stop herself from sitting there, watching in near-morbid fascination as Vicky wadded her napkin and leaned back with a heavy sigh.

"Well, certainly I don't mean any disrespect, but you of all people should understand what a shock it was when he upped and married her so quickly and all. Imagine, Wesley Garrett and little Mara Whitney. Why, the whole town could talk of nothing else. Not that Mara wasn't a dear and I loved her, truly. But she was so frail, so... terribly helpless-looking with those big, sad eyes of hers. Always did look kind of peaked, if you ask me. And certainly not the type of woman one would expect Wes Garrett to... well, you know, get involved with."

Vicky shrugged and glanced down at her hands. Rebecca sat quietly, her expression remote, despite the unpleasant images her friend's words evoked. Mara and Wes. Rebecca and Wes. And what type of woman did people expect he'd become involved with? A foolish one, she reflected, answering her own question.

"Naturally there were some...remarks," Vicky said softly. "Speculations, really, that she might have been... well, in the family way. And then, when she got sick, and so soon after they were married... well..." Her voice trailed off and she shifted in her seat uneasily.

Rebecca swallowed a bitter lump in her throat. "Pneumonia," she managed to say. "They said it was pneumonia."

"Yes, that's what I heard." Vicky glanced up. "But whatever it was Wes— Oh! I tell you, he was like a madman. Wouldn't eat. Wouldn't sleep. Wouldn't even let the nurses sit with her. For days on end, I heard he never left her side. And then, when she died... Oh, Rebecca! They might as well have buried him with her. Looked like death himself at the funeral. That night, I heard, he locked himself away in that studio of his, refused to come out or let anyone in. And then, one day he just packed up and left. Some say he just drifted around after that, trying to forget. I don't know, maybe that's what he did. But I swear, to this day, I don't think I've ever seen another person grieve as hard as that man did. God, how he must have loved her."

She ended the sentence softly, on a low, wistful note and gazed off into the distance, ironically oblivious to the impact of her words.

Rebecca sat motionless, features frozen into a mask of inexpression, pale as death and cold as stone. She couldn't speak; she barely breathed for fear of splintering apart into a thousand screaming pieces.

No! she wanted to cry out. *He never loved her. Never!* Years of insulating herself against the unthinkable wouldn't allow her to consider the notion now. She knew why Wes had married her sister, and if he suffered at all, as Vicky claimed, it wasn't his heart, but his own guilty conscience that panged him so.

He married Mara because he had to, the voice of desperation cried out in her ears. Rebecca clung to it, tenaciously, unable to let go of the "truths" she'd assumed as a protective shield against the memory and the pain of his betrayal.

Mara was infatuated with Wes, Rebecca thought wildly. And he had used her, unscrupulously charmed and seduced Mara into bed, the same way he had seduced her in the barn that day. But their grandfather had found out and forced them to marry—just as he would have forced Rebecca, if she hadn't run away.

But she had run away! And it was Mara who stayed. Mara who became his wife. Mara—dear heaven! Was it possible? Was Wes in love with her sister all along?

Blood pounding like a sledgehammer in her ears, Rebecca fought for outward control as fires of fierce denial raged a fury in her heart. She had to get out of here—now. This minute!

Numb limbs taking sudden life, Rebecca reached for her purse, and mumbled, "Vicky, I have to go. I..." She started to rise, but the woman reached over, touching her hand and stopping her.

"She was asking for you, Rebecca. There... at the last."

Vicky's voice was soft, but the edge was unmistakable, and Rebecca didn't miss the glimmer of reproach that flickered like a blade of steel in her gaze. Vicky looked away and began to toy absently with a bead of moisture gliding down one side of her glass. "She said she had to see you, had to... explain. But what, no one ever knew. Maybe it was nothing. The fever talking, you know. But to her, it was urgent. So much so that she kept on calling, kept holding on even when all hope was—"

"Stop it!" Rebecca choked. "Please! I don't want to hear this. I just couldn't come. That's all. I just..."

"But why?" Vicky demanded in a whisper. "Mara worshiped you. You and Wes were all she had. Why couldn't you come? What on earth could have been important enough to keep you away?"

Important enough! Rebecca longed to scream. Was it enough that she had nearly died trying to protect Mara, trying to keep her from learning of the baby. *Her* baby. Her precious, infant son who was born too early and had died only two days later—one week from the day they'd buried her sister.

It was all she could take—the probing, the reproach, the silent condemnation she saw in her friend's eyes. Suddenly she was on her feet, scrambling to get away, and tipping over a glass of water in her haste.

"I'm sorry, Vicky...I...I have to go. Please. I can't talk about this. I can't—"

"Rebecca, wait!" Vicky called out, but Rebecca was already at the door.

Vision blurred with unshed tears, she burst outside and into the blinding sunlight. She turned to run, and instead collided with something solid. A package fell to the sidewalk. Instinctively Rebecca stooped, snatched it up and thrust it back into the bony hands of the woman she'd bumped into.

"Here. I'm sorry. Please let me by." She hardly glanced at the frazzled-looking blonde as she hurried to move past her. But the woman took one look at

Rebecca's face and stumbled back, staring with startled, brown eyes.

"I'm sorry," Rebecca apologized again. But she didn't turn back, and as she ran for her car, failed to hear when the woman spoke, dazedly...

"Rebecca."

Alma Whitney called her daughter by name.

"FOOL! Fool!" Banging her fist on the steering wheel, Rebecca stomped the accelerator, hurtling her car into a treacherous pace.

He loved Mara. He loved her sister. God, how he must have loved her!

No! Her heart rebelled, as faster and faster the Mercedes streaked, hugging sharp curves and gathering momentum on the narrow, asphalt straights. She wouldn't believe it, she raged. She didn't dare. For doing so meant taking blame and facing a deep-rooted guilt, a reckless thought, a wish made in spite. A wish Rebecca hadn't meant and never dreamed would come true.

But present truth was swiftly gaining a sense of reality, and neither speed nor distance could help her escape her guilt or recapture her fading illusions.

"It wasn't Mara's fault," she cried aloud in torment, frenzied thoughts racing with each twist and turn of the road. Mara hadn't known about the baby. She hadn't known Rebecca loved Wes. She hadn't known, and the fault was Rebecca's. Not her sister's. Not Mara's. No! The blame was hers...and it was Wes she hated. Not Mara. Dear God! She had never meant to hurt Mara. Never meant those terrible, desperate words, whispered through tears in voice of despair, when she read the letter announcing Mara's marriage—and prayed her only sister dead.

Overcome with guilt, Rebecca removed her gaze from the road for a split second. One hand left the wheel to wipe the tears from her eyes. Reaching a hairpin curve, her daring speed became mortal error.

Barreling through the turn, she glanced up too late and horror sucked the air from her lungs. She spotted the truck, the men, the hay...the jackknifed trailer across the road. She stomped on the brake, but the pressure was too great. Tires screeching, the rear end whipped, and the car began fishtailing wildly out of control.

Everything seemed to happen at once. One front tire struck a pothole with a jolt, and suddenly the Mercedes rocked, tipped to one side, balanced on two wheels for a fleeting second, then toppled over on its roof.

In a hair-raising shriek of metal scraping pavement, the car skidded diagonally across the road and crashed to a thunderous halt in the ditch.

Someone was screaming. Rebecca tried to move, but searing pain blazed through the core of her chest. And her head. Oh! How it hurt! She couldn't lift it, and marginally she wondered if her neck was broken. *Stop screaming,* she wanted to shout. But the shrill wail continued, darkness clouded her brain, and she closed her eyes, thinking she had only dreamed the sound of a man's voice yelling down as if through a wind tunnel.

"For the love of God, somebody get her off the horn!"

FIFTEEN MINUTES LATER, the Bronco rounded the same curve, traveling at a much saner pace.

Wes frowned the moment he spotted the man up ahead, standing in the middle of the road and flagging his arms over his head.

"What's the matter?" Alma Whitney asked as she bucked forward in the passenger seat, alarm tremoring her high-pitched voice.

"I don't know." Wes tensed. Beyond the man in the road, he saw the jackknifed truck and the bales of hay that had tumbled off the flatbed, and now lay strewn on the highway. "Looks like somebody needed some help backing his truck in," he muttered and braked, slowing the Bronco to a crawl.

Eyes quickly surveying the condition of the truck, Wes didn't see any obvious damage, but something wasn't right. He could feel it. There was an urgency in the air, a scent. What was it? Smoke? Fuel? Burning rubber?

The smell wafted stronger as a hot gust of wind swept in through the Bronco's open windows. Senses acute to the direction of the scent, Wes shifted his gaze just as a glint of sunlight glanced off the rear bumper of the small silver car, crumpled in the ditch.

"Oh God!" The words were torn from his throat. And the next thing he knew he was out of his truck . . . and running.

CHAPTER FOUR

RUNNING. Seconds were minutes; minutes became hours. Fear knotted his gut. Panic lurched convulsively in his throat and poured off his face in a cold dripping sweat.

Don't let her be dead, Wes chanted under his breath. *Sweet Jesus. Don't let me lose her! Not like this. Not like this.*

He reached the car just as the two men who had witnessed the crash were struggling to wedge a crowbar between the driver's door and the vehicle's crumpled frame. The bar slipped. It wasn't going to work! The realization tore through him, and suddenly he was shoving the men aside, even hurling one to the ground.

Amid the startled gasps of shock and confusion, the expletives vilely questioning the state of his sanity, Wes scrambled down into the wide ditch and dropped to his knees in the mud. Hands cupped to the sides of his face, he strained to peer through the driver's window, which had remained, along with the others, miraculously intact.

"Had to jerk the wires on the horn," one of the farmers explained. But Wes was beyond the point of making a connection between the silenced horn and the too-still form slumped forward against the steering column.

A thousand frantic thoughts hurtled through his brain when he saw her lying there, crumpled and unconscious, blood oozing from an ugly cut near her hairline.

"Stand back!" he yelled and sprang to his feet, daring anyone to interfere. There was no time for deliberations; instinct told him what he had to do. With adrenaline pumping like roaring thunder in his ears, he took a step back, launched himself into midair and with one powerful kick shattered the window to crumbling bits.

Heedless of the glass that scraped and tore at his forearms, he stretched forward and reached inside. Straining muscles and twisting joints in ways they were never meant to bend, he managed to get hold of her. Careful not to drag or pull, he gently drew Rebecca into the crèche of his arms and lifted her out through the narrow, jagged hole.

"Oh, no! Oh, merciful heaven," Alma wailed in rising hysteria. "I knew something terrible was going to happen. I knew it the minute I saw her—bursting out of the café and plowing into me like that. I should have stopped her. But what could I do? Oh, Lord! She might be dying! Why doesn't she come to?"

"Shut up!" Wes snapped, guilt and his own mounting fears making him lash out at the hand-wringing woman riding shotgun on his heels. He thanked God that they were within sight of his house.

Cradling Rebecca's limp form against the solid wall of his chest, he almost ran up the driveway, then crossed the foyer in the large white house, moving briskly with long, urgent strides. He'd known within reason that Rebecca wouldn't be thrilled at the prospects of staying in town for a week, maybe longer. But he'd never anticipated that her reaction would result in near-tragedy. He swore under his breath and instinctively tightened his hold, gathering her closer against him, pressing his cheek to the crown of her head.

"Maybe we shouldn't have moved her," Alma persisted behind him.

Wes swore again and tackled the stairs three treads to a bound.

"I've always heard you aren't supposed to move accident victims. Maybe we made a mistake. Maybe she has internal injuries. Maybe we should have—"

"Should have what, dammit?" Wes roared, reaching the top of the stairs and the end of his patience simultaneously. He halted abruptly outside his bedroom door and jerked his head around to glare at his simpering companion. "And just what did you expect me to do, Alma? Stretch her out on the blazing hot asphalt and wait an hour, maybe two for an ambulance to get here from Rayville or Monroe?"

Alma opened her mouth to reply, but Wes shot her a jaw-snapping look. Dark eyes glittering with silent menace, he mentally dared her to utter another word, just one more syllable that gave too clear a voice to the sound of his own nagging fears.

"Get downstairs and call Doc Hayes," he ordered through tightly clenched teeth.

"Yes...oh, yes, of course!" Alma wheeled and scampered away in a frenzy. Wes hissed a sigh of relief.

But his relief was short-lived as he entered the room. *Internal injuries.* He couldn't shake the fearful thought, and cold chills raked down his spine at the distinct possibility. Why hadn't he considered it before now?

With infinite care, he carried Rebecca across the carpeted floor and eased her down onto his bed. She looked so pale, he thought, her smooth, translucent features appearing almost bloodless against the dark backdrop of the quilted indigo spread. What if Alma were right? He roughed a trembling hand through his sweat-drenched hair. What if it was a mistake? What if he had done her more harm than good by bringing her here with him?

Guilt sank ragged talons deep inside his chest. Mistakes. Wes stepped back from the bed and rammed his fist into the pockets of his mud-encrusted jeans. Making mistakes, he thought, was one of the things he seemed to do best. Second only to his consummate skill at inflicting pain on the people around him. However unintentional, he seemed to have a knack for creating misery and heaping it upon those who deserved it the least.

Or—his eyes slid to Rebecca—not at all.

He didn't want to look at her, but somehow he couldn't stop. His gaze lingered on the stillness of her features, soft and unguarded in unconsciousness. With her eyes closed, the sweep of her lashes lying dark against the pallor of her cheeks, she looked so vulnerable, so innocent, so young. She looked like...

Mara.

With a vengeance only the past had the power to reap, the resemblance cut through him, suddenly, staggeringly, ripping open old wounds... spilling out old regrets.

Wes swung around and stalked to the window. *Don't do it, Garrett,* he mentally ordered, not wanting to compare the experience to anything. He didn't need to remind himself that the past was past, and dead was gone, and that Mara, too, had lain just so—still and pale before she died.

And he'd been helpless. Just as he was helpless now. He couldn't save Mara, couldn't ease her pain. And try as he had, he'd been so utterly helpless to give her the love and the happiness she'd wanted.

Wes closed his eyes, anguish pressing his lids tightly. But even as he willed it with all his strength, he couldn't close his mind to the past that had become so much a part of his life.

Mara. How could he forget the night she had come to him? How thin and pale and childlike she'd looked, standing by the window in his father's house, plucking at a loose button on the bodice of a worn gingham dress.

Her face was ashen, eyes red rimmed and tear swollen. And Wes remembered well the way her chin had quivered when finally she spoke in a voice so soft and low that, at first he'd thought—surely he'd misunderstood.

"I love you," she whispered, then ducked her head to avoid his eyes, a curtain of flaxen hair shielding one side of her face. "I think I've loved you for as long as I can remember. You don't have to marry me. I wouldn't ask for that. But I'm...I'm sick, Wes." Her hand went up to her face, and ever so discreetly, she caught a tear before it could fall. "Doc says I got something wrong in my blood. It . . . it's bad. And the truth is, I don't think I'm gonna get well."

Her confession had shocked him, and compassion, like none he had ever known, flooded every chamber of his heart. He remembered starting toward her, longing to comfort her but not knowing how, or what to say.

"Mara, honey, listen to me. Surely something can be done. There are other doctors, trained people who specialize in . . ."

"No." Her small back went suddenly ramrod straight. "I don't intend to spend what time I have left drugged out of my mind and praying for miracles. All I want—" Her voice broke and she swallowed, struggling hard for control. "I want to know what it's like, just once before I die. Please, Wes. I'm begging you. Make love to me, and I swear I'll never ask for anything more."

It was the irony to end all ironies and Wes could only stare at her, not knowing what to say. He wanted to tell her that this was all wrong, that she was upset, that she didn't realize what she was asking. He wanted to say he was flattered and that he wanted to help her, but he didn't love her and he couldn't...couldn't bring himself to take advantage of her this way. All these things he had meant to say until the very moment she turned and he saw the look on her face.

It was in her eyes. Pain. Desperation. And something else, a resemblance to Rebecca so strong he couldn't believe he'd never thought to notice it before.

Later, Wes thought, he must have gone a little crazy that night. For in that brief second, in that imperceptible blinking of time's eye, Mara became Rebecca incarnate. And suddenly it wasn't Mara, but Rebecca he saw and heard. It was Rebecca pleading, "Help me, Wes. Please, let me stay with you."

Now, turning away from the window, Wes drew a deep breath that was less than cleansing and retraced his steps across the room. At the side of the bed, he stood once more staring down at Rebecca. Her eyes were still closed, and his, shadowed with concern and a deeper, more complex emotion, seemed to move with a will of their own. He touched her gently with his gaze, lingering, as his hands had once done, on the satin-smoothness of her skin, the small, perfect rise of her breasts, the pulsating hollow in the vee of delicate bones . . . her throat . . . her chin . . . her lips. . . .

Her lips. Silent exploration skidded to a screeching halt as Wes's eyes came to rest on the tiny, reddish bruise marring the corner of her mouth. Logic tried to tell him the abrasion was a result of the accident alone. But his heart knew better. And his conscience—that maniacally relentless tyrant of his being—refused to let him forget the brutal way he'd used her, assaulting with kisses, attacking with words, deliberately wounding and hurting her less than twenty-four hours ago.

Good God, man! Wes seethed inside. *Isn't it enough to go on destroying yourself? Must you annihilate everyone else in the process?*

Raging inwardly, Wes commanded his feet to move, his eyes to pull away from the woman he'd wounded. But nothing happened. Instead he remained locked in place, gazing down with unbidden fascination at Rebecca's lips, soft, half-parted in sensual beckoning, as though awaiting a princely kiss to awaken her from the bonds of deep slumber.

And where was this stately prince? The question ironically presented itself to him at the same moment Wes's gaze relinquished control of his senses. His eyes slid from her face to the slender white hand and the ring, the ring branding her unmistakably: Property of Adam Dane.

An acid gall rose to his throat, and he swallowed back something akin—though never admittedly so—to the bitter-green taste of jealousy.

Her fingers were swelling, he told himself, as he slowly knelt down beside the bed. The ring was cutting off her circulation. He was almost sure of it. Lifting her left hand into his own, large tanned fingers gave the slightest of tugs. The ring slipped off with amazing ease and tumbled into the waiting palm that quickly closed around it.

Still kneeling, still holding onto Rebecca's hand Wes looked up and searched her face for any reaction. There was none. No frown. No groan. No sign of awareness. Only the shallow, though steady, rhythm of her breathing assured him that she was alive.

Damn, where is that doctor? With a surge of renewed panic, Wes squeezed Rebecca's hand, gently but firmly, hoping to make her stir. When she didn't respond, he began speaking to her, softly at first. But gradually his tone grew louder, harsher, and within minutes he was shouting at her in a frustrated attempt to convince himself as well as her.

"You're not going to die on me, do you hear? You're going to wake up, and you're going to get better. I won't let you leave me like this. It wouldn't work, don't you understand? Nothing's finished. Nothing's resolved. It never was. We—"

Wes clamped his jaws and clenched her ring in his fist, tighter and tighter, barely aware of the shardlike facets, gouging into the fleshy heel of his palm. He closed his eyes. His rantings were useless. And because he knew he couldn't make her understand, he hung his head between his arms and whispered more to himself than to her. "Before a thing is over, there has to be an end. Rebecca, why did we forget to say goodbye?"

THROUGH THE NEBULOUS BLACK FOG still drifting in her brain, Rebecca couldn't make out the words Wes was saying. She wasn't even sure if she were alive or dead, or lost mysteriously in some strange transcendental state halfway between dream and wakefulness.

But wherever she was, she knew Wes was with her. She'd felt his presence when he'd knelt down beside her, and just now, as he reached to gently brush a strand of hair away from the throbbing ache on her forehead. He was holding her hand and for the moment, nothing else mattered except the darkness—blissful escape. Deeper and deeper she let herself sink into the numbing folds and away from the pain she was, for now, too weak to question.

"HOW IS SHE?" Alma asked frantically, the instant Dr. Ezra Hayes poked his grizzled head out of Wes's bedroom door.

The country doctor, now semiretired, smiled indulgently and patted the woman's hands where she held them, clenched under her chin. "Oh, she's gonna be just fine, Alma. Now, you calm down an' don't look so worried."

"Are you sure, Doc?" Wes stepped toward the door, as the old man drew it shut behind him.

"Of course I am. I'm a doctor, aren't I?" Grinning, he held up his black bag as certifiable proof. "Now, let's go have some coffee and I'll tell you two worriers not to worry another half dozen times."

There were no hospitals or clinics in Hurricane Bluff, and the nearest of either were in larger, neighboring towns, thirty to fifty miles away respectively. "Doc" Hayes, as everyone called him, had left his general practice for his nearby farm, over six years ago. And, as the nearest professional, his neighbors often called upon him to treat minor mishaps, or arrange medical transport for the not-so-minor ones.

"Do you think she needs to be in a hospital?" Wes asked as he handed the doctor a steaming mug of coffee.

"No. She's got a few bruised ribs. Gonna be awfully sore for a while. I put a few strips of adhesive tape around them. Just something to give her a little support."

"But what about that place on her head?" Alma asked, her eyes wide and anxious.

Doc Hayes glanced down at the cup. "Well now, that's what we're gonna have to watch."

He didn't give them any time to panic as his tone changed subtly, and he went on to explain the likelihood of a minor concussion and his prescribed treatment. "A few days' rest should fix her up. No physical exertion. And it'd be a good idea to keep her here, with someone to look after her, for the next week or ten days. Just to make sure she gets along all right."

Wes nodded and glanced at Alma. "Done."

"Well, I guess that's about it." Smiling, Dr. Hayes set down his coffee cup and lifted his medical bag off the kitchen table. "I've left her some pain medication to augment the sedative I gave her. She'll probably sleep through the night. But I want you to check on her hourly. Her condition isn't serious, but if she should develop any other symptoms—sleepiness, nausea, disorientation—that sort of thing—I want you to tell me immediately."

"I will, Doc," Wes assured him, thankful that Rebecca's injuries weren't any more serious, and hopeful that he wouldn't have to call.

As Wes showed Dr. Hayes to the door, the man once more assured him that Rebecca would be fine, and promised he would check in on her again Monday.

When Wes turned to go back upstairs, Alma was standing at the bottom step, sniffling, eyes imploring him, a handkerchief clutched to her breast.

"Wes? What are we going to do now?" She caught hold of his sleeve as he started past her. "We've got to talk about this. I—"

"Later, Alma," he said, effectively cutting her off. Glancing anxiously toward the room at the top of the stairs, he took the steps quickly. "We'll just have to talk later."

"Later" came too soon as far as Wes was concerned. Two hours after Dr. Hayes had come and gone, Alma Whitney was still on the brink of tears.

"I don't want her to know!" she shrilled, leaning forward with a death grip on the arms of her chair.

"Well, I'd say that's about par," Wes muttered. And, not for the first time, he found himself wondering what it was about the Whitney women that kept him on the brink of madness. Uncrossing his legs, he wearily set aside the coffee he'd hoped to savor while Rebecca was still sedated and resting comfortably upstairs.

"I mean it, Wes," Alma persisted. "I don't want her to find out. You've got to promise me you won't tell her who I am."

"Alma, please!" Wes closed his eyes and rested his head back against the sofa. "We've been through this all already."

"Yes... yes, I know." She sprang to her feet and began pacing feverishly from one end of the den to the other. "But it's different now. I can't avoid her. She's here in this house! I'll be fixing her meals, taking care of her, talking to her, and—oh, no! I just can't let her know. Not now!" Alma wailed and threw her hands to her face with a soul-wrenching sob.

"Oh, for the love of heaven, woman! Don't you ever know when to let up?"

Rising to his feet, Wes stalked to the fireplace and turned his back on the source of his most incessant aggravation. For the second time today, Alma Whitney had driven him beyond all points of reasonable tolerance. Now, he gripped the mantel simply to keep his hands from finding their way around his mother-in-law's throat. Why in the name of thunder did he keep her around?

Because you're an idiot, Garrett, Wes castigated himself. *A lead-pipe sucker for any and every wide-eyed blonde with a pitiful look and woeful tale to tell.*

But even as he thought this, Wes knew it wasn't true. Alma Whitney wasn't just any blonde. And that was the whole problem. Sighing, he lowered his head and clenched his teeth to suppress the frustration and anger he always felt whenever he ran up against any situation he couldn't change or control.

"You're her mother," he muttered, as though either of them needed reminding. "Hasn't it even occurred to you that she might eventually recognize you?"

"But I... I've changed, Wes. People change in eighteen years. She was only a child then, and—"

"Don't you think I know that?" His voice was a harsh whisper as he spun to face her. "I've heard it all, and ten times already, how she didn't recognize you in town this morning. But for God's sake, Alma, don't be a fool! Everyone in Hurricane Bluff knows who you are, and it will only be a matter of time before—"

"And that's all I'm asking," she interjected quickly. "Just a little time. Oh, Wes, don't you see? I want a chance to...to get to know her, to be a friend to her, and then maybe I can make her understand. I didn't want to leave them. I was just young and weak and I...I never realized..." Sinking down on the sofa, Alma burrowed her face in her hands and gave way to a piteous round of tears.

"Oh, great. Would you stop it, now?" Feeling a frustrated mixture of helplessness and irritation, Wes rolled his eyes and reached for his handkerchief. This whole idea was so preposterous he couldn't believe he was even discussing it, much less considering it. "All right, Alma. Here. Now, just for the sake of argument let's say I was willing to go along with this harebrained scheme. What do you expect me to tell her? That here in my house is this woman named Alma...Alma Whitney in fact. What a coincidence! Don't you think she might become just the least bit suspicious? She may not know you on sight, but use your head for once, would you? You know damn well Rebecca hasn't forgotten your name."

"I know that." Alma sniffed and clutched the handkerchief in her lap. "That's why I thought...well, it sounds crazy, but it wouldn't be for very long! Oh, Wes, couldn't you just tell her I'm somebody else? You could say I'm your housekeeper and I work for you and my name is . . . uh . . . Alice or . . . Anna or . . . Oh, I don't know! Anybody!" she burst out, tears welling in her eyes again.

Wes stared at her. "Wonderful!" he muttered through his teeth. "An alias, no less. I swear, Alma, sometimes I think they ought to throw a net over you. Can't you see how impossible this is? What if she finds out who you are through someone else? Doc Hayes for instance?"

"I'll talk to him," she insisted.

"Or Son?"

"He's out of town and you know it." Her voice was growing calmer.

Wes shook his head and began to massage the tense muscles at the back of his neck. "It's not going to work, I tell you. Even if I agreed, somebody else would let it slip. It's inevitable, Alma. You ought to know that. In a town as small as this one, no one keeps secrets for long."

"Some manage," Alma muttered, then raised her eyes to met his with a subtle, knowing expression.

Wes straightened slowly, black brows knit together in a forbidding scowl. Through mutual if unspoken consent, there were at least two subjects the two of them chose never to discuss. One was Mara. The other was the portrait he kept hidden away in the tiny back room, leading off from his private studio. Until this moment, Alma had never dared to hint at her knowledge of that painting and what it symbolized, and Wes wasn't impressed with her timing now.

"You're treading on thin ice," he warned. "And right about now, I'd be real careful if I were you."

Realizing she had gone too far, Alma slid from her seat and skeetered around so that the sofa was situated between them. "I didn't mean anything, Wes. It's just that you've got to help me. This is my only chance to make things right with my daughter and I'll do anything—anything—to convince you! Please, Wes, help me and I swear I'll never ask for anything more."

For a moment he simply stood there, staring at her and listening . . . listening in near disbelief to the ultimate irony of her words. Over and over the words repeated themselves in his head. It was a different woman. Different times. But the exact message came through all the same. *Please, Wes... Help me, Wes... Please, Wes...please...* Why did he keep hearing those pleading lines, and repeating the same promises in return?

"All right, Alma," he heard himself say. "I'm gonna give you this one. But you listen and you'd better listen good! You can tell her you're Whistler's mother for all I care. But when it comes to me, you'll mind your own business and keep your mouth shut! Do you understand?"

"Yes . . . yes, of course I will," Alma nodded effusively.

"Good! Then there's just one more thing." His eyes bore into hers. "I know you and Mara talked before she died. I don't know how much she told you, but I'll tell you this: I've waited a long time to settle an old score with Rebecca. Don't try to interfere, I'm warning you, Alma. And after today, you'd better think twice before you ever try to push me into anything again."

His expression assured her that he wasn't kidding. Alma blinked and wrung together her thin hands. "No. I won't. You won't have to worry . . ."

She continued to babble, but Wes heard very little of her parting avowals. In a matter of seconds he was across the foyer and mounting the stairs to the woman in his bed.

WHERE AM I? Rebecca wasn't sure how long she'd been awake before her brain began to function again, however feebly. Her head pounded, and her eyelids felt cemented into place, too heavy to open. Something had happened; she tried to remember what, but she could recall only vague fragments of dreams... voices... faces... and one whose brooding presence had overshadowed all.

Wes. Had it all been a dream? Had she only imagined that he had been with her, calling her name, holding her hand, pressing it to his lips in the night?

Half afraid of what she would find, half afraid of what she wouldn't, Rebecca rolled her head across the pillow, and with an effort, forced her eyelids open.

And then she saw him.

His back was to her as he stood at the window, dressed in Levi's and a crumpled plaid shirt, with the sleeves rolled up and the tails hanging loose from his lean, beltless waist. The early-morning light seeped through the tousled thickness of his hair and bathed his profile in a smoky aura of pale gold.

Dazed and groggy from the sedating effects of an injection she vaguely remembered someone—a doctor?—having given her, Rebecca still wasn't sure if his presence had been real. And yet she couldn't prevent herself from whispering his name.

"Wes?" Her voice was a thick, chafing rasp in her throat, and at the sound of it she fully expected him to disappear before her eyes. But instead he turned, and her eyes widened as disbelief and a thousand other emotions rendered her helpless to do anything but watch him cross the room to her.

"Good morning, Sleeping Beauty. How was your nap?"

"I . . . I thought I'd dreamed you," she murmured, still half-convinced she was babbling to a phantom, until he smiled at her.

"Dreams, huh?" Amusement crinkled the corners of his eyes as he reached for the ladder-backed chair at the corner of the bedside table. "Well, it's nice to know someone dreams about me." Jeans stretched taut over lean muscular thighs, he straddled the seat with ease and leaned forward, forearms resting casually on the upper rung. "But now I s'pose you're gonna tell me it was a nightmare."

Sleepy black eyes gazed down at her with a ludicrous, poor-little-boy expression, and incredulously Rebecca realized he was teasing her. Teasing her! The thought streaked giddily through the befuddled gauze she called a brain, and suddenly she giggled. Was the sound really coming from her? Had she honestly forgotten the sound of her own laughter—when it wasn't strained, when it wasn't forced, when it wasn't for show . . . or cover?

"Ah, you must be feeling better." Wes's smile deepened, and without preamble, he reached out to disengage a single strand of platinum hair caught in the thick web of her lashes.

The gesture was instinctive, the contact accidental. But the moment he touched her, warm knuckles grazing the smooth flesh of her cheek, Rebecca's pulse quickened and Wes seemed unable—or unwilling—to pull his hand away.

"I like it when you laugh," he whispered almost absently and with a kind of bewildered wonderment that thickened his voice and darkened his eyes as his thumb slid to the delicate corner of her mouth.

The fragile smile that had moments before trembled on Rebecca's lips gave way to a far more vulnerable expression. Her heart thudded, her head swam in dizzy confusion, and for the life of her she couldn't remember why she was here—why he was here with her. But it didn't matter, she told herself. All that mattered was written in Wes's eyes. Slowly she lifted her hand and pressed her palm against his stubbled cheek.

The muted sound of chair legs snagging carpet, the creaking of bedsprings as the mattress sagged with a sudden addition of weight, registered only marginally in the back of her mind. All she knew was that her arms had somehow found their way around his neck, and he was holding her, hands framing her face, elbows nestled on either side of the pillow under her head. And his lips... Sweet heaven! How often had she yearned for the taste and feel of them! His lips were everywhere, teasing, taunting, arousing chills that were not chills, but tiny fires dancing along her skin.

"Rebecca." He caught her hair, breathing her name into the warm hollow of her own mouth on a ragged breath that made his voice sound strangely lost and despairing.

His hands moved to her shoulders, and she wrapped hers around his waist, feeling the wrench of hard muscles, straining against his shirt.

This is a dream...a dream, Rebecca told herself, not wanting to think. She only wanted to feel the dark fires smoldering through her, his lips on hers, her arms around him, his body pressing . . . pressing closer . . .

The room whirled and Rebecca felt as if she teetered on the very edge of an unreal abyss. Her head pounded, her sides ached, and yet she felt oblivious to the pain, as though somewhere outside her body her real self stood, condemned to watch herself caught up in a reenactment of the most costly mistake she had ever made.

"Oh God, no!" she choked. Panic gripped her, and suddenly she was fighting, pushing him away and gasping for breath.

Stunned by the violence of her reaction, Wes struggled to restrain her flailing arm. "Rebecca, what is it? Are you hurt? Tell me!"

The alarm in his voice emphasized his contrite and genuine concern. But for Rebecca, the very heat of his touch seemed to act as a catalyst, searing away the final foggy vapors that had until now distorted her ability to think.

Reason rushed back, rationality raged on, and in a flash Rebecca remembered. Son. The accident. Wes's threat to keep her in town. And of course, how dare she forget his perverse need to punish her, branding her with words and a brush of his lips as a woman who couldn't say no.

Well she would show Mr. Wesley Garrett! Damn him! If it killed her, she vowed, she would teach him every nuance of negation.

"Let me go!" she cried, jerking her wrists from his grasp and shoving at his chest. "This is all your doing, isn't it? You sent Son away! And you brought me here. Well, I won't stay. Do you hear me?" Eyes flashing hot with anger and contempt, Rebecca rose up on her elbow and tried to swing her legs off the side of the bed. "You can't keep me here. I'll leave. I'll . . . uh!"

Rebecca fell back with a half sob as her struggles to pull herself up drew a whiplash of pain through her rib cage. Automatically she gripped her sides, but the second her hands reached the spot, sirens of panic obliterated the pain in her head. Taped! Her ribs were taped, and her clothes had been removed, leaving her completely nude except for a man's white shirt. Wes's shirt. Had he undressed her?

Frantic thoughts and questions ran rampant through her mind. What had made him kiss her just now? Had she responded to him, earlier maybe, while her resistance was down and her mind was too muddled to protest? She searched her brain, but couldn't remember if she had made a fool of herself already.

Heart pounding, Rebecca clutched the shirt to her throat, her eyes glaring accusingly at Wes.

For a moment he looked almost puzzled, and then as his eyes seemed to take in the entire picture, he gave a short, disgusted laugh and pushed himself up from the bed.

"Don't worry," he drawled, glowering down at her disdainfully. "I didn't take your clothes off if that's what you're so fired up about. Doc Hayes took care of that, and believe it or not . . ." His narrowed eyes flickered over her impersonally and unimpressed. "The ol' codger wasn't even breathing hard when he left."

Indignation and anger drove a hot rush of blood to Rebecca's face, stinging her cheeks. "Crudeness doesn't become you, Wes," she muttered. "Maybe you should try something that comes more naturally like . . . brutality."

His face whitened, nostrils flared slightly in the tensing of his jaw. "Maybe I will," he grated out. "And meanwhile maybe you should try something that doesn't come naturally. Like behaving like a woman instead of a spoiled child, for a change."

He took a step toward her and their eyes collided in a war of wills, on a battlefront of barely suppressed fury.

Stay out of my life. Silver eyes flashed.

Get out of my system. Black eyes returned.

I can't stand you. She swore to him silently.

I don't need you. He vowed emphatically.

"I want my clothes," Rebecca demanded, severing the lines of their silent communication.

"Why? You aren't going anywhere."

His voice was soft, but his tone implacable, and Rebecca sensed the undercurrent of mockery in his words. Grimacing, she forced herself to sit up. "That's what you think." She slid her feet to the floor.

When she tried to stand her legs were too weak to hold her, and her head reeled sickeningly. Cold sweat breaking out on her forehead, Rebecca collapsed back on the bed, clutching the sheet to her breasts.

"See what I mean?" Wes's tone was harsh, but his touch amazingly gentle as he bent to draw the trailing bedcovers over her bare feet and legs. His fingers brushed the soft flesh of her thigh and, for a split second he hesitated, unspoken words frozen on an indrawn breath.

Rebecca's throat went dry. What was he going to do? Careful to keep her eyes averted, she was all too aware of his imposing nearness, the shadow of his tall body falling ominously across the bed and over her face. Her own breath disintegrated in the shallow constriction of her lungs. And then another question leaped into her thoughts, presenting itself with far more disturbing implications: what did she want him to do?

Shrinking from the inner pressure to delve for deeper answers, Rebecca was relieved when Wes finally straightened. Wheeling around without a backward glance, he stalked to the window and stood looking outside.

Rebecca licked her suddenly parched lips, and eased back against the pillows. Eyes squinting against the now bright sunlight, she watched ripples of tension crawl through the muscles across his shoulders and told herself her discomfort was merely a side effect from the medication. But the sedative she had received hours before could hardly account for the unexpected hammering of her heart, or the tingling sensations that still lingered where Wes's fingers had grazed her bare flesh.

"You can't leave," Wes said flatly without turning around. "Your ribs took a pretty good licking, and that knot on your head isn't exactly the equivalent of a hangnail. Doc says you've got a mild concussion. Nothing too serious, but it could be if you don't follow his instructions."

Concussion! Rebecca stared at the back of Wes's dark head. "And . . . and just what are his instructions?" she asked, alarmed.

"Bed rest. No exertion. And he doesn't want you moved for a week at least. Maybe . . . several."

Horrified, Rebecca's mouth dropped open. "Several weeks?" she echoed. "Why, I can't stay here that long. I have things to do. An estate to settle. A job to get back to. And . . . and . . . a—"

"And a lover, Rebecca? Say it!"

The violence in his voice as he swung around to face her stripped the air from Rebecca's lungs. His back was to the window and, with the yellow light streaming in behind him, she couldn't see the expression on his face. But then...she didn't have to. Wes's tone, his stance, even the shadows that cloaked his features in brooding obscurity told her everything she needed to know. Accusation and condemnation struck a curious balance on the male scales called double standards.

Rebecca glared at him, anger throbbing at her temples, and in that moment she came very close to blurting out the truth. One part of her longed to shout at him that Adam Dane was not her lover, that politics alone was his soul-consuming passion. And—more important—that she wanted it that way.

But stubborn pride held her silent. The moment stretched to a nerve-rending end, and in the following seconds Wes seemed to have lost interest in the matter. Ignoring her stiff expression, he stepped out of the shadows and began striding toward her, unzipping his jeans and tucking his shirttails inside with a casual indifference that grated on every cell in her body. Willfully she trained her gaze on the jutting angle of his jaw, and dared her eyes to stray one inch below the stubbled whiskers on his chin. But through her peripheral vision, Rebecca caught the deft movements of his hands, and her stomach did a funny soft-shoe, as he jerked up the zipper and slicked a quick palm down the taut, denim front of his fly.

"I took the liberty of having your car towed to a garage in Monroe," he announced without preamble, and something in his voice drew Rebecca's eyes to his.

"It's not totaled," he continued, "but the parts have to be ordered, and it's probably gonna take a while. Not many people sport a Mercedes around here. Not very practical, if you know what I mean, for hauling hay... or manure."

The last word he stressed with a mocking twist of his mouth, and suddenly Rebecca had the feeling he was sneering at her. *Let it go,* an inner voice warned. But the nagging ache in her head left her blind to caution, and for some reason—perhaps to cover the hectic seesaw of emotion his nearness created inside her—she couldn't seem to control her need to spite him back.

"What's the matter, Wes?" She deliberately feigned an innocent tone. "Don't you approve of the car I drive?"

Something like surprise flickered briefly across his face before his features turned hard, his eyes narrowed. "Approve?" His brows lifted. "I believe you've already informed me that it isn't my concern to approve or disapprove of anything you do. But since you asked..." His voice lowered a husky decibel. "Let's just say it's not the car I find... unappealing. It's the way you chose to get it."

"What?" Rebecca sat straight up, forgetting her pain, forgetting her dizziness, and wishing for all the world that he was near enough for her to slap his self-righteous face. "You mean you think that I... that Adam... Why you sanctimonious—"

Rebecca couldn't make herself finish. Choking on rage and wounded pride, she forced herself to take deep, even breaths. She fought for calm, and prayed her eyes wouldn't betray the pain of his hurtful insinuations. She told herself she didn't care. It didn't matter what Wes Garrett thought of her, but even as she denied that his opinion was important, she knew she was lying to herself. It did matter. It mattered a great deal.

With a performance worthy of an Academy Award, Rebecca lifted her chin and forced her eyes to look straight into his.

"You think you have it all figured out, don't you?" Her voice was soft, trembling, but strengthened with an inherent sense of dignity. "A little nobody from a nowhere town could only make a living one way, right? Well, you're wrong, Wes. That car belongs to me. I bought it and I paid for it with hard-earned cash...no strings attached. It wasn't a gift, nor was it taken out 'in trade' as they say. I may be a lot of things—" she paused to swallow, to still her quivering lips, then finished in a whisper "—but I'm not for sale."

She met his gaze unflinchingly, but there was something in her face. Something old and terrible that tore at Wes's conscience and drew blood from the very core of his heart. He wanted to tell her he was sorry, but the words got stuck in his throat. He wanted to tell her that he knew she wasn't "for sale," and that he didn't give a damn if she was sleeping with Adam Dane. But how could he say those things? He'd rather cut out his tongue than admit that the thought of another man with her...holding her...touching her, filled him with a blazing fury he didn't understand himself.

Irritably Wes riffled his fingers through his hair. "I didn't mean that remark the way it sounded." His voice sounded rougher, sharper than he'd intended, but it was the closest he could manage toward an apology. "And I didn't bring you here for a sparring match, either. You were hurt, and all I could think of was getting you to safety. Truth is, I don't like this arrangement any more than you do. But as long as you're here, we may as well try to be civil to each other."

Rebecca shrugged, but her gesture caused an unexpected spear of pain along her ribs. With a soblike groan, she sank back onto the pillows, biting her lip to keep from whimpering.

Wes frowned, but resisted the impulse to help her, knowing that if he got too close, if he touched her again, it would only lead to another argument...or something even more volatile. Something neither one of them was in any condition to deal with now.

Using as few muscles as possible, Rebecca finally settled back into a halfway comfortable position. At least she could bear the pain, if she didn't chance a move. "I suppose I should thank you," she murmured then, "for rescuing me, I mean. After all, if it weren't for you, I wouldn't even be here—so to speak."

Wes tensed and Rebecca knew he had recognized her double entendre, and she caught the wicked, black glint of his eyes.

"No problem." He matched her sarcasm with a chilling tone of his own. "Coming to the rescue is one of my favorite things."

"And women in distress is your specialty, I suppose. Or should I make that...distressing women?"

Wes clenched his jaw. Rebecca knew she was pushing him, and yet she felt so defenseless. Words were her only weapons against her frustration, against her inability to control her own situation.

"I don't like this arrangement." His blunt statement kept drifting back to her, reminding her of a

similar sentiment her grandfather had expressed years ago. And for the first time in years Rebecca felt condemned, utterly and unwillingly dependent on the mercy of someone else—a man who resented and despised her as much as, if not more than, her grandfather ever had.

No, she thought. She wouldn't have it. Somehow there had to be a way to get out of here, even if she had to call Adam. Adam! Yes—that was it! That was just what she would do. She would call Adam and tell him what had happened and where she was, and he would send someone to . . . to "handle" it!

"I need to use the phone," Rebecca blurted out suddenly.

"Oh?" Wes had been watching the play of emotion on her face and stood now with his back to the flat of the door, arms folded and ankles crossed. "Sorry," he said, without sounding as if he truly was. "The phones are all downstairs." He didn't bother to add that every room, including this one, was equipped with a plug-in jack and the three extensions could be, and often were, relocated at will. "But if you'd like me to make the call for you . . ."

"Never mind," she said tightly. "I'll wait."

As if he knew exactly whom she'd meant to call, Wes flashed her a satisfied grin. "Suit yourself." He lifted one shoulder and pulled his back away from the door. "In the meantime, I'll have Al—" He caught himself in the nick of time before he uttered her mother's name and strangled back the oath that rushed to the tip of his tongue. "In the meantime," he repeated, "I'll have my housekeeper check in on you. If you need anything, just call. But don't go gettin' any silly ideas about sneaking downstairs. The last thing I need is for you to fall down and break your neck...on top of everything else."

Rebecca gave him a frosty look. "Really, Wes. Your concern is overwhelming. But since you've already made it clear that...how did you phrase it? Oh, yes. That you 'don't like this arrangement any more than I,' why not simply drive me back to my grandfather's farm? I may have a few lumps and bruises, but I'm perfectly capable of taking care of myself. And besides, I'm sure it would be easier on us both if we weren't forced to share such close confines."

"Easier for you maybe, but not for me."

Rebecca's eyes widened. "What is that supposed to mean?"

"It means I promised the doctor I'd keep you in bed. And I intend to..." His gaze dropped meaningfully to the valley between her breast, where gentle curves were revealed above the open buttons on the shirt. "One way or the other."

Clutching the covers to her throat, Rebecca looked at him contemptuously. If anything this only seemed to amuse him.

"Besides," he drawled, his gaze trailing lazily up the slim column of her throat. "I've got a few questions for you, remember? And like I told you," he said, as his eyes came to rest on hers, "before you leave this time, lady, I'll have all my answers, as well."

CHAPTER FIVE

FOR REBECCA, the remainder of the weekend passed in something of a blur, as though someone held her trapped under water. Dr. Hayes had left her pain medication, chalky white tablets that made her drowsy and half sick to boot. She took them anyway. It was cowardly perhaps, preferring nausea to pain, sleep to insomnia. Wes had been right: she wasn't going anywhere soon.

The thought rankled and so did her bitter assumption that as long as she was stranded here, Wes would, no doubt, take full advantage of every opportunity to harass her. To her surprise, however, she saw very little of him after that first morning, when she'd awakened to find herself drugged and half-naked in his bed.

She'd encountered him only briefly Sunday morning when he'd brought her clothes and suitcases from her grandfather's house, and again that afternoon when he'd come in to collect a few of his own things, moving them into the guest room down the hall. Conversation had been minimal and for the time being at least, he seemed content to avoid her.

She should have been relieved, Rebecca reflected. But curiously, she found herself growing tense and expectant, annoyed by the feeling that he was only waiting her out, biding his time for the answers he wanted—answers she was determined he would never hear from her.

By the time Monday rolled around, Rebecca was beginning to recover from the initial shock of her accident. And, as her strength returned, so did her self-possession. Realizing she had let her emotions get the better of her, she became more determined than ever to exercise maximum control. She was stuck here. She had to face it. But surely she was strong enough to withstand a few days, even a week under the same roof with Wes Garrett.

Let him threaten all he wants to, she thought mutinously. He couldn't force her to tell him what she didn't want him to know. And he couldn't hurt her unless she allowed it.

At least they weren't alone in the big house together. And if her cloudy predicament held any glimmer of a silver lining, Rebecca decided it shone in the form of the woman she had come to know as Anna. Wes's housekeeper was bone thin and frowsy and scatterbrained as they come. But it was difficult not to like her; she seemed so anxious to please. And though Rebecca had never taken readily to the company of strangers, there was something about this woman—a faint air of familiarity that seemed to stir some responsive chord inside her. She had noticed it almost from the very instant they met.

"Are you sure we've never met before?" Rebecca inquired for the second or third time.

It was late Monday afternoon. The woman, who was in reality Alma, had just finished helping Rebecca shampoo her hair. They were back in the bedroom now, and Rebecca, seated on a low stool before the dresser, studied the mirrored image of the woman who stood behind her, gently brushing the wet tangles from her hair.

"No," Alma squeaked, straining against a lump of mendacity in her throat. Rebecca had been at Windspear only three days now, but already Alma could feel a relationship beginning to form. Today, they were starting a new week, and now that her daughter was going to be here for at least that much longer, Alma had decided that the present wasn't the right time to give herself away.

She drew a deep breath and tried to sound nonchalant as she added, "I told you before, you just must have a good memory for faces. I didn't think you even looked at me that day in town before your accident. And even then, you couldn't say we actually met."

"No, I guess not," Rebecca said, and glanced away. She didn't really want to recall any detail of that particular day, especially her conversation with Vicky Lynn. "Well...I am sorry about bumping into you like that. I'm not usually so clumsy, and hopefully, not generally so inconsiderate. But I guess I wasn't doing a very good job of watching where I was going."

"Now, don't you go apologizing again," Alma fussed. "I told you there was no harm done."

"But your package?" Rebecca raised her eyes to the mirror again. "I didn't even stop to ask if anything had been broken."

"Well you needn't worry." The woman gave Rebecca a light, rather hesitant little pat. "It was just a new robe. And you can't break a silly bathrobe, now can you? You see," she pursed her lips and lowered her voice as if it were a secret, "my old one had gotten kinda worn and faded and... well, I guess it was getting to look pretty bad. Anyways, Wes—I mean,

Mr. Garrett—gave me some money and insisted that I go on over to Mrs. Thompson's dress shop and buy myself another one while we were in town. 'And for heaven sakes, Anna,' he says to me, 'get something decent this time.' My old robe was sort of satinlike with this furry stuff on the neck? But Mr. Garrett never liked it and didn't want me wearing it. He said it looked cheap, and made me look like a two-bit—"

"Anna!" Rebecca whirled around, causing Alma to catch her breath. "You mean he actually said that? Oh, the very nerve of him! How could you let him say such an awful thing to you?"

"Awful?" Alma frowned, her expression genuinely puzzled. "Why, what do you mean? Mr. Garrett would never say anything awful to me. He's a good man, and he likes me and would never deliberately hurt me. Oh, I know he gets impatient—I do go on sometimes—but he always looks after me, and he never stays cross with me for long."

Rebecca stared at the older woman. Her fawn-brown eyes seemed too large for her thin face, and her features held an odd look that went beyond her momentary expression. There was an innocence about her, a certain naïveté that seemed so incongruous with the miles of experience and lines of age on her face.

Who did this woman remind her of? Stymied, Rebecca shook her head and forced her attention back to their conversation.

"Anna, listen to me," she said carefully. "I understand that you might have a certain . . . respect for Mr. Garrett's opinion. But don't you realize he's insulted you? He has no right to tell you what you can or can't wear. He may be your employer, but he's not your judge."

"Oh, but don't you see?" Alma interjected quickly. "He's teaching me to be a lady. Mr. Garrett puts great store in a woman behaving like a lady. And I don't have anybody else to help me. My parents are dead now, and my husband . . . well, he always was the driftin' sort, never was much count. But Mr. Garrett, now . . . there's a man with a heart. I came to him with nothing and he took me in and for that I'll always be beholdin' to him."

"But that doesn't mean you can't stand up to him! No man has the right to tell a woman how she should live!" It was the truth, but nonetheless, Rebecca was shocked at her own outburst. What was happening to her discipline, her prided self-control? And why did she have the feeling that her words had been spoken not so much for this woman's sake, but rather, in self-defense?

Sighing, Alma laid down the hairbrush and went to stand by the open French doors where a warm breeze wafted in from the small enclosed balcony. The force of it billowed the thin sheers that kept the mosquitoes out.

"You don't like him very much, do you?"

Her voice was soft, the question accusatory, and Rebecca was suddenly sorry they had entered into this topic of conversation.

Turning back to the dresser, she glanced down at the polished surface and began running her fingers slowly back and forth. "No," she answered finally. "I don't suppose I do. But then, I've had a long time to consider all my reasons for disliking him."

A moment of silence passed between them, and then Alma said, "You know, Rebecca, I think you're a lot like your grandfather was. He, too, found it difficult to forgive."

Forgetting her injuries, Rebecca lifted her head too quickly, and the room spun with her sudden move. "You...you knew my grandfather?" She turned to stare at Alma's back.

Alma's spine went rigid, and then she began to shake. Oh now, she had gone and done it! Whenever was she going to learn to think before she spoke? "N...no. No, not really," she stammered guiltily over the lie. Then, seeking to create a diversion, she grappled for a moment with the curtains and reached to close the French doors. "I'll swan! It's no wonder this big, ol' house never gets cool. With the hot air blowing in and the cold air blowing out, that central unit's gonna conk out one of these days. And then we're all gonna bake to a crisp!"

"But, you said..." Rebecca stood up, refusing to be put off. "If you weren't acquainted with my grandfather, then how would you know—"

"Mr. Garrett has told me a few things, that's all," Anna said sharply. "It was a dumb thing to say. I shouldn't have interfered."

Rebecca wasn't so sure the woman was telling the whole truth, but then why would she lie? What did the housekeeper have to gain or lose? Unless she was trying to hide something...or to protect someone. How much had Wes told Anna...about Mara? About herself?

Cautiously Rebecca approached the bed and sank down on its edge. "Well, I guess if Mr. Garrett went so far as to tell you about my grandfather, then he must have told you some other things, too. I suppose you know he was married to my sister?"

Alma hurried away from the windows and went to collect the brush and comb from the dresser. "Yes, I know who you are," she replied as if short of breath. "And I knew your sister, too. I . . . I came to work for Mr. Garrett, the first time, when Mara was ill."

"Well, then maybe you can understand why I'm not overly fond of your employer."

Grooming paraphernalia clutched to her breast, Alma turned, frowning in confusion. "Why? Because he married your sister?"

"No. Not exactly." Rebecca wasn't sure where her words were leading, or why her heart had suddenly kicked into high gear. All she knew was that something inside her clamored for release, and if she didn't let it out, she would explode. "I think he hates me, Anna." The words tumbled from her lips. "He hates me because of Mara. Because I didn't come home when she was sick. But I couldn't, that's all. There were some things...some things that...happened and I . . . I had to stay away. But Wes doesn't understand. He loved her, don't you see? And now he wants to punish me—punish me for her. I think he blames me, Anna. Deep down, I think he holds me responsible because Mara died, and I . . . kept on living."

She was breathless and trembling by the time she finished, and only then did Rebecca realize there were tears wetting her cheeks. Her throat was aching, constricted with emotion, and she could hardly believe she'd revealed so much of herself to this woman, this stranger, who was staring at her now as if she had lost her mind.

"Oh, my God." Rebecca brought up her hands to cover her burning face. "I can't believe what I just said. This bump on my head must have really scrambled my brains. You probably think this all sounds pretty crazy, huh?"

"No. It doesn't sound crazy," Alma answered. "In fact it sounds only too familiar."

Allowing her hands to slide from her face, Rebecca lifted her head to look up at Alma. The woman looked dazed, her eyes fixed and her face drained of its color, as if in a trance. Rebecca caught her breath. "Anna? What is it?"

She reached out and touched her arm. Alma's gaze met hers. Rebecca saw the troubled light in the woman's eyes, and she had the oddest impression that the housekeeper was holding back something she wanted to say, something she couldn't bring herself to verbalize.

"Anna?" Rebecca prodded again gently, and this time the sound of her voice seemed to penetrate the woman's thoughts.

As if coming out of deep sleep, Alma's eyes began to widen, and suddenly she shook her head. "I have to go," she announced abruptly. "Supper. It's almost time to start supper." Whirling around in a dither, she dumped the brush and comb back on the dresser. "Supper will be late. I have to hurry." She spun around and nearly ran from the room, leaving Rebecca staring after her in stunned confusion. What had this strange creature been trying to tell her?

SUPPER WAS FRIED CHICKEN, black-eyed peas and turnip greens. And at any other time Rebecca's mouth would have watered with the sheer anticipation of reacquainting her taste buds with the long-missed and strictly Southern delicacies.

But when Alma brought the tray up to her room, electing not to sit and visit as she usually did, Rebecca found that eating alone suddenly held no appeal for her.

Confinement was beginning to wear her nerves thin, and she couldn't seem to shake the memory of her strange conversation with the housekeeper that afternoon. She remembered how Anna had defended Wes and the peculiar way she'd acted when Rebecca had foolishly poured out her heart.

Still, Rebecca wasn't sorry she had opened up to the woman. Before she had confessed those things aloud, they had been little more than fragmented impressions, subconscious inklings that were not yet full-blown thoughts. Only after she'd put her feelings into words did all the vague pieces seem to come together and make sense. The fates had made a mistake, in Wes's mind at least. And he must have said as much somewhere along the way. What else could explain his housekeeper's strange reply?

"He hates me because I lived. Does that sound crazy?"

"No. It sounds only too familiar."

THE NIGHT WAS UNUSUALLY HOT, and Rebecca couldn't sleep. It seemed to her that she'd tossed and turned for hours, fighting her clinging nightgown and sheets that stuck uncomfortably to her heat-dampened flesh. Giving up at last, she crawled out of bed and went to dash cold water on her face and arms. But the chilling relief was momentary at best, and more than eye-opening at worst. She was wide awake, and thoughts of leaping into another battle with the bed-covers made her groan with renewed frustration.

Convinced she couldn't endure another second cooped up in her room, she reached for the light cotton wrapper at the foot of her bed, but then, almost vindictively tossing it aside, she snatched her satin robe from the closet.

The house was dark and silent. With only the ticking sound of the grandfather clock in the foyer to keep her company, Rebecca, knees still weak and more than a little shaky, cautiously made her way downstairs. She held to the banister, feeling her way as she went and relishing the coolness that seeped up into her palm at the touch of the sleek cherrywood handrail.

It occurred to her then that she hadn't even seen the rest of the house except for a small portion of the upstairs. At least not since Wes's renovations. A sliver of resentment quivered up her spine at the detestable knowledge that Windspear belonged to him. Tomorrow, she promised herself, as her bare feet touched down on the cool marble floor. Tomorrow she would see it all and decide for herself if his restorations had remained true to the mansion's former stately grace and original old-world charm.

Following the dim moonlit path afforded by the slender sidelights that framed the carved oak door, Rebecca crossed the foyer and turned the key that unlocked the dead bolt.

Outside the moon was full, and the night was alive with the droning melodies of tree frogs and crickets and an occasional bass vibrato from a lone bullfrog.

Pearl satin glowed like silver in the night as Rebecca tightened the sash on her ankle-length robe and sat down on the porch steps, lapping the fabric over her knees. She hadn't bothered to tie back her hair, but allowed it to hang, sleek and heavy, long past her shoulders. A gentle breeze ruffled the ends from time to time, and teased her nose with the thick, sweet scents of wild jasmine and honeysuckle and muscadine, riping on the vine.

So many memories, Rebecca thought, as she circled her arms about her knees and drew them tightly against her. So many things that could have been different, if only she had stayed, if only she had tried to change things, if only she hadn't been so terribly afraid... of needing... of loving... of losing.

Relinquishing a dejected sigh, she propped her chin on the crest of her knees and stared out over the dewy, moonlit grounds, the moss-draped oaks and towering magnolia trees.

Strange, she thought, she had seen sprawling estates and mansions in California that seemed almost overpowering, imposing and grand beyond anything she might have only imagined. But how quickly she had learned that ostentatious surroundings were no panacea either for spirit or mind!

But Windspear was different, she thought. Windspear was an island solace in a world gone dark and cold, drawn inward on itself. Windspear was still a wonderland, an enchanted garden created for a fairy or a princess... or a little girl who needed to pretend and dream there were such things, in order to survive in the real world.

Rebecca smiled ruefully. Perhaps her Southern roots ran deeper than she realized. She had seen the West Coast with its crystal palaces and its lure of the sun and the sea. And still she had found no other place on earth that could rival the beauty or the sensual sense of mystery that crouched, like living things in the shadows along the Louisiana bayou—when the moon was full and the jasmines were in bloom.

How would her life have been different, she wondered now, had fate offered her the chance to live and love at Windspear forever?

FROM A DISTANCE, Wes thought, she looked like some mythical goddess of the moon. Or a sea nymph, clothed in the elusive shimmering white of a cresting wave.

What was she thinking? he wondered, leaning his back against the trunk of an ancient oak. Was she thinking of Adam Dane? Were her thoughts as far away as her very presence seemed to be? Remote and unattainable like a dream, like a wish . . . like a sweet, poignant memory a man could hold in his mind, but never in his hands.

Rebecca.

He'd told himself that he hated her, and yet in truth he knew what he hated was wanting her. Wanting her until it hurt. Wanting her until he felt—God! he could not stand another day of keeping his distance, of thinking of her until he thought he would go mad, insane. Sweet mercy, why did she haunt him? And why her? Why only always her?

With a faintly trembling hand and a lingering trace of old habit, Wes reached toward his pocket to locate a pack of cigarettes. It wasn't until the flat of his palm grazed the bare mound of his chest, still damp from a recent shower, that he remembered he hadn't bothered to put on another shirt. Wes shook his head. Old habits died hard, he guessed. And, with the hint of a faintly cynical smile twisting his lips, he wondered if he'd ever stop reaching for what he wanted but didn't need.

His gaze drifted back to Rebecca. And then, with only empty longing to fill his restless aching, he slid his hands into his jeans pockets and slipped out from the shadow of the trees.

Rebecca closed her eyes and turned her face toward the sky. "Make a wish," she could almost hear Mara say. Years ago on many clear, sultry nights so much like this one, when the stars were out and it was too hot to sleep, the two of them used to sit for hours on their grandfather's front porch, watching and waiting for a shooting star to streak its fiery path across the sky. "Make a wish—quick!" Mara would exclaim. Rebecca's reply had always been the same.

"Wishing for things won't make them come true. But if I had one wish, it would be to leave this farm. To run far away and find a rich man who would fall in love with me and want to marry me, but who would never expect me to love him in return."

"But Rebecca, you can't mean that!" Mara had been aghast. "Why ever would you want to marry someone you didn't love?"

Rebecca's gaze lifted to her sister's, and even then her young eyes had held that peculiar antiquity of the world-weary, although she was only a child of ten.

"Because loving is hurting, any way you look at it. I loved Mama, and she just ran away. And Papa? Well, don't matter what I do, can't seem to make him like me much. He thinks I'm like her, all takin' and no givin'. And maybe he's right, 'cause I've made up my mind. I'm never gonna love anybody again. Then it won't hurt so bad when the next one walks out—or stays for duty's sake."

A warm breeze swept her face, and coming back to the present, Rebecca sighed and opened her eyes. She thought of Adam and remembered, now that her brain had finally begun to function free of pain or medication, that she needed to call and let him know where she was. That was something else she would do tomorrow, she decided. And yet, she couldn't help wondering why the prospect of talking to Adam brought her no hint of comfort. Only a deep uneasiness in the pit of her stomach, and a vaguely hollow sense of anxiety that spread like glacial waters through her heart.

Rebecca shivered and pulled her knees closer.

"Well, Mr. Moon." A sad smile crooking her lips, she stared up at the bright, opal ball. "Guess I got my wish after all, didn't I? But somehow it isn't turning out the way I thought it would."

"Maybe that's the trouble with wishing for the moon."

Rebecca jumped up and whirled around in surprise to find Wes casually perched on the wooden railing near the side entrance to the porch. His back was to a whitewashed pillar, one booted foot on the floor for support. And she would have had to have been blind not to notice he was minus one shirt.

A heated rush of blood soared to her face and her stomach drew into a tight, jittery knot. But Rebecca tried to appear calm. She forced her chin up a fraction of an inch and the hand that combed back her hair scarcely shook as she tucked a tendril behind her ear. "What makes you think I was wishing for the moon?" Her tone was a little breathless for all her efforts.

Wes laughed softly. "Why not?" he asked, his voice husky and low like a lover's midnight endearment. "Everyone else does."

Rebecca's pulse pounded in her throat, and she couldn't help wondering what he was up to, as he slipped down from the railing, crossing the porch with the soundless ease of a prowling cat.

"Wishing for the moon is sort of like reaching for the brass ring," he murmured, as he sank down on the step beside and stretched his long legs out next to hers. "We all do it, because there's nothing we want more than the things we think we can't have. Until we get them," he added cryptically, "and then we don't want them anymore."

His body angled toward hers as he propped himself back on one elbow and cocked his head to the side. Moonlight struck the polished onyx of his eyes, and they came alive, glittering like tiny slivers of cut glass. A faintly mocking smile tilted the corners of his lips, and she found herself recalling the way he'd kissed her that first time; gently, hesitantly. She caught herself leaning toward him and saw his eyes narrow.

Oh, Lord! What was she doing? Rebecca jerked her head away and was glad for the darkness that hid the flush of humiliation on her face.

"Well, maybe you wish for things and then don't want them anymore. But that isn't the way it is with me."

"Isn't it?" Wes murmured. "Then maybe I heard you wrong, when you were talking to your friend in the sky just now," he challenged.

He paused for a moment and then shifted his weight, lazily, nonchalantly, half lying on the steps. His body was twisted at the waist so that his hard-muscled thigh pressed dangerously against the soft, upper swell of her hips.

Palms growing sticky with tension, Rebecca clamped her hands together and restrained her impulse to jump up and run. "Maybe you did hear wrong. I don't know what you heard. You shouldn't have been eavesdropping in the first place."

"You're right. I shouldn't have been eavesdropping. But since this is *my* front porch, and I wanted to sit on it, I don't think that constitutes an invasion of your privacy."

His warm breath stirred the hair at her temple, and Rebecca couldn't be sure if the tumultuous emotions that rocked her insides resulted from the mocking drawl of his tone, or from her own realization that he was so dangerously near. In either case, she wasn't taking any chances. Rising to her feet, she secured the sash on her robe.

"My mistake. Certainly, you have every right to do... whatever on your own front porch. So, if you'll excuse me, I think I'll go and leave you to it. Good night." She clipped the words and gave him a smile that was patently insincere.

With a swing of her head, Rebecca turned to start back into the house, but Wes stood up, catching hold of her arm and halting her steps before she ever neared the door.

"I'm sorry, but you can't go in yet. We seem to have a tiny problem here."

His grip though firm was quite painless, and yet Rebecca, well acquainted with the uncertainty of his temper, didn't trust him one single bit. Lifting her chin to meet his gaze, she narrowed her eyes cautiously.

"What problem?" She shivered as she posed the question.

Night-black eyes, sparkling with diamond glimmers of starlight, delved into hers with a lazy daring that sharply disrupted the normal rhythm of her breath. "You haven't paid up," he answered simply. And then, very slowly, he placed his free hand at the side of her waist, gently coaxing her around to face him. "You've heard of toll bridges and turnpikes with pay booths? Well, this is what we call a toll porch."

Rebecca's heart thumped in her throat, but the spell in his eyes held her still as a mesmerist's subject.

"You're at my booth," he drawled, thick and lazy, the sound of his voice drifting to her ears and seeping all through her, like a warm, dark steam, leaving her languid and limp. "So, now, you have to pay, and I have to collect. What do you think might be a fair sum?"

His eyes lowered to the silky satin of her robe at the point where it crossed to cover her breasts. As his gaze touched her, Rebecca had an insane urge to reach down and rub furiously at the spot, as if she feared she might be literally scorched by the smoldering heat in his eyes.

But she didn't do that. Instead she murmured, "I don't know," noting only on some fleeting frequency of thought, that her own voice carried a thready quality of somnolency. "What is the customary charge?"

Wes shifted his weight, brushing her thighs with his, and until that moment, Rebecca thought she had done an admirable job of practically ignoring the fact that he wasn't fully dressed. Not once, since her initial glance and instant registering of the sight of firm pectorals underlying taut, bronze skin, had she allowed her eyes to dip one whit below the strong jut of his chin. Not one time had she let her gaze wander to the narrow path of black hair, which she knew trailed in a provocative line from the V-shaped patch on his chest to his muscle-ridged belly... and below.

But this was tempting the devil! Rebecca clenched her fists to keep her hands from scaling, of their own volition, the powerful planes of his naked chest and arms.

"How about once around the mulberry tree, and then we'll call it even," Wes said, naming his price, to which Rebecca responded with an unsettling pang of disappointment.

The mulberry tree, marking the center of Wes's front yard wasn't really a mulberry at all, but a giant magnolia, loaded with blossoms and waxy-leafed limbs that swagged low to the ground. Bare feet treading the cool grass as she walked along beside Wes, Rebecca wondered if the recent blow to her head had affected her judgment, as well as her common sense. The doctor had instructed her to take it easy. And so, what was she going? Taking a moonlit stroll with a man whose company she found about as relaxing as Little Red Riding Hood found the wolf's.

"You might get stickers," Wes warned, glancing down at her feet, showing pale beneath her robe and against the dark mat of lawn.

"If I do, it won't be the first time," she answered dryly. She felt irritated, but mostly with herself.

Rebecca and Wes circled the yard at a leisurely pace and then started back toward the house, side by side, but each on his own, not touching.

Still, they were close enough that Rebecca heard when Wes drew a lengthy breath as if preparing for a speech. "You know, I've been meaning to ask you something."

Oh, Lord! Here it comes, she thought. Another battle of twenty questions, and all of them asking the same thing: why didn't she come home for Mara.

Rebecca picked up her steps, despite the painful strain the quicker pace put on her sore ribs. "I'm not in the mood for questions."

Wes matched her stride for stride, and then some. Stepping in front of her, he halted in order to block her way. "All right, then. We'll make it an observation. And no, don't turn away. Look at me, Rebecca." He slipped one hand to the back of her neck and forced her chin upward with his thumb. "I want you to look at me when you tell me that you're perfectly happy with your life. I want to see your eyes when you say you're looking forward to your upcoming marriage to your much too old...ah, but very rich Senator Dane."

His back was to the moon, and Rebecca couldn't see his eyes or guess at any expression he might have worn. What did it matter to him if she was happy or not!

"Of course I'm looking forward to my marriage," she declared, pulling her chin from his grasp. "Why shouldn't I be?"

"I don't know," Wes murmured, his gaze dropping to the slim, graceful hand presently working to pull her robe closed.

"Maybe I just can't understand how a woman—so obviously enamored of her fiancé—could fail to notice that she's no longer wearing his engagement ring."

What was he saying? Rebecca jerked her hand from its task and stared down at her bare fingers. The ring was gone! Why hadn't she missed it? Did it mean so very little that she hadn't even given it a thought?

Flustered and angry, Rebecca folded her arms across her chest and glared up at him. "Don't be ridiculous. Of course I knew my ring was gone," she lied. "I was going to ask your housekeeper about it, since you haven't been around to ask!"

He chuckled, a deep throaty sound that sent tingling ripples of sensation up her spine.

"Well, that's a relief," he said, dark eyes dancing in a streak of the moonlight when he tipped his head. "At least we know you're not in a coma or anything. Apparently, you have managed to notice a few things around here."

"Not the least of which is that you can't mind your own business." She started to go around him, but he caught her waist, drawing her back so quickly that she had to put one hand on his chest to steady herself. She had every intention of telling him then that she was becoming pretty fed up with his particularly physical form of conversational detainment. But Wes didn't give her a chance.

"I have your ring," he taunted softly. "And you can have it back anytime you want. All you have to do... is ask."

Rebecca stared at him. What was he trying to get her to say? Did he want her to beg him for the ring? Just because he wanted to get the better of her? Well, she wouldn't do it!

Resentment surged through her, and she turned the tables on him. "Oh, is that how it's done?" she asked in a chilling whisper. "All you have to do is ask. Is that how you've managed to always get what you wanted, Wes?"

"I haven't always gotten what I wanted. Not always."

He straightened slowly, and something in his expression made Rebecca catch her breath. He reached to her hair, and parting the long strands like a skein of yarn with his fingers, spread the pale ends out across his open palm. "Like your moon up there," he said in a strange voice. "Some things forever seem just outside my reach."

Rebecca's heart skipped a tiny beat. "Don't, Wes. Please..." She turned her head and tried to pull away, but he closed his grip, holding a thick length of her hair in his hand.

"Do you want to know something? I've never forgotten the feel of your hair, Rebecca. Not in all these years. The scent, the texture, the way it hangs so thick and full down your back..." His hand slid around to the back of her neck and upward, where he caught the mass of it and held it close against her scalp.

Rebecca's breath evaporated in the heat of a familiar flame that blazed a path of warning through her veins. "Let me go," she whispered, but he wouldn't listen. Instead, he took her chin and gently, oh so gently, drew her around to face him. Instinctively, she braced her hand tighter against his chest.

"Why did you run away, Rebecca?" His eyes burned into hers, as if he would read all that was in her mind. Her lips were only a breath away, and Wes could feel the rush of his heart pounding against the light pressure of her palm. A thousand thunderous emotions converged to form a hurricane in his chest. Driven. He felt driven. "Why...did you leave... without telling me..." *Goodbye!* The word refused to leave his mouth.

Rebecca stared at him, and this time, when she pulled away, Wes didn't try to stop her. He watched her hair slide like silken threads through his fingers, watched her tuck one strand behind her ear. Her hands were shaking. He looked away.

"I...I didn't think it was necessary," she said, words and emotions spilling over, as she struggled to reconstruct the tumbling walls of her composure. "I mean, we hardly knew each other, in...in spite of what happened. I just thought it would be better if we..." *I loved you!* her heart cried out. "If we didn't have to see each other anymore," she said.

For long moments Wes stared out across the lawn. What had he done? She hadn't even wanted to face him. How could he ever tell her that his heart had begged him to call after her that day, that watching her walk away was the hardest thing he had ever done? But he had been too prideful, and too ashamed of himself for what he had done. A virgin. He'd taken a virgin and one who had known so little, had been so inexperienced that she hadn't even known how to kiss. But he had taught her, hadn't he?

"I want you to know something," he said softly. "I went back for you that next day."

Rebecca didn't have to ask what day. She knew. In her heart, she knew and hope soared through every part of her.

"I came to...to apologize."

His words fell like stones in a well, cold and hollow, dousing her momentary elation. She stared at him, a spring of tears hovering in her eyes.

"I wanted to tell you that I was sorry for what happened. I was older, and I should have had more sense. But all I could think of was how sweet and innocent and beautiful you were. And I wanted you—God! In that moment, I think I wanted you more than life itself. But I was wrong, Re.'' He shifted his gaze to her. ''And I'm sorry if I caused you any pain.''

The tears that had been threatening the dam of her eyes, seeped to the corners and began to run in tiny streams down her cheeks. But pride wouldn't allow her to let the tears show. She turned her head aside and wiped them away.

''I'm sorry, too, Wes,'' she whispered, then swallowed hard. ''I'm sorry I didn't understand the rules of the game back then. Now you say yes, now you say no. Maybe if I had been around a little more, I wouldn't have said yes and we'd have both been spared the...guilt. But I was young and foolish and until you taught me, I didn't know that—with you—I was only wishing for the moon.''

CHAPTER SIX

BY ELEVEN O'CLOCK Wednesday morning, under the fierce rays of a blazing hot sun, the temperature was already pushing well into the nineties and climbing higher by the hour.

Even the wind was hot, Wes thought. Heels dragging as he headed out of the paddock area, he tugged off his hat and blotted his face with the back of his arm. Dust, sweat and the smell of horseflesh clung to his clothes and stung his nostrils. A far cry, he thought wearily, from the cool, scented breezes he recalled from two nights past.

Games. The word stalked him like his shadow on the ground. "I didn't know the rules," she'd said, and pain like a knife had sliced him clean through to the bone. Lord, did she honestly believe he'd been playing games back then?

Frowning as he made his way into the shaded breezeway, Wes continued to mull over the things Rebecca had said. It seemed all he'd done since that night they'd spent on the porch, when she'd spoken to him in riddles about wishing for the moon. What had she meant? Wes wasn't sure he wanted to know. But the pain in her voice had been real enough, when she'd admitted she only left Hurricane Bluff because she couldn't bear to think of facing him again.

Pausing at the corner of the stable, Wes peeled off his soiled work gloves, and shoved them more at than in his hip pocket. Was she telling the truth? he wondered. Could he live with himself knowing he was the reason she ran away? The reason she didn't—couldn't or wouldn't—come home when Mara was sick?

Wise up, pal, a cynical voice admonished. *She's the one playing games.*

But she was crying, man, the heart in him whispered. Wes stole a grim glance toward the house. He'd never seen her cry before. Others perhaps, but never her. Proud, invincible Rebecca. Absently Wes rubbed at the back of his hand where the errant tear had fallen. Had she been right? Had he been wrong in his opinion of her? For now he had no answers, but of one thing he was certain. Truth or lies, games or no—whatever was or wasn't to be between them—Wes knew he never wanted to see her cry again.

A PARING KNIFE in one hand, a bouquet of fresh-plucked scallions in the other, Rebecca stood resolutely, trimming the vegetables over the kitchen sink, and blinking back the moisture that watered her eyes from the strong, onion scent.

Dr. Hayes had stopped by to see her earlier that morning. And, despite his grumbling complaints that he'd seen more patients since his retirement than in all his years of private practice, he'd left Rebecca with a thumbs-up signal and his favorite parting words: "You're holding your own."

Encouraged by the doctor's report, Alma required little persuasion before agreeing to attend her planned monthly outing with the ladies from her Sunday school class.

"Are you sure you'll be all right?" she kept asking, right up until the very last moment.

Rebecca had smiled, touched by her concern. "Of course I will," she said reassuringly. "You told me yourself that Mr. Garrett will be in around noon. Now, you hurry on before you miss your ride. And don't forget to phone the garage about my car."

She promised she wouldn't and with one last "do I look all right?" Alma fluffed her hair, squeezed Rebecca's hand, and scurried frantically out the door. Ten minutes later, a garish green van, packed with big-time spenders and bound for the city of Monroe's new Pecanland Mall, sputtered its way out of the drive.

That was three hours ago. Wes had left just after dawn, and now, for the first time, Rebecca had the run of the entire house to herself.

Glancing up from her onion slicing, she stole a glimpse through the kitchen window at a tall, lean man, dressed in hip-hugging, dust-covered jeans, a tattered Stetson tipped back on the crown of his head. The sun was in her eyes, so she couldn't make out his face, and though there had to be a half dozen other similarly garbed cowboys milling in and out of the same area, Rebecca had no trouble singling out Wes. From a country mile away, she knew she could spot that careless, almost reckless stance that seemed too much at odds with the swift, impatient rhythm of his stride.

She watched him disappear around the corner before she turned away. Then she went to check on what she hoped bore some resemblance to biscuits, which were browning in the oven.

The clock in the foyer tolled the half hour, and hastily Rebecca went about setting the table for two.

Her hands trembled as she laid out the silverware. The kitchen grew hotter; her breathing grew shallow. Perspiration trickled between her breasts and down her spine, and with each ticking second panic loomed ever closer.

Why was she so nervous? Reaching for a dishrag, Rebecca toweled her sweaty palms and stepped back to the window. The answer was obvious, she told herself. Without his permission, she had given Wes's housekeeper leave, and no doubt he'd be surprised—in fact, she'd be lucky if that was all—to find her in his kitchen instead. Would he be angry? At Anna? At her?

Sighing, Rebecca tossed the dishrag aside and reached around to untie her apron strings. "Fine time to worry," she muttered.

And yet, in spite of all her surface apprehensions, Rebecca was only fighting a much deeper concern. How was he going to react, when he learned that the two of them were alone? Truly and defenselessly alone together for the first time since the night he'd appeared on her grandfather's front doorstep, sensuously, seductively embodied with the will and the power, if necessary... to destroy her.

A wooden peg on the back wall inside the broom closet served as a hanger for the old, worn cotton apron. Rebecca was just putting it away when the back door burst open in a blaze of blinding sunlight, screen slamming noisily behind.

"I swear, if it's not one thing, it's ten!"

His glance was hardly more than a squint in her direction, as Wes yanked off his hat and turned to the sink, splashing cold water on the back of his neck and face. "Damned pump's going out on that sorry excuse of a well, feedin' the troughs. Sienna Bar's little stud colt's sick with colic. And, as if that's not enough..."

He straightened slowly, his large tanned hands tugging his shirttails free of his jeans.

"Looks like we got big troubles with that bay mare Red Ellis pawned off on me last fall. Been waxing for two days now, and this morning I found her down in the stall. Better call the vet." His voice sounded tired. "I'm guessing we've got us a breeched foal on our hands."

Later Rebecca blamed the heat in the kitchen for whatever brand of madness took hold of her breath and kept her silent as she stood there, staring, half shielded by the closet door, and watching him strip bare to the waist.

Preoccupied and too impatient in allowing his eyes sufficient time to adjust to dimmer, sudden change in light, Wes must have mistaken her for Anna, Rebecca thought wildly. And in that second she wanted nothing more than to make herself known.

Tell him now! Move! Open your mouth!

But even as her brain rapped endless calls to order, her body repeatedly ignored them all. Pulse thudding, feet seemingly rooted to the floor, Rebecca couldn't tear her eyes away, fascinated by the sensuous flow of his movements—muscle and sinew that rose and stirred beneath the sheathlike bronze that was his skin.

And suddenly she ached to touch him, his shoulders, his back—to feel the strength, the warmth, the shifting of hard muscle and flesh under her hands—his arms around her, his mouth on her lips.

Would she have gone to him then? In that interminable second pride and reason seemed only words after all. Nothing mattered but the emptiness she felt inside her, and the need to fill that emptiness. Would she have taken that first step? One step to put him within her reach, to slide her arms around his waist and press her cheek against his bare back as she longed to?

What would she have done, Rebecca wondered, if he had not chosen that very moment . . .

Reaching blindly to shut off the water, Wes turned, his face buried in a hand towel. "Think I'll go upstairs and put on a clean shirt. Might even take a shower just to cool off. No need in you waiting though. Why don't you go ahead and—"

He drew the towel past his eyes and Rebecca saw them open and widen, a look of utter surprise leaping into their lacquered depths. He stopped short, still holding the cloth to his face.

"Rebecca?" His tone was incredulous. Wes threw down the rag with an angry exclamation. "What are you doing down here? Aren't you supposed to be resting? Where is . . . ?"

"I gave her the day off." There was no point in beating around the bush, Rebecca thought. And yet, for all her brave intentions, her voice shook and her declaration sounded more like a criminal's guilty plea.

For a moment Wes only looked at her, distractedly, as if he hadn't heard a word she'd said. And then coming to his senses, he blinked and raked back the raven hair that clung in sleek strands to his forehead. "What? For heaven's sake, Rebecca!"

He snatched up his soiled shirt and began shrugging into it with rough, impatient gestures that would have passed for self-consciousness in any other man. "Would you close that door and stop cowering behind it? Look now, I'm all dressed. Does that make you feel better?"

What she felt was a keen twinge of embarrassment, and—angry with both herself and him for having caught her in such a ridiculous position—a surge of resentment as well.

"I said, Anna isn't here. I gave her the day off. And..." Rebecca slammed the door and stepped from the corner. "I never cower."

His lips twitched and a crooked smile deepened the groove in his sun-browned cheek. "Is that so?" He tilted his head and regarded her with equal measures of amusement and skepticism. "And I s'pose you never faint at the sight of blood, either."

"Only when it's mine," she answered sagely, and wondered how the low, throaty sound of his chuckle could do such crazy things to her insides.

"Good," he murmured, and pulled out a chair from the table, offering it for her to sit. "'Cause if I don't get hold of that vet pretty quick, I may need all the help I can get."

He seated himself across from her, his smile slowly giving way to a dark, troubled frown.

Rebecca, pretending absorption in her meal, watched him covertly through the screen of her lowered lashes, trying to decipher the bleak message on his face.

Was it the problem with the well? She racked her brain, mentally rehashing every word he'd said since he'd entered the room. Was it the sick colt? The bay mare he had spoken of when he first came in? Or was there something else? Something he hadn't mentioned yet?

Maybe he would tell her. She made a casual show of sipping at her iced tea. Maybe he wouldn't. Obligingly she passed him the bowl of mashed potatoes. Maybe she should ask. She glanced up from her salad plate and was stunned to find his eyes fastened on her face. Wes was studying her with that grim, brooding expression she was beginning to know, but found no less unnerving.

Rebecca swallowed, a lump of tension or a head of lettuce. One could be no worse than the other. "What's wrong?" she managed to ask.

"Your hair. It's . . . it's different."

Instantly Rebecca's hand flew up, and only when her fingers grazed the soreness above her left temple did she remember what she'd done . . . and why.

"Bangs," she explained in a word, a wash of color creeping into her face as she self-consciously combed her nails through the newly scissored wisps of hair. "I thought it would help to cover this . . . this globoid mess on my head."

"I like it," he murmured, and something in his voice made her look directly at him. "It makes you look . . . I don't know . . . human." He shrugged. "I guess that's why I've always liked it down. For me at least, it makes you seem real and . . ."

His gaze melded with hers, glittering black to molten silver. "And touchable," he whispered finally.

Touchable. Rebecca waited with bated breath. Heart clamoring in her breast, she was all too aware of the strong, yet sensitive hand, resting on the table, mere inches from hers.

I am real. She longed to cry. *Reach out for me!*

And in a way, he did.

Wes didn't flinch a muscle, nor make any move to touch her hand. But with his eyes, he embraced her. Intimately. Seductively. Binding her to him with a passion and a power she couldn't escape and didn't want to. For in that moment, Wes made love to Rebecca in a way she would never have dreamed possible.

LATER, Rebecca couldn't remember how or when the spell had been broken, leaving her alone in the kitchen once more, and Wes outside tending his stock. She knew only that the experience had left her shaken, so much so that her hands were still trembling as she loaded the last bowl into the dishwasher and flipped the power switch on. Now she didn't seem to know just what to do with herself.

Call your office, a voice in the back of her mind instructed. But she had touched base with California yesterday, which had been the fourth day since her accident, and her first full day up and around.

Diane Herrington had been sympathetic in her assurances that all was well at work, and that Rebecca should take care of herself. A few more days tacked on to her leave wasn't going to matter; she didn't expect the place would fold without her.

When asked, Diane had gone on to say she wasn't certain whether or not Adam had tried to reach Rebecca at her grandfather's farm. He had, in fact, been called away and had flown out early Monday morning to Washington, D.C., for a special meeting with a group of lobbyists for nuclear disarmament. Diane had suggested that Rebecca might try calling him at his town house residence in the capital.

But Rebecca hadn't tried to reach Adam yesterday. And now that same incessantly nagging voice at the back of her mind urged her to pick up the phone.

She walked over to the kitchen wall phone and went so far as lifting the receiver off the hook before she hesitated and hung it up, without ever pressing the first digit.

What was the matter with her? She stared at the beige plastic box on the wall in front of her. Just a few days ago, she could hardly wait to get her hands on a telephone, and now for the second time since yesterday afternoon, she couldn't bring herself to make this one simple call. Didn't she want to talk to Adam?

Of course she did! she assured herself firmly. It was just that...that... She darted an anxious glance at the clock. It was just that it was only two-fifteen here. Washington time was an hour ahead. Chances were she wouldn't be able to catch Adam in at this time of day, anyway. Better to wait until later this evening.

Her decision made, Rebecca turned away and went out of the kitchen, telling herself her troubling lack of motivation to hear Adam's voice had everything to do with time, and nothing to do with her uncertainties about their personal relationship. Nothing whatsoever to do with Wes Garrett, or the emotional confusion his presence inflicted on her senses, on her heart.

CONFUSION WAS ONE THING, Wes thought irritably. Complete ineptitude was another matter.

He was seated behind the tack room on a rickety wooden bench, shoulders hunched and forearms propped on widespread knees. Hat slung low on his frowning brow, he scowled down at the work at hand, a diversion to keep his eyes from straying toward the house.

"One simple knot," he grumbled to himself. "You'd think a pawin' jackass could wrangle a knot from a lead rope."

But the task proved much more difficult than he had ever imagined. The harder he worked, the tighter it pulled and the more complex things became. Just like everything else!

Firing off a foul expletive, he flung the rope aside and slammed his back with a jarring force against the metal wall. He looked up at the sinking sun, down at the baked-gray earth, across the shimmering pasture, and finally in the one direction he'd been avoiding all along.

But the moment he spotted the house, Wes jerked his head around. No, dammit! He squinted his eyes shut and tipped his face upward to the sun. He didn't want to see her. He didn't want to think about her. He didn't want to get close to her, to care about her, to feel like crying when she cried, laughing when she laughed.

Ah, hell! He snatched off his hat and sprang to his feet. He didn't want to spend the rest of his life chained to a memory, unable to commit to any other woman.

He wanted Rebecca Whitney in his bed. And that was all!

Frustrated, he began to pace in a furious round-about fashion. Her accident, his concern over her physical condition, had forced him to postpone his plans for a time. But she was better now. Her strength returning, she was well on the mend. Time was running out, he thought with a gut-gripping sense of panic. But how much time did he need?

Just once. That had been his plan. Make love to her once to get her out of his system. But something was wrong. The scheme he'd imagined as simple and flawless before, worried him now with possibilities of consequences he was only beginning to recognize. No matter how hard he tried, Wes couldn't stop thinking that if he made love to Rebecca once, then maybe he could again. And again and again until...

So what? a cynical voice snapped, and Wes halted abruptly.

So what if once wasn't enough? the same voice probed. A woman like Rebecca could easily become a habit to a man, and he didn't want to be her junkie.

Drawn against his will, he turned again to stare at the house in the distance. What was he going to do? The answer refused to come but the problem, like a two-pronged thorn, embedded itself deeper under his skin.

If he didn't make love to Rebecca, Wes knew he'd never be free. But if he did, if he ever once held her in his arms again—how could he ever let her go?

AT SUNSET the sky waged its timeless civil war with darkness encroaching and the westward front at siege, blazing orange and bloody crimson in the last glory rays of the sun.

Rebecca stood alone, staring out the kitchen window. Anna hadn't returned, and she was beginning to worry. Wes was still at the stables. She studied the dim yellow light and wondered if the others, the men she'd seen this morning, had all gone home by now.

The vet wasn't coming. Rebecca had assumed as much from Wes's numerous trips inside to use the phone, and his grim, tight-lipped expression when he'd stalked from the house for the last time that afternoon.

She drew a dredging breath, and curled her arms about her waist. Eyes trained on the pale glow in the distance that seemed to grow brighter as the shadows grew darker, she tried to imagine Wes out there alone, kneeling perhaps in a hay-strewn stall, seeking to comfort the little bay mare and to coax a new life into the world.

Rebecca closed her eyes and attempted to visualize the sight of a newborn colt. She wondered if it would be dark and sleek, its hair still wet from his mother's womb, when it stood for the first time. Would its legs be gangly and uncertain, appearing too long and out of proportion to the rest of its body, like those of the few young calves she had seen born on her grandfather's farm? She had never seen a mare "give foal" as she'd heard it called. Her grandfather had kept mules, but horses, he'd said, "were good for nothin', save takin' up space and breakin' a man's heart in feed bills."

Well, she didn't know about that. Rebecca did know she still found the idea of being one of the first to gaze in wonder at a new creature just coming into the world exciting.

"I may need all the help I can get." Wes's words flashed through her mind, and Rebecca's eyes flew open. He had been joking of course. What possible help could she offer?

None! she told herself firmly, even as she turned and snatched the largest in a collection of six ornamental baskets from the wall.

"And you're a fool," she muttered and began packing the basket with bread and cheese, fresh peaches and cantaloupe and thick slices of cold roast beef.

Basket balanced between hip and one arm, she shouldered the screen and drew the back door to. What would Wes think of her coming out to him like this? Well, actually she wasn't coming out to him, she quickly corrected herself. She was coming to check on the mare, and to tell him she was worried about Anna and because...

Uncomfortable suddenly, she heaved her bundle to her other hip. For some strange reason—and one she'd probably regret—it made her feel empty and achy inside to think of him out there all alone.

He'll think the worst, a voice of caution warned, as if she needed to be reminded of his low opinion of her morals.

But already she was rounding the corner; it was too late to turn back now. Silently she stepped into the breezeway and into the soft web of light.

The building was an open-ended structure, housing rows of stalls on one side and an assortment of rope and leather tack strung on nails and pegs along the other.

The night air was heavy and the added heat from a string of overhead bulbs steeped the airless quarters with the thick, steamy scents of damp soil and old leather, sawdust and hay. Rebecca drew a deep breath and started down the narrow aisle.

"Wes?" she called. Glancing at each stall as she passed, she was surprised to find most of them empty. Aside from one huge, black beast, who greeted her with a snort and a wary shake of his head, a chestnut mare with a foal at her side were the only inhabitants to be seen.

Surely he's in here somewhere. She paused and noticed for the first time a stall door standing ajar near the far end of the building. "Wes? Where are you?" she called out again, and this time, she heard him answer.

"Down here."

His voice came from the direction of her gaze. And quick to follow was a high-pitched whinnying sound, and the muffled noise of a mild scuffle.

"Easy, girl. Easy," Wes spoke gently to the restless mare. Rebecca deposited her basket on a nearby bench, and made her way toward the sound of his voice.

She found them in the open cubicle, the mare lying flat on the ground. Wes sat hunkered back on his heels near the animal's flanks, his expression looking bleak and drawn.

"How is she?" Rebecca asked softly as she squatted down beside the stall.

"Not good," he frowned, reaching out to stroke the horse's quivering neck. "If that colt doesn't turn, I'll lose 'em both for sure. If it does, I'll be lucky to save one."

His tone held a soft, but weary note of resignation, and Rebecca turned to stare at him, her eyes wide with concern.

"You mean one of them might die?" She hadn't thought of that, and the idea both shocked and dismayed her. "But if the colt turns..."

Wes shook his head. "There's still the danger of hemorrhage," he explained grimly. "Either way I'm 'fraid we're gonna lose this little lady."

The mare gave a smothered groan, and as if to refute her owner's prediction made a halfhearted attempt to raise her head up, straining back toward the pain knotting her side.

"Settle down, now. Easy, babe," Wes coaxed in soothing tones, and the animal submitted to lie flat again, winded but subdued, under the pressure of his hands.

"Oh, Wes," Rebecca whispered, pity clawing at the muscles in her throat. "Isn't there something we can do?"

She raised her head to look at him, her eyes overbright, and Wes was both surprised and shaken by the expression he saw there. He'd accused her once of indifference, but the compassion on her face was real, and he tore his gaze away, wondering why the realization distressed him so.

"If the vet were here," he began to say distractedly, glancing again at the little horse, "he'd probably section her, but he's in Tallulah and won't be back till morning." Wes sighed at his luck. "Sometimes when a mare gets down like this, she'll wallow around and try to turn the foal herself. But so far, she hasn't done that and if something doesn't happen pretty soon, I may have to do it alone."

"Will that work?" Rebecca asked anxiously, eager to accept even a remote possibility that the mare and her offspring might be saved.

Wes answered dismally. "It's not as easy as it sounds. I guess we'll just have to wait and see."

They sat silently for a moment longer, and then Wes rose to his feet, flexing his knees and running his hands down the hard-muscled length of his thighs. "May as well let her rest a while." He gave the mare one final pat, before stepping clear of its forelegs to join Rebecca outside the stall.

Her own actions were considerably slower as she, too, started to rise. Dr. Hayes had seen fit to remove the supportive tape from her ribs that morning, and the stress reminded her sharply of the soreness she still felt.

"Here." Wes smiled and offered her his hand.

She accepted it unthinkingly, slipping her fingertips into the warm strength of his palm. He drew her up effortlessly, but once she had straightened he surprised her by suddenly tightening his grip, when she would have pulled away.

Her eyes flew to his, but they were filled with brooding shadows that gave no indication of his thoughts.

A shiver raced through her. "I . . . I'd better go in," she mumbled, but felt incapable of moving toward the door. Caught fast in the glittering spell of his gaze, she thought that even the air conspired to hold her to him, it was so charged with emotions that left her weak and dizzy for breath.

"How 'bout a walk?" Wes asked at last. His tone was almost light, but his fingers increased their pressure, and his eyes never left her face.

"Where to?" It didn't matter, she didn't even know why she'd asked.

Then he beseeched her, his voice a husky whisper, "Please, Rebecca..." It was all the explanation she needed.

CHAPTER SEVEN

THEY WALKED IN SILENCE, touching only when the beaten path from stable door to pasture fence became rough or uncertain, and then Wes placed his hand near the small of her back.

It was a simple courtesy, something Adam had done a dozen times in the past. But when Wes touched her, his body so near she had only to turn to find herself in his arms, the gesture became decidedly more intimate. Rebecca couldn't decide if she was relieved or disappointed when they reached the fence and she felt his hand slip away.

"It's nice out this evening. Not as hot," Wes said idly, as he moved to lean his elbows on the rough cedar gate. The sun had long since set, but twilight lingered in the summer sky, and a gentle breeze sifted through the taller weeds and grass, and the few trees that stood along the fence.

"Yes, it's very nice," Rebecca murmured, raking back a tendril of hair with a suddenly shaky hand. She didn't know why she had agreed to come out here with him or why she didn't just turn around and go back into the house where she belonged. But something in the way he had looked at her in the kitchen that afternoon had made a mockery of her resistance. Now was her chance to prove, to herself as well as him, that the incident hadn't affected her in the least.

Surreptitiously her eyes slid to his profile.

"I didn't expect to see you outside tonight," he said, his husky voice drawling out his words, low and lazy. "Figured you'd be plumb tuckered out from all that work in the kitchen today. Never knew you had all the makings of such a good cook."

He spoke without looking at her. But Rebecca could have sworn there was a marked trace of smugness in the crooked tilt of his mouth, as if he knew very well she was looking at him... and that she was pretending not to.

Indignation stung her, and she glanced quickly away, wondering why she would even let anything as insignificant as his expression disconcert her. "I'd imagine there are a lot of things you don't know about me," she said. "Not the least of which being that I'm an excellent cook."

"Yeah?" One dark brow lifted as he slipped her a curious sidelong glance. "Then maybe you'd like to enlighten me. Tell me about all the things I don't know. Truth is..." He turned, partially facing her, one shoulder propped against the broad, wooden gatepost. "I've always wondered what makes a woman like you tick."

His tone was casual, as was his indolently lounging stance, yet Rebecca thought Wes's eyes narrowed fractionally, looking deceptive and full of scrutinizing intent. Still, it was difficult to tell. He had picked up his hat, on the way out of the stable building, and the brim rode low, nearly obscuring his already sun-dark features. Especially when he cocked his head slightly to one side as he did now.

Rebecca's breath caught in her throat. As she looked at him, a picture from another time sloughed off some cell within her memory and layered itself atop this current one, shaking her with the sensually potent similarities between the recklessly swaggering Wes Garrett of then, and the wary, enigmatic man of now.

A feathered ache of longing teased her. Promptly denying its distressing effects, if not its presence altogether, Rebecca shrugged and slid her hands into the pockets of her denim skirt. "I... I'm sorry, I... uh, seem to have forgotten the question. I must have been... thinking of something else."

Though she was careful to keep her eyes averted, Wes was just as careful to keep his own leveled on her face.

"I was merely suggesting," he reiterated with mockingly exaggerated patience, "that you might catch me up on yourself. How's life? How's business? Is it true that pie tastes sweeter off the upper crust?... you know, that sort of thing."

Rebecca bit her tongue and suppressed a rise of anger. She should have known this was coming. In the week, minus a day, since she and Wes had first set eyes on each other again, there had been, she was certain, fewer than a dozen civil words exchanged between them. And the majority of those simply because they'd been forced to rise to the mutual cause of enduring a meal together, devoid of any unnecessary gnashing of teeth.

Whatever had made her think, Rebecca wondered now, that anything had really changed—or ever would—between them!

"My life is what I've made it," she answered with a cool indifference she didn't feel. "Business is business, and I'd imagine pie tastes about the same, regardless of the angle, and provided you're willing to take the salty in with the sweet."

"Salty, huh?" Wes clicked his tongue, and gave his head a shake. "Now, I ask you—is that any way for the bride-to-be to talk? Why do I get the feeling all's not well in paradise? Maybe ol' Adam isn't taking care of his homework."

Rebecca glared at him. Her temper was rising and she was glad of it. Given a choice she would rather deal with his vulpine sarcasm, than his momentary lapses into kindness any day. The former was much less threatening.

Lifting her chin, she said evenly, "I'm not even going to try to justify that comment. I didn't come out here to discuss my love life with you."

"Then why did you?"

"Why did I what?"

His question threw her for a moment, but he looked only vaguely interested in hearing her reply as he thumbed back his hat and folded his arms patiently across his chest.

"Why did you come out here tonight?"

Rebecca gave him a near-blank look. "Because you asked me to," she admitted, failing to follow his train of thought.

His eyes glittered wickedly. "And do you always do what people ask you to, Rebecca?" A mocking smile tugged at his lips, but his tone was oddly serious.

Rebecca's own lips tightened. "Hardly ever."

Their eyes locked for several seconds, swords struck, shields in place, each protected and yet armed, equally prepared to strike in the senseless, but timelessly human battle for the upper hand.

"I think you're missing my point." Wes was the first to drive a fissure through the solid wall of tension which seemed to imprison them. "I was wondering why you came out to the stables earlier? Was there something you wanted?"

Raising one hand to dash back a suddenly particularly annoying wisp of hair, Rebecca decided she wouldn't touch that remark with a ten-foot pole. "You didn't come in for supper." She lifted a shoulder just to make certain he knew that she couldn't have cared less, one way or the other. "But I was coming out to talk to you, anyway, so I brought you something to eat. There's some leftovers and a couple of beers in a basket in the building. In case you're interested." She sniffed and shrugged again.

"Well, that was mighty nice o' you, Miz Whitney," he drawled, and Rebecca wanted to slap his smirking face.

Instead, she remembered her vow not to let him affect her this time. She smiled sweetly and matched her tone to his. "You can be assured, Mr. Garrett, that while my concern for your welfare is genuine, your nutritional fortitude was not my principle concern when I sought your company this evening."

Wes's eyes sparkled with a temptingly reckless glint, and he seemed to be smothering a full grin. "Then, pray tell, Miz Whitney, please. Don't keep me in suspense. What prompted the fly to join the spider in his parlor?"

A grin tugged at her own lips, but Rebecca refused to let it show. "I was worried about Anna," she informed him. "She hasn't returned from her shopping trip yet. And I was beginning to worry. I wondered if you knew when we might expect her?"

Dark eyes sobered for a moment as Wes regarded her with a strange look, almost as if he were searching for some hidden motive on her face. But he sighed after a few seconds, and though his eyes remained slightly guarded, his tone was light. "Now, how would I know? You're the one who gave her the day off."

"Well, I just wished she'd come on in, that's all. You know, I've really started to like her, and that big house gets awful lonely without someone to talk to sometimes."

As soon as the words left her mouth, Rebecca regretted having said them. She glanced at Wes and it was as if she saw shutters slam shut.

"Yes, it does get that." He dropped his arms from his chest and turned again to face the gate, sliding one foot through the crack above the bottom slat.

"You know, when I first decided to buy this place, everyone around here said I was crazy. The house wasn't worth fixing up, and the land no good for farming anymore."

"So why did you buy it?" It seemed the most likely and natural question in the world, but something twisted in Rebecca's chest, and she wondered suddenly if the property had been some sort of wedding present for Mara. She tried to remember if Vicky Hodge had said precisely when Wes had purchased the rambling old house that she had always secretly thought of as her own.

Wes pulled off his hat and idly ran his finger over the crease in the crown. "I don't know," he answered truthfully. "I couldn't afford it at the time. But somehow it seemed like the only thing to do. You see, I had this strange notion that I'd lost a piece of myself somewhere. And that it had something to do with this place. I guess, I thought if I bought the house and the land, and everything that went with it, I'd find whatever that thing was, missing from my life."

He glanced out over the darkening field. Rebecca's eyes followed the direction of his, and for a second, she could almost imagine the shadowed outline of an old barn roof. But of course she couldn't. Even if it were daylight and that old barn was still standing—which she doubted—Rebecca knew it couldn't be seen from here. Still, she couldn't explain the sudden escalation of her pulse. Had Wes remembered the existence of that barn when he bought this place?

Rebecca inhaled deeply. "And did you?" she asked, her voice decidedly reedy. "Did you find the missing link?"

Wes laughed shortly and glanced down at the scruffy toe of his boot. "No," he answered softly. Then turning his head, he added, expressionless eyes probing straight into hers, "But I'm still looking."

Rebecca's heart leaped to her throat. She swallowed quickly and glanced away, pulling her hands from her pockets and locking them around her waist.

Wes laughed, low and huskily, a sensually disturbing vibration that had little to do with her hearing. From the corner of her eye, Rebecca saw him abandon his hat to a fence post within his reach. And something told her, the spider had only been spinning webs, until now.

"And what about you, Re?" He turned halfway to face her, further assaulting her defenses with his personal diminutive of her name. "When do you think you're gonna find what you've been looking for?"

She eyed him cautiously. "I...I don't think I know what you mean. I don't feel as if I've lost anything, and therefore I'm not looking."

"No?" He gave her a sly, mockingly quizzical look. "Then why don't you tell me the real reason you came back to Hurricane Bluff? And don't say it was because of selling the farm and all that. 'Cause you and I both know a good lawyer and a power of attorney could have saved you the trouble—and the time."

Rebecca shifted uneasily. She'd been able to list a number of reasons for returning to this town when she had. But she wasn't about to discuss them with Wes. "Maybe I don't know any good lawyers," she said. And then, hoping to turn the tide of the conversation, she added flippantly, "Perhaps you're interested in recommending one?"

Something menacing and remote flickered like lightning in the jet of Wes's eyes. "How about Adam Dane? He used to practice law, didn't he? Until he decided to start making his own."

That was the final straw! Rebecca turned on him, eyes flashing. "That was completely uncalled for! You know, I'm getting tired of you taking potshots, and making lurid innuendos about a man you don't even know. You're so good at setting yourself above and beyond everyone else, judging the world by your own twisted standards. Just who do you think you are?"

She hadn't realized that sometime during the delivery of her impassioned tirade she had arrived at a dangerous position: toe to toe with Wes. With a lightning-quick movement, he caught her shoulders, wheeling her around, and pinned her between the wooden gate and himself.

"I'll tell you who I think I am." His eyes blazed into hers. "I'm the man who's gonna kiss you, like you've been needing to be kissed, since the day you got here."

He didn't give her time to resist. His mouth descended on hers, capturing and swallowing the whimpered protest that rose in her throat. She tried once to swing her head, but he released her arm and caught her jaw, splaying his fingers against the base of her skull, still kissing her.

His other hand encircled her waist, and he pulled her to him, until she fell against his chest, the hard length of one muscled thigh positioned between her legs.

And still he kissed her... drugging her.

Warm. Wet. His mouth widened, completely covering hers, even as his tongue moved seductively, rhythmically, back and forth across the resisting line of her lips.

Chills swept through her, and dark waves of sensation moved with heavy languor through her lower limbs, weighting and weakening her. Her arms slid to his back, and moaning, she opened her mouth, no longer certain who was kissing whom.

"Oh, God, Re..." Wes gasped, pulling away only long enough to swallow convulsively, before his mouth sought hers again.

Rebecca groaned and moved her hips. The blade of his pelvis dug into her waist, and the rigid heat of his wanting pressed against the soft mound of her belly. Her lips clung wetly to his, and when he lifted his head, pulling back a second time, she nearly cried out in breathless torment.

But instead, it was Wes who murmured anguished questions against her ear: "Why do you torment me,

Rebecca? Why do you make me want you, when I don't want to want you?''

His words might have been her own, but they hit Rebecca like a stinging slap in the face, filling her with humiliation. She shoved hard against his arms, and he let them drop almost immediately, leaving her to stand alone on shaking legs. She grasped the fence rail for support.

''I don't care if you want me or not! I've never tried to make you feel anything for me,'' she cried. ''You started this, and—''

''And you weren't exactly resisting,'' he charged angrily.

''I was! I—''

He pressed his thumb to her lips, cutting her off. His hand slid to the nape of her neck. ''You were responding, Rebecca. Admit it. It isn't over between us yet. And it never will be until we finish what we started years ago.''

His eyes dropped to her mouth, his thumb gliding to the corner of it, his face so close she could taste the moist heat of his breath on her lips.

''No,'' she rasped, her pulse pounding erratically in her throat. ''I don't want anything to do with you. Why can't you just leave me alone?''

''I'm afraid it isn't that easy.'' His eyes found hers again, and they narrowed dangerously as his hand came to rest at the base of her throat. ''I've waited for you, Rebecca Whitney. Eight long years. I've waited to find out what it was about you that's stayed in my memory. Whatever hold you've had over me, I want it broken—now. Finished, once and for all. And there's only one way to do it.''

Still watching her face, he trailed his fingers lightly over the neckline of her white peasant blouse. "I want to make love to you again, Rebecca." His tone held the same intensity as his dark, probing gaze. "Something happened between us that day—something more than just sex. And until we find out what it was, or make it happen again, the past won't be over for us."

Rebecca stared at him, pretending she hadn't felt his fingertips graze the upper swell of her breasts. She couldn't believe what he was asking of her. But more than that, she was afraid to let herself read any false truths into the words he was using to persuade her into his bed.

"You must be crazy," she said. "And a fool on top of that, if you think I'd even consider becoming involved with you again."

He stared down at her a moment longer, a muscle ticking in his jaw, and from the looks of his expression, Rebecca expected some angry retort. But as usual, he surprised her. Stepping back with a careless shrug, he lifted his hat off the fence post. Almost at the same instant, the beam from a pair of headlights struck the treetops in a lazy arc.

"Looks like your friend made it after all," he said, sliding on his hat. "Maybe now you won't find it so unpleasant to stay in the house."

The casual change in his attitude irked her. One moment he was trying to seduce her, and the next he acted as if she had been deadweight in his way! "Yes, maybe I won't." She turned on her heel for the house. But he caught her wrist before she could take a single step.

"I want you to think about what I said, Rebecca. Ask yourself why you really came back. And remember what I told you. It isn't over yet. We can end it together... or not at all."

I WANT to make love to you. Think about it, Wes had said. And despite Rebecca's firm resolve that she would do nothing of the kind, it seemed she could do little else.

She thought about his invitation all that evening as she and Alma sat on the boot of her bed, laughing and talking like two young girls, discussing clothes and prices and stores.

"And what about this one? Do you like it?"

Alma held up the second dress of two she had purchased at the mall. The first had been a bold Hawaiian print of brightest red and deepest violet. The second one, also, lacked subtlety. With its startling geometrical designs of fluorescent orange on polished black cotton, Rebecca wondered if the fabric designer had ever thought of doing billboards... or uniforms for road gangs.

She smiled at Alma. "It feels nice. Soft and kind of silky."

Soft and silky. Rebecca thought of the way Wes's lips had felt against hers, the silken touch of his fingers as he'd caressed her breasts. Unwanted images leaped into her mind, and she saw her blouse slip down her shoulders, strong, sensitive hands cupping the fullness of her breasts, and a dark head moving lower... lower, lips parting...

The image disappeared and she dropped the dress as if it had burned her.

But that was not the end of it. Later that night as she lay awake, staring up at an empty ceiling above a bed that was built for two, Rebecca thought about it again. She thought of the first time Wes had touched her, of the heat and the hardness of his hands, of the tender way he had looked at her and stroked her hair from her face, when his body joined hers the first time.

Would it be the same? she wondered. If she and Wes made love again, would he treat her with the same gentle care? Or would he be different, more forceful, less hesitant than before, because they were older? So much had changed, and she wasn't the same wary innocent anymore.

Only a woman, Rebecca thought, who was trying very hard not to get hurt.

ALMA WAS IN THE KITCHEN, slicing bacon, when Rebecca came down for breakfast the next morning, and the woman's heart nearly burst with pride at the sight of her daughter. It never failed to amaze her that two people as plain as she and Luke Whitney were could've produced any child so beautiful.

"Morning, Anna," Rebecca said, reaching for the coffeepot.

"And good morning to you," Alma sang. Catching the smile in Rebecca's eyes, she thought again of how her daughter reminded her of Luke. Luke Whitney, the carnival man, who had vowed to love and protect her when she was only sixteen. And he had done that. Right up to the very day he'd picked up and moved on without her.

A rueful smile crooked Alma's lips. "Want some breakfast?" She glanced at Rebecca, as she lit the fire under a black iron skillet.

"No thanks," Rebecca murmured absently. Gazing out the window, she watched as a large panel truck backed up to the stable doors. "Who's that?" she asked Alma.

"You don't want to know. Those guys are worse than vultures. Can't wait for a horse or a cow to stop kicking before they're here, ready to cart it off. Heard someone say they sell 'em to a man who grinds them for dog food." Alma shuddered. "Makes my skin crawl, just to think of it."

Rebecca sat down with her cup, her eyes wide. "The mare? The mare that was in labor. Did she—"

Alma shook her head. "Lost them both. And I tell you, Wes was fit to be tied this morning."

She sighed and wiped her hands on the faded apron she wore. And, though it was the farthest thing from Rebecca's mind at the moment, the gesture caught her eye. For one flashing instant, there was something almost overwhelmingly familiar about the woman.

Rebecca thought she might have said something if Alma hadn't turned to the stove and Wes hadn't chosen that moment to come striding through the back door.

"Breakfast is cooking," Alma told him with a particularly adoring smile, which Wes didn't bother to return.

"None for me," he said, his eyes flickering to Rebecca's, though he directed no greeting toward her. "I'll be working in the studio today. Got a couple of pieces I need to finish for a show in Dallas next month. Coffee's all I'll need."

"Well, what's the matter with everyone this morning?" Alma exclaimed in exasperation. "Isn't *anybody* hungry?"

She wheeled from the stove, just as Wes paused at the kitchen table where Rebecca sat, looking up at him.

"I'm sorry about the mare," she said, and wondered why her voice quivered as though she were about to burst into tears.

"Yeah, me too," Wes mumbled, but his mind seemed someplace else. "Rebecca, I..." He started to say something, but caught himself up at the last minute. "Never mind," he muttered impatiently and brushed past her, turning into the hall.

Seconds later Rebecca heard the door to the studio open, shut and the sound of a dead bolt. Her eyes slid to Alma's. She half expected the housekeeper to ask, "What's going on between you two?" Instead, the woman flushed and instantly busied herself with the fierce task of scrambling eggs in a bowl.

"He, uh...doesn't like to be disturbed when he's working," Alma explained nervously. "Doesn't even like anyone in there dusting or straightening things. Says he likes to find things where he left them."

Rebecca lifted her coffee cup to her lips. "Makes sense," she murmured against the rim, pretending disinterest. Wes was an artist, she reasoned silently, and no doubt, like any other creative professional, he needed time and privacy for his work.

And yet, despite the soundness of her logic, she couldn't help recalling the comment Vicky Lynn Hodge had made on the day of her accident, about Wes locking himself alone in his studio after Mara had died. And the image that thought conjured hurt her now, as it had then. How much might have been different between them, if she had been here to comfort him and share in his grief when he'd needed her?

Uncomfortable with her own thoughts, Rebecca sought refuge in the diversion of motion. Rising up from the table, she had just started across the kitchen to refill her coffee cup when the telephone rang. Alma reached for it automatically.

"Hello?" she answered airily, lifting one shoulder to brace the receiver against her ear, while her hands were still busy.

Rebecca wasn't really paying attention, but from the corner of her eye, she saw the woman stiffen and sensed by her manner that something was wrong.

Her face as colorless as the eggshells she'd just tossed into the disposal, Alma turned to Rebecca. "It's for you," she choked, her eyes round as saucers.

"Me?" Rebecca took the phone from Alma's outstretched hand, a dart of panic jolting her heart for a brief moment at the woman's expression.

"It must be Adam," she said, speaking her first thought aloud. Her second raced only through her brain. What was wrong?

"Rebecca. Hi, it's Vicky."

Instant relief washed over her at the sound of Vicky Lynn's voice, but Rebecca saw that Alma still looked somehow desperate and inexplicably green.

"Yes, Vicky. How are you?" Though speaking into the phone, Rebecca frowned in puzzled regard of Alma.

"Well, I've been meaning to call you, ever since I heard about your car wreck. Are you okay? I mean, I heard that you were hurt and all. But nothing too serious from what I gathered. I heard you were staying over there. And to tell you the truth, I've just been dying to know how you're all getting along."

As usual, Vicky lit right in, talking as fast as her jaw muscles allowed the words to escape from her mouth.

Rebecca sighed and Alma inched closer, slightly stooped as if she'd had thoughts of stealing in to overhear all Vicky was saying.

Again, Rebecca frowned. "We're fine, Vicky. My car got the worst of it, unfortunately. But I suppose I'm lucky that I came away with only a few bumps and bruises."

"Well, I should say so!" Vicky exclaimed. "And I've been worried, really I have. You were so upset when you left the café that day, I thought maybe— Oh, my God!" she gasped suddenly, then shouted to one of her son's. "Bobby Joe! Don't you dare hit your brother with that!"

From her end, Rebecca could hear muffled sounds of an altercation still going on in the background as Vicky returned her attention to the line. "I'm sorry, Rebecca," she said, apologizing for the abruptness of the interruption. "Summertime makes the natives restless. What were we saying?"

Rebecca wasn't sure.

"Oh, yes," Vicky continued cheerfully. "What I've been trying to say is that I hope it wasn't anything I said that caused you to go out and have an accident?"

The lilt of her voice made the statement a question and Rebecca answered it as such. "No, of course not." She saw no purpose in putting blame on Vicky, when the fault was hers for letting her emotions distract her away from her driving.

"Oh, good," Vicky breathed in relief. Then she hastened to add more excitedly, "Now, we've just got to get together. I tell you, I'm dying to know how you took the news. Maybe, we could make it for lunch at my hou—" A background scream interrupted her sentence, and it sounded to Rebecca as if the cold war between the woman's two sons had erupted suddenly into blood-for-blood battle.

"Billy Frank!" Vicky shrieked. "Stop biting your brother! Turn him loose. Do you hear me?" And then, to Rebecca she shouted—above howls of pain and crashing objects—"I can't talk now. But I'll call or come by. Maybe Sunday. We'll talk then." And the line went dead, on the tail of a horrid threat: "I'm gonna tell your daddy!"

For several moments, Rebecca simply stood there, staring, dumbfounded, at the phone in her hand.

"Wh . . . what did she say?"

She glanced up, and Alma inched forward, her eyes agog with a terrified expression that was as much a mystery to Rebecca as the conversation she'd just had.

"I'm not sure," she answered honestly, shaking her head as she hung the phone on the wall. "But I think I'm having lunch with somebody's daddy."

THE CENTRAL AIR CONDITIONING in the big house hummed incessantly throughout the day. But just as Alma had predicted, the overworked unit proved no match for the pitiless bombardment of heat from the outside. The early mornings downstairs were bearable, but by late afternoon the upper floor became little more than a stuffy hibernation chamber, a place to get in out of the sun.

Not bothering to undress, wishing she didn't have to think, Rebecca collapsed on the bed and turned her eyes to the setting sun.

I want to make love to you. Wes's admission continued to tempt and torment her. Why couldn't she put it out of her mind?

The heat made her drowsy, and she let her eyes shut, forcing herself to think of Adam. Maybe she needed to try to phone him again. Maybe something had happened and Diane had forgotten to give him her number here. She was a little surprised that he hadn't taken the initiative to call her himself. But she knew, also, that if he was busy he probably wouldn't make the effort to do so until the weekend, and it was only Thursday.

Sighing, she tried to picture his face, but his features refused to materialize and she was too sleepy to recall them. At least that's what she told herself.

But in her mind's eye, another man's image presented itself with vivid clarity...

"You were responding, Rebecca." She could hear Wes insisting, see his dark eyes glittering like polished stones. *"Admit it. It isn't over between us yet."*

No, she thought, *I'll never admit it.* But moments later, just before she drifted off to sleep, she did admit it. To herself at least. Wes had been right. She had responded to his kisses as always, with a passion she'd never experienced with any other man.

IN THE ELEGANT TOWN HOUSE overlooking the Potomac River, high above the capital city's gleaming lights, Adam Dane held the telephone slightly away from his ear, listening indulgently to the rantings on the other end.

"But just you wait until I get ahold of him!" Cliff Gordon was shouting. "This is the second time that s.o.b.'s shafted me. When I'm through with him, he won't be able to win a race with a three-legged dog spotting him a mile."

Adam chuckled at the younger man's rather profound gift of metaphor. "Take it easy, Cliff." His silky-smooth baritone voice was, as always, calm and commanding, and ever so slightly condescending. "I'm sure if the congressman canceled at the last minute, as you say, he had a good reason for doing so."

"Yes, and we both know what it is," the young politician said. "I'll lay you money he's off the wagon. Not that I care if he pickles his liver, but I'm trying to conduct a campaign here. I was promised a few decent endorsements!"

"And I'm sure you'll get them," Adam said easily. "When did you say this . . . event is to take place?"

"Monday night, and that's the whole problem. I can't get anybody else on such short notice. But how am I supposed to tell a hundred people at five hundred a plate, that Congressman Benchman got drunk and took a rain check? He was the keynote speaker, dammit!"

Adam strolled into his bedroom, the cordless phone still held to his ear. "Tell you what," he said, stripping off his silk tie and expensive suit jacket. "I'll make the trip myself and you can owe me one. It just so happens I've finished my business here, for now, and I've something to take care of in your area anyway."

Tossing his suit coat over the back of a Queen Anne chair, Adam spotted the piece of paper, peeking out from his breast pocket. "Seems my publicist," he said carefully, withdrawing the transcribed message he'd received from his Los Angeles office the afternoon before. "Seems she's had a bit of an accident, and won't be returning to the office as soon as I had hoped."

"Your publicist?" The younger man's voice peaked curiously. "Well, I'm sorry to hear that. Hey, didn't I hear something about you and her...and marriage?"

"Perhaps you did. Our engagement is no secret," Adam replied. Offering no further details and evidencing little change in his matter-of-fact tone, he steered the conversation back to business. "I can be down there, say..." He glanced at the time and date on his watch. "No later than six on Sunday evening. We can discuss the preliminaries then. Now, does that satisfy you?"

"Why, yes. Of course," Cliff agreed and then at Adam's request, promised he'd have his office call and reserve a suite for two at the New Orleans Hilton.

Seconds later the connection was severed. Adam slipped out of his shoes, sank down on the bed and punched out another number.

On the third ring, a man answered crankily, "Yeah?"

"Max, get the jet ready," Adam instructed his pilot. "We're through here, but we're not going home yet. I have to be in New Orleans Sunday, and I've decided to make a stopover along the way. Locate the nearest airport to a place called Hurricane Bluff, Louisiana. We leave at seven sharp in the morning."

CHAPTER EIGHT

IT WAS LATE in the evening when Wes emerged from his studio and started up the staircase as if each step were a living testimony to the singular power of will.

"But you haven't eaten!"

That infernal female voice rang in his ears, attacking, as usual, from behind.

"Surely you must be hungry. I could fix you a sandwich or... I know! I'll heat up that cabbage casserole, and..."

"Please!" Wes protested. His stomach shuddered at the very thought.

Halting midway up the flight, he turned to face his nagging concern as she stood, looking up at him from the ground level, swathed in an audacious bundle of blood-red fleece.

The robe, Wes concluded astutely. And not just the regular run-of-the-mill kind, either, but a Liberace-style masterpiece complete with capelet. A garment, no doubt, any one of your normal, flamboyant-type Canucks would be more than proud to call his own. Wes shook his head. It'd be a miracle if she didn't smother to death, or go blind from the sheer reflection.

"I don't mind now. I'd be glad to fix you a plate of something."

With uncommon valor, Wes pulled his eyes away from the crimson tide and managed to limit his next comment to the polite refusal of cabbage casserole.

"No thanks. I appreciate it, but I'm really not hungry." He started to turn away then and resume his upward progress, but when Alma continued to stand there, imploring him with an anxious look, one hand conspicuously stroking the ungodly red fluff at her bosom, Wes couldn't help the wry smile that tugged at his lips.

"Your new robe?" he asked casually, as if he didn't know.

Alma flushed and replied, her tone slightly breathless, "Why, yes. Do you . . . like it?"

He swallowed hard and nodded. "It's...ah...nice. You look real . . . nice," he lied. Alma beamed in the light of his approval. And, though his compliment might have lacked a little something in sincerity, Wes's smile was genuine as he added softly, "You worry too much, you know that? Now go on, and get yourself some sleep."

Amazingly—since she did this only a small percentage of the time—Alma minded what she was told and trailed off in her imperial mantle to her small bedroom, the only one on the ground floor. It was an airy little nook, located off the larger formal dining room. During Mara's illness, when Alma had moved in the first time, she had taken it mostly because there had been no other place for her. At the time, Wes had just begun the renovations on the house, and those on the upper floor had not yet been completed.

Later, after Mara died, Alma—so clinging and yet always in search of greener pastures, in hope of finding some "kindly man" who would love and take care of her—had moved out. After that, Wes had closed the house and taken to the road himself for a while.

Looking back on that time now, Wes could admit he really never knew why he'd felt so compelled to leave Hurricane Bluff. Even now, he wasn't certain if he had been simply running away. Or if—like Alma—he had been searching for something, or someone, instead, drifting from place to place, hoping to find a greener pasture, a lifeline to cling to, and a friend on God's earth able to help him shoulder the tremendous burden of his own mistakes.

But, as Wes had soon learned, his burdens were strictly his own and peace of mind was not to be found outside the man himself. After a few years, then, when the running brought him nothing and the searching turned up about the same, he had come home to his roots. And, like hot gum on a soft shoe, Alma had soon followed in his tracks.

And now, since it looked as if she planned to stay—heaven only knew why he let her—Wes had tried repeatedly to convince her that she would probably be more comfortable in one of the rooms upstairs.

But Alma refused to hear it. "A man needs his privacy!" She was adamant. Wes had the sneaking suspicion that this had been her way of assuring him she would be neither seen nor heard should he decide to entertain any "lady friends" in the privacy of his home.

But Wes had never felt compelled to bring any woman into his home. The idea reeked of change and to some degree, commitment. For this reason, he habitually limited his intimate relationships to women who demanded nothing more than a pleasant evening or a weekend at the most. Then, he always managed to find some discreet, sometimes romantic hideaway. But he never confused lust with love, affairs of the flesh with those of the heart. And he never once wanted any woman in his own bed. At least—he paused at the door of Rebecca's bedroom—not until now.

He reached for the knob, but froze. Pain struck his chest, hard, brutal, the kind he didn't need, the kind he was afraid of, the kind he had tried to pretend didn't even exist. He stood suspended for a moment, joints locked, hand extended. And then, very carefully, eyes squeezed tightly shut, he eased his hand away from the doorknob.

Gradually the pain subsided. Fluidity returned to his limbs, and turning on his heel, Wes clipped off the distance to the room down the hall in something just short of a dead run.

REBECCA AWOKE abruptly and sat up on the bed with a start. Her heart was pounding. The front of her blouse and her face were drenched with sweat. She had been dreaming—she realized it now—terrible, frightening nightmares of running in place; of thick, tree-tangled marshes and bogs that sucked at her heels, the calfs of her legs, every attempt at struggle only embedding her deeper.

"Crazy," she muttered to herself, shaking her head. Whatever had possessed her to become so caught up in a silly dream?

Allowing a moment longer for her pulse to calm, she got out of the bed and went into the bathroom. Stripping off her uncomfortably clinging garments, Rebecca soaked a rag with cold water and pressed it to her throat, closing her eyes, relishing the coolness. She filled the sink and sponged off her face and body. This heat! she thought. Years of living in southern California had almost made her forget the sweltering humidity that plagued Louisiana in the summer months.

When she'd finished washing up, Rebecca clicked off the light and walked naked into the bedroom.

It was dark outside now. There was no clock in her room, and she had no conception of the time. But moonlight shone in through the paned doors where the sun had been earlier. Enough that she could manage her way to the closet. Enough that she caught a glimpse of her own reflection in the mirror, above the dresser as she passed.

Why did she stop? Why did she feel, in that moment, almost sinisterly compelled to turn around and look at herself, a slim-flanked stranger, with full hair that hung to her waist, wide eyes that held no color and ivory-pale skin. Too pale.

Perhaps, she thought later, it was the lingering remnants of the dream. Or maybe the sayings were true about moonspells and madness. But whatever sensation took hold of her, as she stood there, staring back at her own reflection in the polished silver glass, she couldn't help noticing the way the gauzy, white light caressed her bare shoulders, her breasts and thighs, but left the private, more feminine parts of herself dark in shadow, untouched. Empty.

Caught up in the strange spell of the moment, Rebecca lifted one hand to her nipples and touched herself lightly. Her breasts felt swollen and heavy, painfully so, and their tips oversensitive, throbbing when her fingertips brushed them.

She closed her eyes, letting her head fall back. And just for a moment, she allowed herself to pretend it wasn't her own hand, but Wes's that touched her skin, seeking to soothe away the itchy, aching sensations pent up and crying out for release.

But pretending wasn't enough. With a sigh, Rebecca let her hand fall away. She opened her eyes and looked again at the pale, haunted face in the mirror. No, it wasn't just a physical release she craved, but emotional liberation from a memory that had taunted and tormented her, for as long as she could remember—like a dream that taunts the dreamer, like a desert image that torments the one who has taste for water, but has none to drink.

An odd shudder ran through her and suddenly she felt removed from herself as if, without conscious thought, a decision had been made for her, and now there was nothing left to do but see it through.

There will be no love in this, a sane voice cautioned.

She went to the closet and reached inside.

He doesn't love you, the voice continued to protest. *There'll be no vows, no cherished words of commitment to cling to when this night is over.*

It doesn't matter, she thought, silencing the voice. *It will be finished.* No more restless longings for things that might have been. She would put her past to rest at last.

One trembling hand closing on the hangered shoulder of the gown she sought, Rebecca drew it out of the closet: it was a glittering web of antique lace, with Victorian-style sleeves and a high, sheer neck, secured at the throat with a blue satin ribbon, five tiny pearl buttons at the breast.

It was part of her trousseau, a gown that had been meant for her wedding night. Strange, she still couldn't imagine how it had gotten mixed up among her things. She had packed it by mistake, or at least she'd thought it had been a mistake. Now, she wondered.

She wasn't a bride. But when Rebecca touched the soft, gossamer fabric of the gown, when she slipped it over her head and felt its shimmering folds spilling down around her, caressing her bare hips and thighs, she experienced a curious mingling of emotions. Apprehension was coupled with the ache of anticipation, and her every action seemed controlled by some force outside herself. Surely every bride had felt this way, she thought, moments before she committed herself, body and soul, to another human being.

But she wasn't Wes's bride, she reminded herself seconds later as she stood in the hall, staring up at the oak barrier of his door. She was only a woman who had loved him long ago in a dream. And now, for the sake of her sanity, Rebecca told herself, she had to wake and put the dream behind her.

LYING ON TOP of the covers, bare-chested but still in his jeans, Wes had almost dozed off when he sensed someone else in the room. It was a feeling, a presence, a subtle fragrance that teased his nostrils and awakened every cell and nerve ending in his body with a sudden awareness that made him ache all over.

Wes sat up slowly, his eyes searching the darkened room. At first his gaze found nothing, and then a hint of movement caught his eye…and he saw her. A pale, gossamer shadow standing by the door, staring at him from a long, billowy cloud of moon-drenched hair.

Wes's heart convulsed and then leaped wildly in his chest. His first impulse was to reach for the lamp, but something, some inner signal stopped him. And instead he sat perfectly still, listening only to the driving beat of his heart and a silent litany to God, as he prayed he wasn't dreaming.

"I've come," Rebecca said softly, and the same haunting aura that seemed to surround her was there in the whisper thinness of her voice.

Wes held his breath, afraid to move. But his eyes strained through the darkness, searching and finding hers.

"I've tried to stay away," she went on in that same barely audible voice. "But you were right. I can't forget. And if either of us is to survive, I know there can be no other way. We have to end this...whatever it is, that exists between us."

She had yet to move from her place by the door, but stood in the shadowed light of the moon, pale, rigid, close and yet, Wes thought, still so far away.

He searched his brain, his heart, to find some words to answer her, to take away that distant look that fixed her eyes like glittering stones, blank crystals inside her face.

But words wouldn't come. There was so much to say. So little time. And his mind was too numb with wanting her to spend it wasting moments in futile search of explanations that couldn't begin to describe all he felt in his heart. Soundlessly, he rose from the bed and went to her.

Rebecca watched as Wes approached her in the misty haze of moonlight with the same fluid movements she recalled from another time.

"Rebecca." He whispered her name and took her icy hands inside his warm ones. She trembled, and again he whispered, the soft fan of his breath a sweet disturbance against her cheeks. "Don't be afraid. I want you here."

If she'd had cause to believe, in view of her surrender, that Wes would insist on seeing her humbled, defeated before him, a casualty in the war of anger and bitterness they had waged against each other, then she was wrong.

He was neither rough nor demanding, but infinitely gentle as he led her to the bed. And, when she was seated on its edge, he knelt down before her, still holding her hands, his thumb caressing her bloodless knuckles.

"I want this to be right," he said, his head bent, his raven hair shot through with dark streaks of indigo.

Rebecca had to struggle against her impulse to disengage her hands from his, to reach out and stroke the thick, glistening strands.

"I want us to go slow." The husky sound of Wes's voice called her attention back to words he was saying, and the grim, yet almost yearning note that seemed to inform his tone. "I've waited forever, Rebecca... for you and this moment, and I don't intend to lose it, or ruin it now, by rushing through it. But..."

His grip tightened on her slender hands, and he lifted his head to look at her. "But, when this night is over, I want us both to be sure we knew what we were getting into this time. And when it's done, it will be ended... for good."

Under any other circumstances, or with any other man, Rebecca would have found his presentiments callous, her own participation in such a liaison unthinkable. But these were not other circumstances, and Wes Garrett wasn't just any man. He was the key to her future, the locking bolt on her past. And yet, as she looked down into his dark, glittering eyes, she knew that, had he been none of these things, nothing to her beyond the man that he was, it would have made no difference. He was still Wes. And she wanted him. Wanted him so that for this night she would risk whatever she had to risk, gamble at any price. Tomorrow she would count her losses. Tonight, she told herself, tonight she would think of nothing but the moment.

"I understand," she spoke in answer to the silent question lurking deep in Wes's searching gaze. "And my answer is still yes. Yes, I want this. One night to say goodbye, because there can be no more between us. I belong to someone else, and yet whatever bonds you say have kept you tied to me couldn't hold you any tighter than I, myself, feel bound."

He held her eyes for a second longer, but Rebecca thought his features had gone suddenly ashen, frozen in the pale wash from the moon. But then, as if he had been waiting only for the final reassurance of her words, he rose up and walked across the room.

She heard him lock the bedroom door with a tiny click that seemed to seal their fate. When he came back to her, reaching down to draw her up by the hands, his liquid movements caught the light, and Rebecca was again aware of the sleek, bronze hardness of his body, of muscles that stirred like cords of steel beneath his skin. And her fingers burned to touch him.

"Rebecca." Wes whispered her name again, as if to reassure himself that she was really here, after all. One hand freed itself from hers, and he touched her face lightly, his fingertips brushing the slim arch of her brow. "You are the most beautiful woman I have ever known."

His hand moved to her temple, and his gaze followed it there. "The kind of woman a man could kill for."

He traced the high swell of her cheekbone. And then very slowly, his eyes glued to workings of his hand, he drew his fingers down the length of her face to the clean, tapered line of her jaw. "Or the kind who could kill a man . . . if he wanted her too much."

He tipped up her chin, and their eyes met and melded in the tentative exchange of once-veiled, but now tenderly revealed, emotions.

"And you, Wes?" Rebecca asked softly, her voice trembling. "Are you the kind of man who could die from . . . from wanting a woman too much?"

She hadn't meant just "a woman." Instead, Rebecca wanted to know if he had ever felt—could ever feel for her—as she did for him in that moment, a hunger so deep she thought she could easily die from wanting him.

Wes's eyes moved slowly, scanning her upturned face; wide, silver eyes, dark with desire; fair skin, slightly flushed, and the thin wisp of bang that made her look so vulnerable, so touchable.

"In your case," he answered huskily, lifting a tress of hair from her shoulder and touching it to his lips, "I think I'm as good as dead, already."

The intensity of his gaze, coupled with the uncertain force of her own emotions, rocked Rebecca so that she had to take a small step back to steady herself. Behind her she felt the bed against the calfs of her legs. Her heart leaped inexplicably, and something—close to panic, she thought—must have flickered in her eyes, for she saw in Wes's expression a sudden wariness that hadn't been there before.

"You're in too deep to back out now," he said, his voice low as he cupped her elbow to help her right herself.

"I know," Rebecca whispered, and ironically she thought of the dream that had awakened her earlier, with its visions of entrapment and the feelings of sinking helplessly, hopelessly away.

A premonition? What did it matter when she was already lost? Gazing up at him in the darkness, she lifted one slender, white hand and pressed her palm to the stubbed hollow of his cheek.

"You don't have to worry." She smiled softly, and the light in her eyes gave credence to her tender promise. "I'm not going anywhere."

The poignant honesty in her expression squeezed at Wes's heart and filled him with something more than simple wanting.

But he did want her. So much so that he could hardly control the tremor in his hands as he reached up and gently—prolonging each second, savoring each brush of his knuckles against the flawless warmth of her skin—untied the slender ribbon at her throat.

Rebecca's heart fluttered wildly at the tantalizing contact and a shallow sigh escaped her lips.

Wes drew a steadying breath, and then, with painstaking care, his fingers moved to unfasten, one by tiny one, the pearl buttons, nestled between her breasts.

As the last button was undone, Rebecca arched her neck. The moonlight struck the ivory sheen of her throat and interacted with the shadows to mark the valley where her throat left off and the soft swell of her breasts began.

"Oh, God, Re," Wes groaned, sliding his hands inside the opening he had created and cupping her shoulders. "You are so beautiful. So beautiful." He lowered his head and pressed his lips to the soft undercurve of her jaw.

Chills shivered down her arms and Rebecca moaned softly, turning her head from side to side, languidly offering him greater access to that sensitive, vulnerable part of her throat and neck.

"So sweet. So perfect..." Wes murmured huskily, his lips moving against her skin, his heated breath suffusing her body with a molten, slow-burning flame.

Slow, he'd said. He wanted them to go slow. And yet Rebecca didn't think she could bear the torture of waiting much longer. Her knees felt rubbery, no longer capable of supporting the sudden heaviness that weighted her limbs like a hot, sluggish fluid. Her body ached for the feel of his, and she slid her arms around his lean waist, pressing against him, molding her palms to his naked back.

"Oh, Wes." She closed her eyes and burrowed her face into the hollow of his chest. His skin was warm and smooth, and she opened her mouth, tasting its salty moistness, nipping at the sprinkling of dark hair, drawing one hand across his ribs to his pelvis.

Wes's heart thundered violently, testing the walls of his chest and the strength of his restraint. He cupped one hand to her head and lowered his chin, planting small kisses near her brow and the corner of her eye.

Rebecca lifted her head and buried her lips against the base of his throat. When her tongue flicked into the shallow basin there, Wes groaned, and his hand at her back tunneled upward, under the weight of her hair. Curling his fingers into its shimmering fullness, he tugged back her head until she opened her eyes and looked up into the black smoldering flame of his gaze.

"Tell me," he commanded, his voice roughened with passion, mesmeric with seductive potency. "Tell me what you want."

"I want...I want you," Rebecca breathed, and even her own voice sounded drugged and thick, as if it didn't belong to her. As if it had been someone else who whispered, "I want you to make love to me as if you really loved me, and as if this were our first time together."

Her vulnerable expression as much as the unexpectedness of her request tore through Wes with the speed and the impact of a stray bullet. His heart twisted and he crushed her to him, squeezing his eyes tightly shut and lifting his head as if in fervent, impassioned prayer.

"Rebecca, oh, baby. Oh, God, if only you knew. If only you knew how much I..."

Then, suddenly he felt that pain again, that tender, tearing agony deep down in his chest, that made him ache to say words and make promises he couldn't keep, even as he wished—*wished* it were their first time, and that it was within his power to take them both back; to erase all the other meaningless hours of their lives, all the years they had spent apart.

But these things were not within Wes's power. He knew he couldn't sweep them back in time, couldn't erase or change any part of their lives. But he could answer her request. And beyond any shadow of doubt, he knew it wouldn't be difficult to make love to Rebecca as if he loved her. For her sake and...for his own.

His hands returned to her shoulders, but this time Rebecca sensed the slight tension in his fingers as he set her a small distance apart from him. And then, his eyes holding hers, he inched the gown down and down the length of her arms, until her breasts sprang free and the garment tumbled in draping folds around her slender hips.

Wes froze. In fact, it seemed to him that time froze altogether, sealing only the two of them alone in another place, an ethereal world, as he stood, staring at her, his private vision finally flesh before his eyes.

The moonlight painted a slanting ribbon across one side of her face, illuminating her breasts and striking the crest of one slender hipbone.

Wes's eyes drifted over her, as if by sight alone, he could inhale, absorb her wholly into his craving senses. His gaze feasted on the fullness of her firm breasts and their small rose-tipped peaks, thrusting upward. Below, shadows descended over the flat of her stomach, becoming darker where they slipped into sensuous mystery beneath her gown.

Wes's pulse quickened. His memory had not done her justice. In reality she was more beautiful, even than he had remembered. And never had he remembered desiring her more than he did now.

"Come here," he murmured, reaching to draw her into his waiting arms.

Rebecca went willingly, molding herself, as he molded her, to the heat and the hardness of his body. When his mouth took hers, his lips were warm, gentle, persuasive, and infinitely tender, as she had known they could be. Softly, he wooed her lips apart. Nudging. Nipping. Slicking the tip of his tongue across the outside of her mouth, and then seeking dark entrance inside.

Rebecca moaned and sagged against him, her pliant breasts yielding against the solid strength of his chest. The rough denim of his jeans chafed her lower belly, creating a sensual friction that sent a flurry of sparks tingling to the very center of her womanhood.

"Oh, Wes... I need you," she pleaded, incapable of controlling the instinctive rolling motion of her hips or the desire that nurtured it.

"Wait, love. Easy..." Wes whispered. His body throbbing to know every inch of her, and yet wanting their time together to last as long as possible, he eased down on his knees in front of her. "Rebecca, oh, love. Believe me, I've never, never wanted another woman as I have you." He laid his cheek against her abdomen, and then turned his head, burrowing his lips into the soft, mounded flesh of her belly.

Rebecca gasped and strained against him, thrusting her hands into the raven silk of his hair. "Wes, oh... No one has ever..." But she didn't finish. Her gown shimmied to the floor and her breath disintegrated as Wes strung a fiery streamer of kisses from hip to hip and all places in between.

Rebecca swayed and gripped his shoulders, red-hot sensations rushing to set her skin afire, until she thought surely even her bones would burn.

"No, Wes... Please." She coaxed him up and he hugged her to him, his bare flesh as hot to the touch and fevered as her own.

"Re... Oh, love, you don't know how long I've waited, wanted you." His voice shook and his heart pounded in double time with hers.

"Yes, I do. I do," she breathed, then dipped her head and rained kiss after kiss across his chest and down his taut abdomen. Her hands found and reveled in the muscled ridges of his ribs and stomach, even as her lips traced the black line of hair from broad chest to hard belly. When she stooped to nip with her teeth the paler flesh just above the waist center of his low-riding jeans, Wes's stomach tightened involuntarily.

"Oh, baby, baby..." he moaned, crazy drunk with sensation. "You'd better come here," he warned between rasping breaths. And then, with a crooked smile that was part relief, part regret, he slipped his hands to her waist and guided her upward.

Rebecca's arms encircled his neck as he folded her into his tight embrace, his mouth taking hers once more, fiercely this time.

When both were breathless, Wes raised his head and Rebecca reached out to touch his face. "I've tried so hard," she confessed, trembling fingers caressing his brow. "So hard not to think of you. Not to want you."

"I know. I know," he whispered, thinking of his own unsuccessful attempts to chase her memory from his mind, his desire for her from his body. But now, she was his, and with each passing moment, each kiss, each touch, Wes was finding increasing difficulty in maintaining control over his rapidly escalating need.

Very gently, he reached up and caught Rebecca's hands, planting a kiss on each of her wrists, before pressing them to her sides. "Stay here," he rasped, moving from her and into the shadows on the darker side of the room.

Surprised and left shivering, without the heat of his body to keep her warm, Rebecca reached instinctively for the gown at her feet.

"No," Wes said, his voice coming from the corner beside the bed.

Rebecca stared through the shadows, searching out his face. "Wes? What is it? What's wrong?"

"Nothing. I just want to look at you," he murmured huskily. "This time I want to see every inch of you. Your hair . . . your face . . . your body."

He clicked on the lamp, and soft yellow light spilled into the room like a fragrance.

It was then that Rebecca saw he had shed the rest of his clothes, and she caught her breath at the sheer masculine beauty of his body.

For one suspended moment, they stood facing each other with no shadows in between, heart to heart, man to woman, equally vulnerable and unashamed. And then, Rebecca smiled and reached out for him. "Wes," she whispered.

And he went to her, lifting her up into his arms and out of the circle of her gown.

Her arms curled around his neck and she buried her face in the strong curve of his shoulder, remembering another time when he had swept her up and carried her to lie beside him in a bed of dry straw.

But this time was different. This time when he eased her down on the bed, when she sensed his weight pressing down beside her, it wasn't sticks or hay chaff she felt snagging her hair and prickling the flesh at her back. Instead she felt the soft cotton of a down-filled spread gently, intimately caressing her skin as Wes's hand had begun to do.

And this time she wasn't afraid. Not like before. Now there was no apprehension, no wonder or fear of the unknown. Only an ever-growing need to possess and be possessed, to lose herself and yet, rediscover all she needed in the arms of the only man she had ever really wanted.

And with every touch, he made her want him more.

His face was dark and his eyes glittering, fever-bright with the heat of passion. It was the same light Rebecca knew shone in her own eyes.

Wes slid his hands to her breasts. But when he touched, he didn't knead or cup or rub her tender flesh. Instead his hands...his hands adored her. There was no other word for it. And his lips did not just kiss her; they cherished her, loving her body as if it were a temple created for all that was good and clean and right with the world. And he alone knew of it. And treasured it.

His lips swept her face, her breasts, her stomach. And her heart wrenched with overwhelming emotion, tenderness and desire. His hands stroked her thighs and his fingers slipped ever so gently and easily inside her, sending ripples of pleasure scorching through her veins. Her hips writhed upward, straining for his touch, but wanting even more.

"Wes, oh, Wes...please. I want you. I need you, now," she moaned. And just when she thought she could stand no more, he rolled on top of her, pinning her with his weight.

"Rebecca," he groaned against her lips. "My love. My distant star. My sweet, beautiful obsession."

When at last he entered her, Rebecca had to bite her lip to keep from crying out because of the sheer intensity of her emotions, and the pleasure he brought her.

She clung to him desperately, matching the thrusting rhythm of his hips, and pressing her heart against the sweet thunder of his.

Higher and higher he lifted and carried her along on a dazzling whirlwind of passion. And yet it was so much more than passion. Quicker and quicker her body rose to meet his, as they melded and became one together, spark to flame, entities lost in the essence of a total and all-consuming fire.

"...leave...don't...this time..." Wes murmured broken sounds against her ear, but Rebecca was beyond the point of making sense of his words.

"Wes!" she cried out his name, and emotions exploded like a blinding light inside her.

A second later, Wes moaned and drove one final thrust, hard and straight, into the deepest part of her. His body convulsed and he sought her lips, driving his hands into her hair and spilling words of sweet rapture and fulfillment into her mouth.

Rebecca held on to him, and warm tears filled her eyes. She drew a shuddering breath, and then silently, while her arms still cradled him and he was lost to the final sublimeness of the moment, she surrendered to him, through mind and body, three words that came from her soul.

CHAPTER NINE

FOR A LONG WHILE neither spoke, and Rebecca lay very still, not daring to stir for fear Wes would move likewise and the moment would be shattered.

And she wanted it to go on forever.

She wanted to spend the rest of her life in this room, in this bed, with Wes's arms around her; his hands caught in her hair, and the warm weight of his body, covering hers protectively. How long had she waited, dreamed of this very moment? Yearned for it, in spite of the fact that she had told herself it would never happen again?

Wes sighed; she felt his breath on her shoulder, and warm feelings of contentment fluttered through her. Even as Rebecca silently acknowledged her feelings, the serenity of her emotions, she could feel the present slipping from her grasp, fleet-footed, like a thought. Why did it always seem true happiness could not be held for much longer than the span of the second it takes one to think: I am happy?

Slowly, Wes shifted his weight, easing to her side. And with the same reluctant knowledge of inevitability, Rebecca opened her eyelids and urged her senses back to reality.

The lamp was still burning. She had forgotten that. And its gentle glow dusted the shadows with burnished gold. *Why is he so quiet?* She lay on her back, concentrating on pinpoints of light, wishing she could read her lover's mind. *What is he feeling?* He was looking at her, she knew it. *Why doesn't he say something?* Hearts, beating in time, seemed to thunder through the room and vibrate through her body. *Doesn't he know? Can't he see he's killing me with his silence?*

Hesitantly, she turned her head to look at him. He lay on his side, facing her, his eyes open but downcast. Rebecca lifted her hand, one finger reaching out to trace the deep groove in his cheek.

"Wes?" It was a question, a sudden, burning need for some kind of reassurance she couldn't seem to put into words.

At her touch, Wes groaned and caught her hand, covering it with his own. Closing his eyes, he drew her palm to his lips. And for long, heart-stirring moments, he simply held it there, pressed to his mouth, as if to memorize every line, every hollow, the curving spread of slender fingers, fixing in his mind the impressions he felt against his skin.

It was a warm, sensual, intimate gesture, a message that might have carried the hopes of a thousand tomorrows.

Or the certainty of a single goodbye.

Which did it mean? Rebecca's heart wrenched. Didn't she already know?

"Rebecca..." he breathed, releasing her hand. It was a poignant song, a sweet caress—the music he made of her name. "You make me feel so free. So alive."

Raising up on one elbow, he looked down at her face and began to stroke the damp hair away from her forehead and throat. The roughness in his soothing gesture was inherently male, and yet poignantly gentle in the conspicuousness of restraint.

Rebecca watched him. His eyes were smoky, and dark lashes weighed heavily on lids already drooping sleepily in the afterglow of their loving. But this time—thank God—she saw not a trace of the sobering emotions she'd half expected to find, because she had seen them all before.

No, this time was different from the last time they'd made love together. They were adults now, not restless youths. And there was none of that old, painful awkwardness between them, no grim regret, no apologies, written in the depths of Wes's eyes.

Now, there was only peace. It seemed to emanate from him, visibly softening the hard lines of his face and making his features appear younger, almost boyishly vulnerable when he looked at her, when he touched her—the way she had asked him to—as if he loved her.

Emotions clogged her throat, and suddenly Rebecca was seized with an unbearable sense of finality. Tears sprang to her eyes, but before she could blink them back, a bitter sob slipped from her lips, destroying any hope of control.

"Oh, baby, no! Don't cry..." Wes begged, reaching for her and gathering her to him, though she tried to pull away.

But to her horror, Rebecca couldn't seem to stop herself. Her whole body shuddered with the sudden, violent crumbling of inner walls and the rushing release of long-banked emotions.

Wes cradled her against him, her face buried against his chest. "Don't cry, Rebecca. Please. I don't want to make you cry." His tone was agonized as he caressed her shoulders and kissed the tangles from her hair, and tried to wipe the tears from her eyes and her cheeks. "It doesn't matter, love. Nothing matters. I'm here. I won't hurt you. I lo...I..."

Good Lord! What was he saying? Wes wasn't sure he knew. He knew only that it tore him up inside; he couldn't stand to see her like this, and that he was willing to say or do anything—*anything!*—to dry her tears, to keep her safe in his arms.

Anything? a small inner voice challenged, mocking him.

REBECCA WASN'T CERTAIN exactly how long she'd cried or at precisely what moment the tears had subsided, giving way to a round of dry, gulping sobs.

It was all over now, she thought. And now, he would send her back to her own room, out of his arms, out of his life.

Oh, God! Please, not yet! she silently beseeched. *If I never ask another thing in this life or any other, please let him hold me here for just a little longer, until I can find the strength, the courage to leave him on my own.*

She waited, scarcely breathing, listening to the heavy thud of his heart against her ear. And then, by some miracle she felt his arm tighten around her. Sighing, she closed her eyes and fell asleep.

WES COULDN'T SLEEP. As exhausted as he was, one part of him was half-afraid to give in to the grogginess that made drivel of his brain and transformed the task of holding his eyes open into a test of endurance and will. If he slept, he might wake up to find as he had so many times in the past, that he'd been only dreaming after all.

Reluctant to let her go, he continued to hold Rebecca's sleeping form in his arms, making a pillow of his body until his shoulders ached and his fingers grew numb from lack of circulation. What are a few fingers? A small price to pay, he thought with a wry smile as he gazed down into her tear-stained face.

The smile faded from Wes's lips, and his dark brows knitted together in a brooding frown. Why had she cried? She hadn't cried before, even though it had been her first time and he'd known, by the look in her eyes then, that she was hurting inside.

Was she sorry? Sorry they had made love again? The thought coiled into an aching knot in the pit of his stomach. He drew a deep breath and closed his eyes, toying absently with a silken strand of pale hair that had fallen across his chest. Dear Lord, he prayed, don't let her be sorry. Not for this. Not for what we just shared together.

Rebecca moaned softly and stirred in his arms. Wes shifted his weight, allowing her to nestle down between his side and the undercurve of his arm.

He reached for the covers, drawing them tighter and more securely around her. She sighed and snuggled closer, a faint smile lending a wistful curve to her sensuous mouth. She was so beautiful, he thought, even when she slept. And her warm body fit so perfectly against his. Wes couldn't help wondering what it would be like to have her wake up beside him in the morning—every morning, for the rest of his life.

No! an inner voice shouted. That wasn't in the bargain. He'd given himself permission to make love to her. Once. Just once. He'd told himself he had needed no more than that to purge her from his system. And so, he was purged. Wasn't he?

"I belong to someone else." The truth of her words clawed at his heart. *One night to say goodbye.* Wasn't that the promise they'd both made? To free themselves of each other?

"Oh, damn!" Wes threw up one hand and splayed it across his aching head and eyes. When was he going to admit the truth to himself? Free of her? He didn't want to be free of her! He wanted her to stay with him. He wanted her strength and her beauty and, yes—even that infernal wall of ice she carried like a shield around her, until temper or passion got the better of her...

And he wanted that passion. He wanted to make love to her and to keep on making love to her, not once in a night, but a hundred thousand times in a hundred thousand nights. And in a million different ways.

So what are you going to do, Garrett? the relentless voice taunted. She's engaged, or have you forgotten that? She reminded you clearly enough. And even if she isn't in love with Adam Dane—like you want to believe—what can you offer her that he can't give her ten times over?

Wes sucked in a deep breath, dragging his hand down his face. It was true and he knew it. The modest measure of wealth he'd acquired wouldn't stack up, like a hill of beans against Mt. Rushmore, when compared to the kind of money Adam Dane had been born to possess.

And, the voice reminded him ruthlessly, hadn't Mara said that Rebecca had always sworn, if she ever got out of Hurricane Bluff, she'd find herself a rich man and marry him in a second?

Well, she'd found the man, all right. Adam Dane. Wes jerked around to glare at her sleeping face, as if she had any idea of his raging thoughts.

"Well, what do you want me to do, anyway? Get down on my knees and beg?" he accused so loudly it was a wonder she didn't wake up. But she continued sleeping soundly, and Wes sighed, tightening his arm around her shoulders almost involuntarily.

Rebecca stirred and murmured something soft and incoherent, her head tipping back to rest on the cap of his shoulder. Her lips were slightly parted and tempting in invitation. Forcing himself, proving that he could ignore temptation if he chose to, Wes dragged his eyes from Rebecca's lips. He turned to the lamp, and with his free hand, clicked it off.

For a long moment, he lay in the darkness, waiting for sleep. But the drowsiness he had felt earlier had vanished in a puff. Suddenly now, his eyes were wide open and his mind, working overtime and seemingly divided in half, prodded him with hard-put questions.

Well, are you going to? Would you really beg her to stay, if you had to? a part of him asked hopefully. *Hell, no!* came the sharp reply. *You're not gonna beg, are you, Garrett? Because you know what begging means. You've seen it up close, haven't you?*

Yes.

Wes closed his eyes and threw his arm over his face, trying to block out the images and the voices in his mind.

Far off in the distance a train whistle blew, long and lonesome. The sound carried for miles through the clear country night.

Had there been a train whistle blowing that long-ago night? Or had his sleepy, child's mind confused the sound with that of the planes that were always flying over the house? He had been only six years old. His father, a retired navy fighter pilot, was working for a commercial airline. It was long before his family had moved to Hurricane Bluff. Back then, they—his mother and father, he and his kid brother—had lived in New Orleans, not far from the airport, and sometimes at night the sound of the planes woke him up.

But on this night it hadn't been planes. It was voices . . .

"He's not your son!" Wes had heard his mother shouting. "*Brent* is your son," she said of their younger child. "But Wes . . . oh, my God, James. Are you so blind? Or is it because you just don't want to know the truth? No, he doesn't look like you, and he never will. Because I was pregnant already. Do you hear? Wes wasn't premature. I was pregnant with him when I married you. And I married you only because his real father wouldn't have me."

A surging rush of old bitterness coursed through Wes's body, causing him to shudder.

He should have left her, Wes thought now. His father should have walked out and left his mother high and dry on the spot. But James Garrett hadn't done that. In fact, it had been his mother who'd threatened to leave. And Wes, sleepy, frightened and not quite understanding all he was overhearing, or why his parents were shouting at each other, had cowered behind the door, afraid to leave and yet afraid to make his presence known.

It was then that he had seen his father—or the man he had thought was his father, that big, strong man who loved to laugh and could carry both Wes and his brother, Brent, on his shoulders at the same—he saw that man drop down on his hands and knees and crawl, literally crawl to his mother, sobbing like a baby, begging her not to leave.

Wes swallowed and lifted the weight of his arm from his face. No. He turned his head to gaze at Rebecca. He would never beg her or any other woman, or man for that matter, for anything. He had his pride, and while that might not be much, it was more than his father ever had.

Oh, his mother had stayed all right. And after that they left New Orleans and came to Hurricane Bluff, where his father started up what turned out to be a very profitable crop-dusting business.

But nothing was ever the same in the Garrett household, after that night. And from that moment on, he had watched as his father grew to hate his mother with deep, cancerlike venom, that seemed to spill over on all of them, making them pull apart and build walls against each other and around themselves.

That, Wes thought, was what came of wanting something too much. Yes, he wanted Rebecca. But no, he wouldn't beg her to stay. He would ask her. Maybe. Maybe tomorrow. But he would never beg. Never.

Wes glanced at the clock. It was two minutes to midnight. He needed to try and get some sleep. Maybe things would look a little brighter in the morning. He glanced at Rebecca. She smiled in her sleep. And, despite himself, Wes smiled, too.

"Tomorrow," he murmured. Giving in to temptation, finally he bent his head and touched his lips to hers. "Tomorrow, we'll see." And then he closed his eyes, taking comfort in the sweet warmth of the woman beside him and the promise of a new day...a new hope.

LYING IN THE SANCTIONED WARMTH of Wes's arms, listening to the soft rhythm of his breathing and his heart beating strong beneath her hand, Rebecca stared into the fluorescent glow of the digital clock on the nightstand. Numbers...minutes melting, passing, turning one into another, as if time was of no consequence.

But it was, Rebecca thought despairingly. It was four in the morning and already the night had given up, surrendered to a new day...without promise, without hope.

Silently, careful not to disturb the man who slept so peacefully beside her, Rebecca slipped out of the bed and crossed the room to the bedroom window.

Four in the morning, she thought, gazing through the strip of glass revealed between the velvet drapes, and yet it didn't look much like morning. In the dead light of the moon, tall oaks and spider-limbed willows threw lonesome shadows across the lawn. The darkest hour is just before dawn, she thought, remembering the old truism. A time when the whole world lay still and cold, barren as if all the life had been drained from it; the way she felt inside...away from Wes.

Rebecca shivered and glanced down at the floor, searching for her discarded gown, something to help ward off her chill. She didn't see the gown. Instead, her gaze fell on a man's plaid shirt, which appeared as if it had been tossed carelessly toward the chair in the corner. It hadn't quite made it.

She squatted down and scooped it up. Slipping her arms into the sleeves, she didn't bother with the buttons, but pulled the front around her, wrapping herself in the fabric and her senses in the poignantly lingering scent of the man.

Her eyes filled with tears. Rebecca shook her head. No! she thought impatiently. She wouldn't cry. She had done that all last night, while her emotions were still raw, too close to the surface to suppress. And what good had it brought her? A few more hours? Precious minutes?

Borrowed time in Wes's arms.

But wasn't that all she'd ever had?

Closing her eyes, Rebecca sighed and leaned her head against the window. She'd been a fool to come back here. A fool to try and pretend that her feelings for Wes had been anything more than a kind of fixation—a young girl's infatuation and a woman's bittersweet remembrance of her first love.

First love. Dear God! As she thought the words now, Rebecca wondered how she could have been so utterly blind, so stubborn. Why had she refused to admit the truth she'd always known? Wes Garrett was much more than her first love. He was her last love, her only love, this man who made love as if it possessed him. And yet, even then, even as he'd held and kissed her, desperately, fiercely, his body claiming hers, he had called her his obsession, and vowed that he only wanted to see it ended between them.

Oh, God! Why him? Why did it have to be Wes? If she had to fall in love with someone, why couldn't it have been Adam? Adam who wanted to marry her and give her everything she'd ever wanted. Everything but the man she loved. Oh Lord, what was she going to do?

SHE WAS GOING to leave him.

Wes knew it. Just as surely as he had known the very instant she'd slipped from his arms and out of the bed. He'd listened to the restless treading of her bare feet along the carpet. And even before he'd opened his eyes to find her staring out the window, anxiously awaiting the dawn, he had known he wasn't going to ask her to stay. Because he was afraid. Of wanting too much. Of being controlled by emotions he couldn't control. Emotions that could very easily bring him to his knees... if he wasn't careful.

Sliding quietly out of the bed, Wes searched the floor for his jeans.

Rebecca heard the faint creaking of the bedspring and turned just in time to see Wes ease the form-fitting Levi's over his narrow hips. Her heart turned over, and she thought he must have sensed her eyes on him, for his hands became still on either side of his waist. And then, slowly, he raised his head to look at her.

Their eyes locked, dull silver meeting lusterless black across the room. It had seemed small and cozy last night. But now in the break of day, and outside Wes's arms, Rebecca felt dwarfed, bereft, soul-bare in an emotional desert, and swallowed up in sweeping starkness.

They looked at each other, and then, with a wry twist of his lips, Wes closed the zipper on his jeans. "Morning's here, I guess." He shrugged expressively. But the eyes that held hers remained carefully blank and steady, indiscernible.

"Yes. I guess it is." Rebecca smiled weakly, determined that he wouldn't see how suddenly panicked and desperate she felt.

"I, uh..." Wes glanced away. What was he supposed to say? Gee, I really enjoyed that last night? Maybe we'll get together and do it again sometime? That is if you're still around. Which you won't be. Will you?

Will you? His eyes swung back to hers, and anguish hit him, like a vile hand, making a lunge for his heart, twisting it savagely, nearly taking his breath with pain. He whirled on his heel, blindly, instinctively, turning his back on Rebecca's gaze, driving his hand through his hair.

"Wes, what is it?" Rebecca had glimpsed the pain on his face just before he swung away and it frightened her. She started toward him.

"Nothing. It's nothing." He motioned her away, averting his head as if to say: don't come near me. "It's just a headache. That's all." *And it started in my heart and now it's eating me up, and if I fall apart, I don't want you to watch.*

Rebecca halted in midstride, interpreting his turned back and refusal to look at her as rejection in its most blatant form. Her heart writhed, but she couldn't say his attitude surprised her. He had promised her nothing. And she was determined to take what he gave with some dignity, at least. Drawing a breath, she pulled herself up and squared her shoulders.

"Well, I guess I'll go now."

Wes said nothing, but Rebecca saw him stiffen and she was instantly stricken with a bizarre sense of her own words. Had he noticed, too? How could such an ordinary statement suddenly sound so brazen? Like a cue. Like a line a streetwalker might use to remind a customer his time was up. Why wouldn't he turn around? Wasn't he even going to look at her?

Wes closed his eyes. He didn't dare turn and look at her, for fear he would cry out something wild and stupid and desperate. Because that was the way he felt. Wild with panic and rage at himself. Stupid because his heart wouldn't listen, when his head tried to reason that she was only leaving the room, not the universe! And yet, Wes couldn't shake the desperate terror embedded in his soul. When Rebecca walked away from him this time, she'd be taking his universe with her.

"Wes?" Rebecca whispered, but Wes winced in pain as if she had screamed instead. "Could you . . . would you hand me my nightgown?"

Don't go, he wanted to cry out. *Don't leave me.* But his mouth formed the words "Sure. No problem."

The ivory confection of lace and pearl lay on the floor beside the bed, discarded where they had left it only a few short hours ago. Turning, Wes scooped up the garment. The scent of her body engulfed him, and suddenly he was overcome with aching desire, and rage.

"Here it is. Take it!" he shouted, shoving the gown into her hands. "And you're right. You may as well be leaving now. So there's the door. Don't let it hit you." He indicated the exit with a fling of his hand, then turned to the nightstand drawer, yanking it open with a bitter curse. "Why in hell isn't there ever a cigarette in this house anymore!"

Rebecca stared at him, so stunned for an instant, she hardly knew what to think or feel. Throwing her out! He was throwing her out! Amid the scrambling overload of mental circuits in her brain, she managed to grasp that one clear thought. And it hurt like nothing before ever had.

Her eyes flooding with tears, Rebecca did not walk, she ran to the door. Frantically fumbling with the lock, she failed to notice the sudden cessation of Wes's mad pillaging of the shallow drawer. Until his husky voice sounded behind her.

"Wait a minute," he commanded, but it was only the odd note of uncertain challenge in his tone that stopped her. "I think you forgot something."

Rebecca let go of the doorknob. Intuitively, she knew even before she turned to look at Wes's outstretched hand, that he was holding her engagement ring. When she did look, her gaze merely skimmed the jewel's glittering surface before her eyes met his.

"Take it," he whispered, his voice rasping and his dark eyes bloodshot.

Why was he doing this? Rebecca searched his face, feeling somehow this was a test. What did he want of her? What was he trying to prove?

Their eyes locked, and the tension of conflicting emotions—those expressed and those pleading for outward release—seemed to swirl and rise up between them, like ghost soldiers, fighting long-lost battles on long-surrendered ground.

Slowly Rebecca reached out and took the ring from Wes's hand.

IT WAS ALMOST LUNCHTIME, hours after Rebecca had left him for her own room, before Wes found either the physical or emotional strength to come downstairs. Alma was already in the kitchen, snapping beans, when he stalked in, heading straight for the coffeepot, as if his intent were to rip it apart.

Alma took one glance at his shocking appearance—the tousled hair, bare chest and feet, low-riding jeans haphazardly zipped; not even buttoned at the waist—and she knew something terrible was wrong.

"What's happened?" She watched the haggard way he dropped himself into his chair and slumped down over a cup of stale coffee. "It's Rebecca, isn't it? Something's happened to her! She didn't come down for breakfast and when I went up to her room, she wasn't there and I was afraid..." Her voice trailed off, and she shifted uncomfortably. "Wes? Was she with you all night?"

"That's none of your business!" Wes exploded, slamming his fist down on the table with a force that made Alma jump. Suddenly he felt as if all his anger, all his pent-up frustrations had broken loose at once, and were tumbling in on top of him, smothering him. And there was no way out. "Just leave me alone," he murmured. Dragging himself from his chair, he crossed the kitchen aimlessly, his steps halting only when the cabinets presented a barrier he couldn't walk through. "Please, just leave me alone."

Alma sank down in a nearby chair, one hand pressed to her breast, her eyes wide with fearful uncertainty and concern. "Wh... what did she do? This is about Rebecca, isn't it? Did you... You didn't tell her about..."

"No," Wes sighed wearily. "What's between her and me has nothing to do with you."

Even though his back was to her, Alma could almost imagine the look Wes wore on his face, brooding, dark and half-bewildered. It was the same expression that always seemed to appear on his face when the subject was Rebecca.

Plucking nervously at the stitching on her blouse, Alma ventured a rare show of daring. "Do you want to tell me about it?"

She braced herself for the worst, expecting another loud outburst. But strangely it didn't come, and Alma watched in concern as Wes—arms stiff, palms flattened to the countertop—bowed his head and slumped, dejected, like a banner without a wind.

"She's gonna leave me, Alma."

The raw pain in his quiet voice seemed to intensify its husky rasp, and he spoke as if each word were a strangled torment in his throat. "There's nothing I can do. I've tried...everything. I can't make her stay. I can't watch her go. I can't..." He sucked in a weary breath and straightened, letting his head fall back, his eyes closed. "I can't live this way." He expelled his breath slowly and turned to face Alma. "I'm going up to the cabin for a few days. Tell her Son's on his way back, and I'll send one of the stable boys for her car. It's ready, you know. I just didn't... Well, I haven't had a chance to tell her yet. She'll be gone when I get back, I guess, so just tell her I said..."

His teeth caught the inside corner of his lip for a second. Strange, he thought. The word just wouldn't come. And then, with a short, kind of disbelieving little laugh, he shrugged and said, "Tell her...bon voyage."

Alma got up and went to him, putting her hand on his arm. "Wes, you said you've tried everything, but you never told her what Mara said, did you? And you haven't told her the whole truth."

Wes glanced down at the floor. "I don't see any reason to bring Mara into all this now. God knows she had her share while she was alive. And as for the truth—" he turned his head to look at her "—don't you think it's about time *you* leveled with her?"

There was nothing vindictive or threatening in his tone. Alma knew he was only being frank, yet she blanched.

"Oh, Wes, I can't. I can't. I..."

"You're gonna have to." He reached to cover her trembling hand with his own. "When Son gets back, you know what's going to happen. That estate's gotta be settled. There's interest and taxes to be paid to the state. We might stall Son, but we can't ignore the law. You're in the will, Alma. You're alive and you're here and she's going to find out. Re can't sell her part without your consent, and you can't keep yours without giving yourself away."

"But, what can I say? I don't know what to say. She won't understand. She'll blame me. She'll hate me, for sure. I know it!"

Alma fell against him, collapsing in tears. Reluctantly, but gently, Wes slid his arms around her and patted her as he would a sobbing child. "It's gonna be okay. Okay? You're a big girl, and you can do this because you know you have to."

"No! I can't do it!" Alma insisted, her voice muffled and hoarse from crying. "Not without you. Please don't go, Wes. Stay here and help me. I won't know what to do if something goes wrong and you're not here, and there's no phones up at the lake, so I can call you."

Wes put his hands on her shoulders and held her at arm's length. "Alma, I can't stay. I've already told you that I—"

"Well, then you're no better than me, are you?" she cried. Twisting away from his grasp, she stumbled across the kitchen floor and plopped down with a jolt into her chair.

"What? What did you say?"

Alma refused to look at him. "I said that you're no better than me, because you think I shouldn't be afraid to tell her what I've got to say. That a long time ago, I made a terrible mistake. But then, you—you just want to run away! And do you know why?" She swung around to face him.

Stunned, Wes shook his head. Her rantings were beginning to make sense and were hitting a little too close to home.

"Why?" he heard himself ask, and a rueful smile edged her lips.

"Because you're afraid, too. You're afraid of being hurt. Of admitting how wrong you've been in blaming her for your own mistakes."

"No, that's not true. I'd never do that," he protested, but his objections rang hollow, even to his own ears.

Was that what he'd been doing all these years? Blaming her for his own mistakes? Blaming her because he'd married Mara, but hadn't loved her and never could? Blaming her because she'd left him. And would again.

Yes, he thought. He blamed her. It was the only way he could remain sane. He had to tell himself he hated her, to keep from loving her.

"I'm going upstairs to take a shower." Wes changed the course of their conversation with the same force he used to halt the direction of his thoughts.

"But we haven't settled anything!" Alma tagged along behind him. "Are you going to the cabin or not?"

He never had a chance to answer her. The sound of the doorbell chimed through the hall.

"I'll get it," Wes said, forgetting his state of undress until the moment he drew open the door.

"Mr. Garrett?" the slightly graying, extremely distinguished-looking man in the tailored suit inquired.

Wes nodded. The man smiled and extended a well-manicured hand.

"I believe we have a friend in common, sir. I'm Senator Adam Dane."

CHAPTER TEN

THE GRANDFATHER CLOCK TOLLED. Twelve slow, reverberating gongs muffled Alma's stunned gasp and gave Wes a few seconds to recover from his own initial shock. Cold rage was quick to follow.

"Senator." He accepted the man's handshake, but he did not return his smile. "I wasn't aware that we were expecting you." It was the understatement of the year.

On the landing above them, Rebecca stood frozen, clinging to the stair rail, staring in disbelief at the scene below.

"Adam!" she managed to choke out, and at once three pairs of eyes swung to lock on the bloodless features of her face.

There was a moment of ominous silence in which no one seemed to know just what to say. But Wes rose to the occasion, stepping forward like a well-mannered host, only a bitter smile to mar his gallant show.

"Well, if it isn't our mutual friend." His voice was low and his tone sarcastic. "Why don't you come down and join us, Rebecca? This is your party, after all. And it appears your guest has arrived. Just in the nick of time."

She saw the sardonic flicker of challenge in his eyes as his gaze went from her to Adam.

Poised and confident, exuding an air of old money and influence, Adam Dane looked merely amused at the tension that crackled around him. A curious smile curved his lips as he came forward to greet Rebecca, who moved on shaky legs down the stairs.

"My dear, it's so good to see you." He took her limp, icy hands in his and brushed his lips against her cheek in a chaste kiss, which for all its chastity was nonetheless effectively staged. "I should have phoned ahead, of course, but I was so anxious to see you. And a little frantic, I'm afraid, when I'd learned of your untimely accident. You're well now, I trust?"

Rebecca stared at his handsome, tanned features, noting the suave smile and the cool blue eyes, tempered with just the right amount of concern, gazing steadily into hers. Did he suspect anything? she wondered wildly. Confused and unnerved by his surprise appearance, all she could think of was how horribly humiliating and hurtful it would have been for all three of them if he had arrived only hours before. And though she had showered, coiled back her hair and dressed sedately in mint-green slacks and a cool summer-floral cotton sweater, she felt...exposed, as if she were still wearing nothing but Wes's shirt, as if guilt had been stamped in bold red letters across her face.

Her cheeks burned and she eased her hands from Adam's, trying not to think of the situation he might have caught her in had he arrived just a few hours earlier.

"I'm doing quite well now, thank you, Adam," she replied with a forced smile. And then, averting her eyes, "Have you met everyone?" She turned to Alma, who all but cringed. "This is Anna, Wes's housekeeper. And of course—'' her gaze darted to Wes and her face caught fire ''—this is—''

''We've met.''

The harshness of his tone cut through Rebecca's needless introductions and made her realize, more than ever, the mortifying awkwardness of her situation. Only Adam seemed unaffected, exhibiting complete control.

Smiling innocuously, his gaze shifted to Wes. ''Yes, and I understand, Mr. Garrett, that besides having the pleasure of making your acquaintance at last, I also owe you a debt of thanks.''

Fierce black eyes flashed warily into speculative blue ones, but Adam's smile remained calm and fixed.

''When I stopped in town to get directions, I was fortunate enough to encounter a young woman—Vicky Lee something—who told me where I might find you all. And, she explained that you—may I call you Wes?—that you were the one who pulled Rebecca from the car's wreckage. Anyone would have done that, of course, but to offer her your own home in which to convalesce? You are to be commended, sir.'' Adam's gaze lowered to Wes's bare chest. ''Such chivalry. And in a brother-in-law?''

He was fishing, but his barb drew blood. Rebecca's eyes flew to Wes. His face was dark and suffused with rage. Alma gave a strangled cry and whirled around, heading in a flurry for the kitchen.

''Did I say something offensive?'' Adam looked with innocent surprise, first at Rebecca and then back to Wes.

''Offensive or not—'' Wes's eyes squinted dangerously ''—I believe you made your point. And now if you'll excuse me, Senator?'' He nodded to the man, but his eyes merely flickered contemptuously over Rebecca as he stalked past her without a word.

WES DIDN'T COME DOWN to join them for a late breakfast on the veranda. Rebecca wasn't surprised, but relieved. Although she had wanted to see him, longed desperately for a chance to explain—if only for her heart's sake—that last night had meant more to her than any one-night stand, she realized also that now was hardly the time. With Adam here, it was all she could do to maintain some semblance of her old self-control, the calm, carefully erected exterior Wes could decompose with a glance.

"Your brother-in-law has a nice place here," Adam commented. Taking a sip of his coffee, he leaned back against the cushioned wicker settee and stretched out one arm casually across the back.

"Yes," Rebecca answered absently. She was seated beside him, but found herself growing increasingly nervous and uncomfortable in his presence. Leaning forward on the edge of her seat, she gazed across the emerald, sunlit grounds as if for the last time.

Adam watched her, blue eyes resting easily on Rebecca's pensive features, appraising her without seeming to. "I thought you didn't like it here."

His smooth baritone voice carried no accusations, but his words were a gentle reminder of all the things she had told him about Hurricane Bluff.

But she hadn't told him everything. At least not about Wes. She licked her lips and swallowed. "Attitudes change, sometimes."

Adam smiled benignly. "True. But it's been my experience that the essential person never does. Perhaps you should consider that."

Rebecca stared at him. If she hadn't known better, she'd have thought he was warning her against something. But what? Herself? Wes? That was absurd, she told herself. He couldn't know how she felt about Wes. She had told him only that she had cared something for him a long time ago, but that it had ended when he had married her sister. Which until now, had been the truth. And, even if Adam had hired someone to check into her past, as Rebecca suspected, he would have learned only that she had borne a child out of wedlock. A child who had not lived, and whose birth certificate had stated: father unknown.

"How long will you be staying?" Rebecca asked, deliberately changing the subject.

Adam handed her his coffee cup to refill. "Overnight if you think I might persuade your Mr. Garrett to put me up. I'm flying down to New Orleans in the morning for a speaking engagement Monday night. And I'd like to have some time to discuss a little business with you, first."

"Oh?" Rebecca tried to sound interested, although business was among the least of her concerns. Surely he wasn't serious, she thought in a heart-pounding rush of panic. Though she was well aware the closest motel was an hour's drive back, Adam couldn't possibly stay the night here. In this house? With her and Wes? All three of them under the same roof?

No! her brain tried to reason. Wes would never agree to that. But then, how could he refuse if Adam asked point-blank?

With shaky hands, she passed Adam his cup, somehow managing not to spill a single drop of the scalding contents on herself or him. "I'm almost afraid to ask what kind of business would bring you all the way down here, when calling would have been a lot easier. Diane gave you the number, didn't she?"

"Yes, and I would have tried calling, but since it turned out that I was coming this way, I decided I'd much rather see you in person."

Leaning forward, Adam reached to squeeze her hand. "You could come with me to New Orleans, you know. I told Max to keep the jet's engines warm, when I left him at the airport in Monroe. We could leave any time you'd like."

"I don't think so," Rebecca said nervously. "You'll be busy, and I . . . I still haven't taken care of my own business here."

"Ah, but darling, how much longer can it take? And I have never been too busy for you, have I?" He slipped his arm around her shoulder and leaned toward her. "We could make an event of it. Call it a honeymoon rehearsal, and I'll take you to Antoine's, Bourbon Street, the Top of the Mart. Have you ever seen the ferryboats cross the river at night, or watched the streetlamps blink on in the French Quarter from the top of the International Trade Mart?"

"No. I've never been to New Orleans," Rebecca answered truthfully.

"Then come with me." Adam pressed closer, his fingers trailing the back of her hand. "You'll love it, Rebecca. I will make you love it."

Rebecca couldn't stand any more. She pulled away from him. "No, Adam! I can't. I just—"

But Adam was looking at her hand. "Rebecca, why aren't you wearing your ring? Don't tell me it's been lost."

Color flooded Rebecca's cheeks. "I...I had to take it off. After the accident. The doctor. I don't think he wanted me to wear any jewelry. Circulation..." Her voice was speaking, making up excuses, all the while her brain was saying, "Tell him the truth, tell him that you are not in love with him and that you can't marry him, not after last night...with Wes."

And she meant to, she really meant to.

"Adam, I don't think I can go through with this. There's so much to say and yet I..." She looked into his eyes, but the words suddenly tangled in her throat.

Adam only smiled. "Shh, we won't discuss the matter now, if it upsets you," he said. "The ring is unimportant. It is what it stands for that counts. But you are well now, right? And there's no reason why you shouldn't wear it. For my sake, darling, and because it suits you so well, find the ring and put it back on."

Rebecca had opened her mouth to protest, when he surprised her by grasping her shoulders and pulling her to him, kissing her with an ardor that was so out of character for him and their relationship.

She must have closed her eyes, a purely reflexive action, for when she opened them again, Adam was pulling away, an almost smug look of satisfaction curling his mouth.

And then she saw Wes, lounging in the shadow of one of the fluted columns, his features implacable, chiseled in stone.

"Sorry to intrude on this romantic little reunion, but I have work to do and I'd like a cup of coffee first. If you two don't mind?"

As he spoke Wes moved to the small patio table and reached for the coffeepot. Filling the china cup, he grasped it like a mug and lifted it to his lips, ignoring the frivolity of the matching saucer.

Rebecca was speechless. She didn't know what to think, what to feel. Adam's peculiar behavior disturbed her, but then so did Wes's presence. Her eyes grazed his, but she looked away quickly and found Adam watching her.

"I understand that in addition to being something of a local artist, Wes, you also raise horses, am I right?" Adam spoke to the man he had addressed, but his eyes were trained on Rebecca.

Why won't he stop looking at me like that? she asked herself.

Wes sauntered over to the edge of the porch. "Last time I looked there were a few head in the pasture."

Adam smiled again at Rebecca. "Well then, it seems we have yet another thing in common." He pulled a thin cheroot and lit it with a gold lighter from his pocket. "I've an interest in a horse or two myself. Thoroughbreds," he said, leaning his head back and blowing a stream of smoke toward the ceiling. "What about you? Get to the tracks much?"

Wes regarded the older man without expression. "I've been to Louisiana Downs a time or two," he answered. "But I raise quarter horses, not Thoroughbreds."

Wes's gaze drifted to Rebecca and she knew Adam noticed, for he picked that moment to reach over, taking hold of her hand again.

"Ah, but they race quarter horses, too, don't they? Ever run any of yours?"

She was living in a nightmare. Rebecca was convinced of it. Otherwise she wouldn't be sitting here with Adam holding her hand and Wes looking on, while the two men exchanged meaningful glances and played cat-and-mouse games with each other.

Draining the last of his coffee in a swallow, Wes set his cup down on the porch rail. "My horses are bred for stamina," he said casually. "Not speed. Most are trained for cutting cows. Some are just for riding. A few are bred for show. But—" his eyes met Adam's "—I don't get into any races. Some things are better left untried."

She might as well have not existed, Rebecca thought as she watched the two men lock in some kind of silent combat. And yet, she had the feeling they were talking about more than just horses. It was as if they were carefully gauging each other, getting ready for a race between themselves.

"Cutting broncs, really?" Adam was the first to break the silence. "I wouldn't know much about those, I'm afraid. I'd have thought most cattle ranchers today relied on more modern methods of corralling their herds."

"Mostly, they do," Wes agreed. "But some people prefer old ways to new."

"My point precisely," Adam said. Uncrossing his legs, he stood up and glanced down at Rebecca. "Didn't I tell you, darling? Some things never change."

But Rebecca was inclined to argue. Adam Dane seemed to be literally changing before her eyes. Were her feelings for Wes so obvious that he had taken one look at her and realized the possibility of a threat? If that was the case, Rebecca thought bitterly, she could have saved him the worry. Clearly, Wes felt nothing but disgust and contempt for her.

"Well, I've got work to do." Without so much as a glance in her direction, Wes started down the steps.

Adam called after him. "I'd be most interested to see how you run your operation here. Would you mind if I went along with you?"

Wes made a half turn on the steps. He took one look at the meticulously groomed salt-and-pepper gray hair, the perfectly tailored suit, the shoes that were no doubt Italian, and the corners of his mouth crooked despite himself. "Won't bother me, but your shoe-shine boy might not take kindly to the results."

Adam laughed and turned to Rebecca, pressing her hand to his lips. "I'll see you later, darling." He smiled and reminded her, with a discreet rub of his thumb on her ring finger, that Adam didn't like to lose.

"I GET THE FEELING you aren't very pleased to have me here, Mr. Garrett," Adam said, as the two of them left the paddocks and strolled toward the stable building.

Wes saw no need to comment. To agree would be rude. To disagree would be lying. He let the statement stand.

"My fault, of course, for dropping in uninvited." Adam took Wes's no comment in stride. "I'm afraid it was unforgivable of me. But then, as I was in the area..."

"You don't have to explain or apologize to me, Senator," Wes said curtly. "Hurricane Bluff isn't Washington. Around here, people drop in when they feel like it. Most of them don't wait to be formally announced."

"Southern hospitality." Adam seemed amused. "What a different world we would have if everyone practiced that charming custom."

"Yeah," Wes mumbled, himself unamused.

"Mornin', boss."

He nodded to one of his ranch hands, coming out of the building, ignoring the curious looks from every man they passed.

"So, these are your stables?" Adam stated the obvious as they moved into the barnlike structure, where Wes had lost the bay mare and her colt two nights before. "It's not very large, is it?"

"Doesn't need to be," Wes replied. "We pasture most of our stock. The stalls are for sick animals, those we've cut to sell, or troublemakers that need to be separated from the rest of the herd for a while."

"And what about this one? What's he in for?" Adam reached to pat the big black stallion that had frightened Rebecca a few nights ago. But the beast flung his head and backed away, stamping his hooves and banging his rump against the wall behind him.

"This one is a troublemaker," Wes answered, reaching into his shirt pocket for a sugar cube. "He likes to race. Don't you, boy?"

The horse shook his head, sending his glossy mane flying, and eased forward cautiously to nibble from Wes's hand.

"Nice looking animal. What's his name?" This time Adam didn't try to touch him, but stood casually aside.

"Blackjack."

At the sound of his name, the horse pricked his ears and threw his head over the stall door, waiting for another treat.

"Very nice," Adam repeated and pulled out another cheroot, offering it to Wes.

"No thanks." Wes shook his head and gritted his teeth as the tempting smell of tobacco swirled around him. "I quit."

"Really?" The gold lighter clicked, then disappeared once more into Adam's pocket. "You know, I am always amazed at people with such patience and willpower. Myself, I have very little when it comes to depriving myself of something I want. Sometimes I say to myself, Adam, these things are going to kill you. But then, I think... ah, but what good is living, if a man must spend it fighting himself for the pleasures he desires. So you see, I am a very weak and worldly man."

Wes's eyes narrowed suspiciously. "I have the feeling you're trying to tell me something, Senator. But unfortunately, I'm not good at riddles. So why don't you just come out and say what's on your mind?"

Adam's brows lifted. "Very well, then. I'm going to be frank with you, Mr. Garrett—Wes," he corrected, smiling. "I was opposed to Rebecca returning here in the first place. But I understood that there were some... problems she needed to work out before she would be content to become my wife." He paused, flicking the ashes from his thin cigar. "You see, Mr. Garrett, I've been a bachelor by choice, and a cautious man by nature. When I decided to ask Rebecca to marry me, I had her investigated."

"Does she know that?" Wes interrupted, feeling suddenly as if his distrust and dislike for Adam Dane, even before he'd met the man, had been justified after all.

Adam looked at him steadily. "No," he answered truthfully. "I never told her. But as it is, I probably know more about my future wife than she knows about herself."

"So, where's the problem?" Wes had to restrain himself from punching the guy in the nose. Weren't there laws against such an invasion of privacy?

"The problem is that when I want something, I never settle for half. I want Rebecca. She intrigues me. But I don't intend to share her with any ridiculous fantasies or ghost men from her past. Now, do I make my meaning clear?"

Wes glowered down at the shorter man, his temper on an even shorter fuse. "I think so. Are you warning me to stay away from her, Senator?"

Adam laughed. "Certainly not! I wouldn't put it that way at all. Let's just say that competition interests me. But no matter how favorable the odds, I always consider my opposition. And..." He glanced again at the stallion. "As a good politician, I've learned to never discount the strength of a dark horse."

Wes scowled. Adam smiled and gave Blackjack a pat. The two men understood each other.

IN THE SOUTH, there is an inbred code of honor among the men, and male pride is spoonfed in stiff doses from date of birth. Knowing this, Rebecca thought, it shouldn't have surprised her when Wes, appearing as if he couldn't have cared less—and maybe he didn't—had granted Adam permission to stay overnight at Windspear.

Upon hearing the news, Alma had instantly taken ill with a blinding headache and had gone straight to bed, leaving the problem of preparing dinner for the rest of them that evening, to anyone who cared to try. Rebecca had offered to take care of it, but Wes had informed her flatly that he was perfectly capable of seeing that everyone got fed. The evening meal had become a matter and an issue of male pride.

Thus, later that evening, Rebecca dressed for dinner with all the enthusiasm of a convicted felon preparing for the chair. The dress she chose, from the few she had brought with her, was a willowy, royal-blue jersey with a draped cowl neck. The fitted bodice dropped to a low waist that clung to her slender hips. Soft folds of fabric flowed to a handkerchief hemline, striking her at midcalf. The effect was one of quiet elegance, graceful in the simplicity of understatement.

Her shoes were low-heeled sandals, and she wore no jewelry, except for the tiny sapphire studs in her ears.

And the ring.

With trembling hands, Rebecca slipped it out of the small velvet bag she kept tucked in her purse whenever she traveled. Despite Wes's imperious command and Adam's subtle but resolute suggestion, Rebecca found she could hardly bring herself to slide the brilliant diamond back in place.

For in fact, it was out of place. Yet tonight, she told herself, she would wear it one last time to save argument.

Downstairs, the clock struck eight and Rebecca knew they were waiting for her. Silver eyes grew stormy gray as she turned from the room, but the remoteness that masked her features was as impenetrable as the diamond she wore.

The formal dining room, though seldom used, was nonetheless splendid and spacious. Decorated in regal Georgian style, candles flickered and chandeliers glittered off the rich, cherry-paneled walls.

"Ah, Rebecca, darling. Here at last." Immaculately attired in dark slacks and a white dinner jacket, Adam came forward to greet her as she entered the room. "And breathtaking," he added softly, "as always."

He was smiling solicitously, as if he meant to kiss her, but this time he did not. Instead he caught her hand and lifted it to his lips, a suave, staged gesture as his bright eyes leveled with hers above the sparkling token of his affection.

"Intelligence and beauty," he murmured in a meaningful tone. "An irresistible combination. Wouldn't you agree, Mr. Garrett?"

There was a slight taunting edge in the offhandedness of Adam's address, but Rebecca failed to note it. All other thoughts were obliterated at the mention of Wes's name. Her gaze traveled past Adam to the younger, taller man.

Wes returned in a gravely voice, "When my guests are as influential as you, Senator, I'd be a fool not to agree." And then he added, nodding to Rebecca, "Ma'am." He saluted her with an impervious glance and a casual tip of his brandy snifter.

The white linen-draped table, which might have easily accommodated twenty, was set for only three.

"Maybe I should go see if I can help in the kitchen," Rebecca offered, anxious for any excuse to use as an escape from the brooding, dark eyes she could feel boring right through her.

Adam handed her a glass of white wine. "Nonsense, my dear." He reached to brush the curling hair from her shoulder, his hand trailing possessively, then, along her spine to her waist. "It seems our friend here is *also* a man of great influence. Our meal is being catered. Gumbo, oysters rockefeller, red and black fish. Creole cuisine from one of the finest restaurants in the South. My mouth is watering already." Again Adam turned, smiling at Wes. "Once more, I must thank you, sir, for putting yourself to such trouble on our behalf."

Adam's condescension was showing. Rebecca saw it, and she knew Wes saw it, too. If it affected him, however, he hid it, commenting with a careless shrug and the slight narrowing of his black eyes, "My uncle owns his own restaurant in Shreveport, Senator. And the trouble, I'm sure, was all his."

They were standing in a quaint little cluster now, Adam having steered her toward Wes and the small sitting area that faced an unlit hearth.

Standing so close to Wes, Rebecca couldn't help noticing that while he had not conceded to formal dresswear for the evening, he had never looked more handsome in plain navy slacks and a pale blue knit shirt.

Rebecca thought she could almost feel the tension that seemed to emanate from him, despite his casual, negligent manner. The sensation made her tense, too. What was he really thinking? she wondered. Did he hate her more than ever now? Or worse, did he feel nothing for her at all?

The men went on talking, conversing as if she wasn't present, and Rebecca was only too glad that they did not bother to include her, much of the time.

She kept her eyes downcast and forced herself not to stare at Wes, although it was all she wanted to do. She wanted to make him look at her, to plead with him to forgive her, to understand. But instead, she occupied her gaze with the bubbling wine in her glass and her mind with the constant wish that the floor would open up and swallow her.

Dinner was at nine, catered by a young, red-vested waiter who Wes explained was a second cousin twice removed on his mother's side.

Adam, persuasive and charming at his purposeful best, related anecdotes and lavished compliments on first the waiter, and then Wes, proposing toasts to his knowledge of fine food and good horseflesh.

Lounging back in deceptive ease at the head of the table, Wes feigned a fair degree of amusement. He spoke and smiled, if rather mockingly, in all the appropriate places. But once or twice Rebecca caught the hardened look in his eyes, and she knew he wasn't as relaxed as he seemed.

The young man acting as their waiter refilled her wineglass and she drank it as if it were water, pretending to eat only for appearance's sake. She had already made up her mind that tonight she would tell Adam the truth. And she told herself she needed the wine to bolster her courage.

But her courage was already waning by the time dinner was over. Adam rose and went to pull out her chair, bending as he did to place a kiss on her cheek. Her eyes flew to Wes, but he continued to avoid looking at her.

"Superb meal, stimulating conversation and a lovely woman to complement it all. What more could a man ask?'' Adam remarked as the three of them moved into the study for café au lait and more brandy.

Wes said dryly, ''Not much.'' And for the first time in several hours, his eyes settled on Rebecca. She hadn't been prepared for his direct gaze and her hands began to shake, rattling the cup and saucer in her lap. She set it aside hastily, but not before she had drawn Adam's slightly questioning glance.

Snapping the lid on his lighter, he squinted his eyes against the pale stream of smoke. ''Are you all right, dear? You look a little flushed.''

Rebecca tried to smile. ''I'm fine. Just a little tired, that's all.''

''Well, we'll fix that.''

Without allowing her time to protest or to consent, Adam put his hand on her elbow and drew her to her feet. ''I think a walk is in order. Wes? Do we have your permission to wander around your lovely grounds?''

''By all means,'' he said, turning to the bar. ''Make yourselves at home.''

There was bitterness in his husky tone, and Rebecca could almost imagine that he'd scowled as he reached for the brandy decanter. But then, she was being propelled out of the room and into the heavy night air.

''I'VE MISSED YOU.'' Adam was the first to speak, his tone silky soft as they paused in deep shadows of a moss-draped oak. Feeling drained and alone, despite the company of the man beside her, Rebecca made no reply. Idly, she plucked a pointed leaf from the tree, and proceeded to strip apart the green from its veins.

Adam watched her for a moment, then slipping his hand under her chin, he tilted her face so that she was looking at him. "It might be nice to hear you say you've missed me, too."

"Oh, Adam, I have missed you," she said, and it wasn't a lie. She was fond of him, and she respected him, and she never wanted to hurt him. But she couldn't marry him.

"Adam," she whispered, lifting a hand to his face, hoping he would understand what she was about to say. "You've been good to me. I love working for you and with you, and I wouldn't want to lose you as a friend. But you see, I..." Her voice trembled and her eyes filled with tears. "Adam, I just can't marr—"

"Shh, don't say it." He pressed his fingers to her quivering lips, and then drew her gently into a comforting embrace. "I know, my darling. I think, I have always known from the first moment I saw you that here was a woman who had loved almost to the point of self-destruction, and loves still, though she won't admit it, even to herself."

"But, Adam..." Rebecca tried to lift her head, but he cupped her neck and held her closer.

"No. You will be still now and let me speak. I won't connive or play coy games with you by vowing words of endless love and adoration. But I'll tell you in truth that I admire and respect you as I have no other woman. And I want you for my wife, Rebecca. No matter what, my feelings haven't changed."

His arms loosened slightly, and Rebecca, her hands against his chest, gazed up in question, looking into his shadowed face. "But, Adam, doesn't it matter to you that I don't love you? That I love—"

"Stop it now." Again he interrupted her, sharply this time. "I don't want to hear his name. And what matters to me is that you are an intelligent woman and will make the only practical choice in the end."

Rebecca stared at him. "What are you saying? If you're asking me to choose, I'm trying to tell you that I've already decided. I love him, Adam! I love him, and I can't . . . I won't marry you!"

He shook his head, smiling with exaggerated patience as if she had been a child.

"Rebecca, darling, can't you see that you're distraught? And this is why I refuse to let you breach your promise to me, until you've had the time to think things over more rationally."

Something in his tone clicked inside Rebecca's head, and her heart began to pound. Her eyes narrowed. "Breach of promise, Adam? Are you threatening me?" The idea was so insanely ludicrous, she could have laughed aloud.

"Oh, my dear, sometimes you still amaze me with your charming naïveté. Sue you? Good God, no, I believe I'm a bit more civil than that. No, all I ask is that you wait. Don't be so hasty with your emotions. I'll be leaving tomorrow, and you?" He smiled indulgently. "Stay, if you choose. Business can wait for a while. You see, I'm not a difficult man. I give you leave to stay for as long as it takes to disengage yourself from this infatuation with our rather austere Mr. Garrett. Then, when this thing is done, come back to me. I will be waiting. And, if you still feel the same in a week, two weeks from now . . . then we'll talk."

Rebecca couldn't believe her ears. Forget your job, he was saying. There are others to take care of it. Have your little fling. What does it matter? she translated his words and Rebecca was so shocked, so mortified by his casual attitude that her mouth dropped open. But she couldn't manage to utter a word of protest, even when Adam drew her into his arms and kissed her.

Wes had seen it all.

From the window where he stood, reduced to a voyeur in his own home, he had seen Rebecca caress Adam Dane's smiling face, watched his arms go around her and saw the way her slim body swayed, arching like a willow limb against him, her head thrown back as if in ecstasy.

Jealousy surged through him in the form of a molten hot rage. Restless fingers tightened on the fragile glass in his hand, forgotten, until the very moment the crystal exploded in the pressure of his grip.

"Dammit!" he swore, slinging brandy and glass slivers off his hand. "Alma—Anna! Whoever you are!" he called irritably to the woman who was nowhere about. "Bring a rag for this mess, would you?" He was staring at the floor, when a single drop of red blood hit the carpet beside his foot. "And a Band-Aid," he added in a softer voice.

CHAPTER ELEVEN

IT WAS WELL AFTER ELEVEN when Adam escorted Rebecca to her bedroom door.

"Sleep well, my darling," he murmured, his tone silky smooth and cool as the good-night kiss he brushed against her forehead. She stood there numbly, watching him move down the hall to the guest room Wes had so punctiliously allotted him.

Turning into her own room at last, she stripped out of her dress and sank down on the bed. "Sleep well," he had said, as if she hadn't a worry in the world, as if her mind were not jumbled and confused. She was disgusted with herself and angry with the two men who seemed to have taken some perverse pleasure in the evening, behaving like opposing prime ministers sparring at a summit parley.

She had been almost in a state of shock throughout, but now Rebecca felt humiliated and enraged. *Fools! Both of you!* she wanted to scream. And Adam! Adam was deliberately trying to make everything more difficult. What was the matter with him? Why wouldn't he listen to her?

Wearing only her slip and panties, Rebecca snatched on her robe and tied the sash with a vicious yank. Too much was going on in her head and she felt she couldn't stand being cooped up in her room another second.

Downstairs she turned toward Alma's room. At least the housekeeper was a woman, Rebecca thought. Someone who wasn't trying to drive her insane.

But as she drew level with the room that was Wes's studio and saw, by the crack under the door, that a light burned inside, she realized it hadn't been Alma, but Wes she had wanted to see all along. Lifting her hand, not allowing herself time to consider her actions, Rebecca rapped lightly on the door.

"Wes. Wes, are you in there?" She paused to listen, and for a moment there was only a stark, dead silence. Then she heard the sound of movement and footsteps inside, and the door was snatched open, but only partway.

"What do you want?" Wes growled impatiently, almost as if he had known she would come and was prepared to get rid of her.

"I wanted to talk to you," Rebecca whispered, knowing that her voice sounded weak and pathetic. She didn't care. "I couldn't at dinner, but . . . please, Wes. Please let me in."

His darks eyes held hers steadily as he seemed to consider it. Finally he swung away from the door. "I don't have anything to say to you." He turned his back to her, striding into the interior of the room. But he left the door to swing open. Rebecca stepped inside and closed it behind her.

"But Wes, we have to talk. Please listen to me. I didn't know Adam was coming. I—"

"I don't want to hear it," he interrupted, his voice flat. "I've had just about all the talk of Senator Dane I can stomach for one night." He stooped and picked up a paint-soiled sheet from the floor, tossing it carelessly over an easel in the corner. "Now, if you'll excuse me, I have every intention of drinking myself into a stupor."

It wasn't until Wes reached with his left hand for the whiskey bottle on a small table nearby, that Rebecca noticed the white bandage on his right.

"Wes? What's happened? You're hurt."

Despite her earlier anger, concern now shook her voice and she reached for him instinctively. He jerked away.

"Spare me your sympathies. It's only a scratch." He plopped down in a barrel chair. "And if you've got something to say, I wished you'd say it...and get out."

He sloshed three fingers of straight liquor sloppily into a glass and lifted it to his lips, eyeing her over the rim.

Rebecca stiffened automatically, the heat of his mocking gaze threatening to consume what few defenses she had left. "I just wanted you to know..." *I love you. Oh, God, please! Don't do this to me.* "...that I'm sorry for all that's happened. I don't know what else to say."

In truth there must have been a million things she wanted to say, like: *why can't I make you love me? If you still want me, can't that be enough? Why can't you see that I can't bear the thought of losing you again?*

A rueful smile curled the corner of his lips. "There's no reason for you to apologize. We wanted to make love. We did. Now it's over. Thanks for everything." He could have kicked himself for adding the last in an off-handed, gratuitous way.

There isn't anything else to say, Wes thought. *Prince Charming has arrived for Cinderella, and you're right back where you started, loving a woman you're never going to have.*

Rebecca didn't flinch at his words, although they hurt more than she could ever say. Thanks for everything? Oh, God, how could he say that? Did the love she'd given him last night mean so little?

"I wish... I wish you wouldn't hate me." Despite her efforts, tears welled in her eyes. She clasped her hands together in front of her and stared down at them, watching her knuckles turn white. "I've decided to go back to the farm tomorrow. I had hoped we could at least part friends."

"Friends!"

It was the final blow to an already wounded heart. The final injury adding insult to a flagging sense of male pride.

Slamming his glass down on the table, Wes sprang to his feet and crossed the room in three angry strides. "Let's get something straight. I don't want to be your... friend." Eyes ablaze, he caught her shoulders, leaning his angry face into hers. "I don't want to be anything to you. Or you to me. Do you understand?"

Rebecca's body seemed to burn all over with pain and humiliation. She twisted away from him. "Yes, I think you've finally made yourself clear. It's just my mind slipping, I guess. I seem to keep on forgetting there's only one thing you've ever wanted from me."

There were tears in her eyes, and Wes had to struggle with his desire to crush her to him and kiss them away. But he couldn't do that. Sighing, he dropped his hands to his side, and turned away from her, massaging his aching head.

"I'm sorry, okay? Let's call a truce." He raked a shaky hand through his hair. "What either of us wants doesn't really matter now anyway." He was standing beside the covered easel, and she saw him run a finger over the stained sheet. "Tomorrow is Sunday. Son will be back on Monday. You'll be leaving town after that, and I've decided to get away myself for a while."

His mood changed so quickly it took a moment for Rebecca to comprehend what he'd said. "When... when are you going?"

He turned and gave her a long look, but she could read no expression in his eyes. He shrugged and murmured, "I'll be gone when you get up in the morning."

Rebecca felt the blood ebb from her face. "Will you be back soon?" Her voice trembled, and she bit her lip, despising herself for asking, when in truth she was afraid and didn't want to hear his answer. What she really meant was "Will I ever see you again?"

They looked at each other and slowly, very slowly, Wes shook his head. "No," he whispered. "No."

And then nothing else.

"But why?" Rebecca cried, tears clogging her throat until she thought she would choke. But she couldn't let it alone. She couldn't let him go. "Why do you have to do this? Why? I don't understand! What have I done to make you hate me so much? If I've hurt you somehow, then can't you see that you've paid me back ten times over! When will it stop? Where will it end?"

"Dammit, don't you realize that's the point?" Wes's face twisted with frustration and pain. "There isn't any end for us. And the only way we can stop hurting each other is to stay away from each other!"

"That's not true."

"Yes, it is. And you know it." He reached up, touching her face, and for a moment Rebecca thought he might kiss her. But instead he only gave her a slight twist of his mouth that might have been a smile, except for the look in his eyes. "I don't want to hurt you anymore, either, Re. That's why it's better if I go."

Her throat constricted. "But I told you, I'm leaving, too. I don't want to force you out of your own home."

Wes sighed and let his hand drop away from her face. "Don't worry about it. I just thought it'd be better if I weren't here while you were getting ready to leave. I'd get in the way probably." He smiled again, and a glimmer teased his eyes for a second. But then he sobered. "Try and be happy, okay?"

She nodded, afraid if she opened her mouth to speak she would cry.

Wes let his eyes roam her face and her hair. He sucked in a breath, filling his lungs. "I'll see ya."

This time Rebecca didn't even bother to nod, and only when she was certain he was gone, did she turn to leave the room, wishing with every step she were dead.

"WELL, DARLING, I guess this is it."

Standing in the shade of the broad veranda, adorned in his wheat-colored suit, a panama hat held loosely in his hand, Adam Dane looked as if he had been cast for the leading role in a David O. Selznick film.

Rebecca stood beside him, watching the two young stable boys who worked for Wes loading Adam's luggage into the trunk of his rented Volvo.

"If you need to reach me, I'll be at the Marriott until Wednesday," Adam was saying. "After that it's back to Los Angeles. Gelsey Howard is giving a dinner party next weekend, in honor of Judge Goldthwait's appointment. Shame you won't be joining us, darling. How long do you think it will take to have this estate business settled?"

He gave her no chance to reply, but rushed on, patting her hands solicitously as she held them clutched together in front of her. "No matter. As we agreed, you may take all the time you need. But don't be too long now. Wouldn't want to get the press stirred up, would we? In the meantime, I'll give all our friends your regards."

Rebecca merely looked at him, her eyes dark and expressionless. "Yes, Adam," she murmured dryly. "You do that."

At her tone, Adam raised an eyebrow, but his smile never wavered, despite the fleeting glimmer of disapproval in his gaze. "Now listen, darling..." He put one finger under her chin and tilted up her face, as though he were speaking to a child. "If you need anything, you know you've only to call. If you can't reach me, you know Diane can run me down. And please, dear, do try and get some sun. You look so washed out—bad for the press shots. We wouldn't want them to think you're ill. In fact, I'm going to insist that you phone the L.A. office and have Mrs. Richards make you an appointment with Dr. Cassavettes. These country doctors are fine for treating scrapes and bruises, but I'd feel much better if you were to have a checkup with a real professional. The first thing when you get home now, okay?"

Rebecca only smiled, her expression noncommittal. She hadn't the slightest intention of phoning Adam's secretary or his personal physician for that matter. Neither of them could help her now with what she knew she had to do. Involuntarily, her fist tightened on the small velvet pouch she held, concealed by the folds of her skirt.

"She's all ready to go, Senator," one of the teenagers called out with an airy wave, as the other slammed the trunk and the two struck out, side by side, in the direction of the barn.

"Come. Walk me to the car."

Allowing Adam to take her arm, Rebecca strolled beside him to the graveled drive where the Volvo was parked. He released her only when he reached for the door and slid in behind the wheel, looking up at her from the driver's window.

"You won't forget me now, will you, darling?"

White teeth gleaming, perfect and polished in the morning sun, he gave her one of his infamous off-the-record grins. But Rebecca was in no mood to return it.

"No, Adam. I'll never forget you. But I can't marry you." There—she'd said it straight out.

Adam threw back his head and squinted his eyes for a better look at her. "Oh, good God!" His tone rang sharp with exasperation. "I thought we'd settled all that. And now, when you know very well I've a plane to catch in less than an hour, you hit me with this again! Well, I'm sorry, my dear..." He rammed the key into the ignition and revved the engine to life. "But I simply do not have the time—nor the inclination—to deal with this ridiculous matter now! We'll discuss it later, if we must, at home in L.A., as we agreed."

"No, Adam." Reaching inside the open window, Rebecca caught him by the shoulder and forced him around to look at her. "We'll talk about it now, not later, because I don't know when...or even if...I'll be back in L.A. But one thing I *do* know. I don't need any more complications in my life right now, no more loose strings left dangling."

Adam's mouth fell open, his face flushed. "Loose strings?" He all but snarled, and for the first time since she had known Adam Dane, Rebecca saw his control slipping. "Do you know who you are talking to?"

Ignoring the obvious, she shook her head, refusing to fall into an argument with him. Her mind was made up and nothing could change it. "I'm sorry, Adam," she said softly, then tossed him the velvet pouch, with the ring inside, so that he had no alternative but to catch it before it struck him.

"Rebecca..."

She cut him off, lifting her hands to her lips in a prayerlike pose. "Please, believe me, Adam, I never wanted to hurt you. But, if I married you, I'd be committing myself to doing just that. And you would end up hating me more for it. I'm sorry," she repeated.

Adam drew a weary breath. "You're making a big mistake, Rebecca. Can't you see what you're throwing away? I have money, power. With me you could go your own way, manage your own life and live like a queen in the process. And what can this...this brother-in-law person offer you? Love and kisses, Rebecca? Is that what you think will make you happy?"

He lowered his voice, his tone becoming mocking. Rebecca flushed and looked away.

"Ah, my poor dear. I had imagined you to be more sensible and above such nonsense. Love?" He shook his head. "And what is that but a silly word? A tool to manipulate others. But love is fickle." His eyes met hers. "Money is not. I'm a very rich man, Rebecca, and I've learned that it isn't love but money that makes things happen. Marry me, and if you want this Garrett fellow, I'll buy him for you...just to show you that I can."

Rebecca stared at him, a cold sickness rising up in her throat. She had always known that Adam possessed a certain...cynicism, a characteristic that seemed as inherent as discriminative genes among the privileged few. But until this moment, she'd never realized how deeply ingrained that nature was. Until this moment, she'd never thought of Adam as unfeeling.

"Goodbye, Adam," she said softly and stepped back from the car.

For several merciless seconds, he silently challenged her to reconsider. But Rebecca said nothing, and after a while he shrugged.

"Well, then—I hope it works out." His tone indicated his doubts, but a half smile formed at the corner of his mouth. "And need I say, whether it does or doesn't, I'm afraid you're out of a job?"

Of course, Rebecca had expected that. She nodded slowly. "I understand."

And then, after a few more moments, Adam shook his head, set the car in gear and drove away.

"BUT, I DON'T UNDERSTAND. Why do you have to leave *now*?"

Alma's voice quivered in a rising wail of emotion as she watched Rebecca carting her small armload of clothes from the closet to her suitcases, lying open on the bed.

Rebecca drew a breath, on the verge of tears herself, deliberately turning her back on the desperation in the woman's brown eyes.

"I can't explain. I just have to get away from here. Please, just accept that. And don't make this any harder for me than it already is."

"It's Wes, isn't it?" Alma pinched and twisted her hands together mercilessly. "He's said something to upset you. I know, because last night I thought I heard—" She stopped herself, her color rising. Her hands abandoned each other for the buttons on her blouse. "What did he tell you, Rebecca? Was it about me? Did he—?"

"Oh, Anna, please!" Rebecca closed her eyes and tried to calm her twanging nerves. "Just leave it alone, can't you? It's in the past, and I just need some...some time to try and figure out what I'm going to do."

That didn't answer her question and Alma looked more distraught than ever. "But what did he say? I mean, why are you so upset?"

Rebecca folded her eyelet blouse and threw it into the suitcase. "What difference does it make? I'm leaving and that's what he wants."

Alma bit her lip and frowned. "Did he say that?"

"In so many words." And so many ways, Rebecca thought painfully. "He left his own house to keep from having to be around me."

"Oh, I don't think that's the reason he left."

Rebecca's eyes lifted to Alma's, and she started to ask her what she meant, but ultimately decided more talk would only slow her down. Besides, she didn't need an interpreter to tell her why Wes had left. He had made it clear to her, himself, that he never wanted to see her again.

Paying little attention to what she was doing, Rebecca snatched another garment from the bed, intending to fold it and toss it into the suitcase, until she realized what it was. Her heart wrenched and the tears she'd been fighting to hold inside burst forth with a sob, which was muffled as she buried her face in the gown of ivory lace. "Oh, Anna, I love him. I *love* him! What am I going to do?"

Sharp relief dawned on Alma's small features, and she went quickly to comfort her only daughter. "Oh, is that all it is?" she said lightly. "Men! They're so hardheaded, sometimes."

"Hardheaded?" Rebecca wanted to laugh, but it hurt too much to try. "If only it was that simple."

Alma lifted one thin hand, and after a moment's trembling hesitation, reached to brush a tear-wet strand of hair away from Rebecca's cheek. "I think he loves you, too. He's always—"

"No! You don't understand," Rebecca stormed, jerking away from Alma's reach. "He doesn't love me. He despises me. He's even implied that I can be bought. Sexually, do you understand?"

Alma looked horrified. "Noooo! You're wrong. I know he would never think that."

"Then you don't know him. And you never knew my mother," Rebecca said bitterly. "He thinks I'm a tramp, just like her."

Alma swayed and threw her hands to her face, a soblike sound escaping her lips. Rebecca wheeled around just in time to see the woman's eyes filling up with tears.

Rebecca frowned. "Oh, Anna, I'm sorry. I shouldn't be talking that way with you." She realized suddenly that she had been so concerned with her own problems, she hadn't stopped to think about upsetting this woman. About how fond the housekeeper was of Wes. "You've been so good to me, and now look what I've done. I've gotten you all upset, too."

Paling slightly, Alma swiped at a tear. "N...no, you haven't. Don't mind me," she said, darting a nervous glance at Rebecca. "I just don't want you to leave, that's all."

Rebecca placed a comforting hand on one bone-thin shoulder. "I have to go, Anna. I don't want to. But there's so much all mixed up with Wes and me. I can't even begin to tell you all—" Her voice broke in an involuntary sob, and Rebecca clutched a hand to her throat, as if she could call back the sound, hold back the strangling pain.

Alma's faint brows drew together. "Don't cry," she tried to console. "Maybe you just need someone to talk to. Someone who really wants to understand."

"No," Rebecca choked, averting her eyes from the woman's troubled gaze. "These are things I've carried for so long inside. I don't think I could let go, if I tried."

"You might be surprised," Alma encouraged, restlessly wringing and tugging at her hands. "And believe me, I know how hard it is to tell someone else how you feel."

Rebecca lifted her head, meeting the older woman's eyes. Soft, brown eyes that seemed to offer tender comfort and compassion unconditionally. And suddenly Rebecca needed someone...this woman...to understand.

Fresh tears swam in her eyes. "Oh, Anna," she whispered, because she could manage no more of a sound. "I had a little baby, a boy."

Alma's eyes widened incredulously.

"He died nearly eight years ago. He was only two days old."

A strange little whimper slipped past Alma's lips and tears glistened in her eyes for the daughter she had abandoned, and the grandchild she would never know. "I'm sorry," she breathed, her voice a feeble tremor, racked with years of guilt. "If only you knew how much."

Rebecca wrapped her arms around herself, chilled by a gust of aching remembrance that swept across her heart like a bitter wind. "There were problems," she said, her tone hollow, her eyes glazed with distant shadows. "The labor was difficult, and the baby's heart was weak. They tried but they couldn't save him. He was just too small, they said. Not strong enough for...this world."

"But that was..." Alma took a step forward, frowning. "That was about the time Mara..."

"Yes." Rebecca raised her eyes to Alma's. She took a deep, steady breath and tightened her lips to keep her chin from quivering. "When my sister was dying, I was miles away, giving birth to an illegitimate child." Her mouth twisted. "Wes's child."

Alma's face went white with dawning shock, and Rebecca searched her expression for any signs of condemnation or rejection. But she saw none. In spite of the woman's obvious surprise, her eyes still held tender compassion, and even affection.

And suddenly, as if the burden of a lifetime had been lifted from her shoulders, leaving her numb and weary from the strain, Rebecca's knees folded under her. In slow motion, she sank down on the edge of the bed and leaned her head against the headboard. Long moments passed, and then she felt the sagging of the bed as Alma sat down beside her. The woman's arm slipped around her shoulders. But they didn't talk anymore. And after a while, feeling a grateful sense of cool relief wash over her, Rebecca closed her eyes and slept.

Alma sat very still; it was an effort for her, but she didn't want to wake Rebecca. And she needed a moment to think. Her heart was still pounding in her newfound knowledge, and her brain ticked with the worry of what to do with it. And then it hit her. A light clicked on in her head, alerting all her senses, and she knew exactly what to do.

Gently, and with all the care of a doting mother, Alma slipped her arm from Rebecca's shoulders. And, with her mind made up, it took every ounce of her shallow restraint to tiptoe from the room. Only when she reached the stairs, did she bolt into a wide-open run.

"Merciful heaven!" Alma shrieked, seconds later, as she tore out across the backyard. Waving a scarf like a red flag over her head, she raced for the paddock area.

It was Sunday and they were working only a skeleton crew. But Alma spotted Wes's foreman, coming out of the office-tack room. "Come on, Hank." She nabbed the lanky ranch hand by his shirtsleeve and proceeded to drag him, struggling, to his pickup truck.

"Hold on, there, Almie. Where we goin'?" Hank balked, even as he heaved himself into the cab.

"I gotta find Wes!" Alma declared, tying her scarf on her head and giving the ends a determined yank. "We'll try the cabin, first. If he's not there, we'll check at Buster's."

"But Almie," Hank protested, sticking the keys into the ignition. "That place is all closed up on Sunday."

Alma shot him a withering look. "Never you mind about that. The ol' coot'll open for me, or rue the day he didn't!"

She slammed her back against the seat. "Now, step on it," she ordered, pointing her eyes dead straight ahead.

Hank shrugged. "Whatever you say." He cranked the truck and pulled it out of the drive, spinning gravel in all directions.

One of these days, Alma thought, she was going to buy a car... and learn to drive it.

RIDING A TALL STOOL over a beer-ringed bar, Wes took the last drag off his cigarette and snubbed it out in a dirty, black plastic ashtray.

On a hot night, when the lights were low, the smoke thick and the house so packed nobody noticed that the country-and-western band wasn't nearly as talented as it was loud, The Bottoms Up Saloon wasn't a bad place to be.

But in the stark light of a Sunday morning, Wes decided as he glanced up at the neon woman—"bar-ing" the joint's name for propriety's sake—he'd have been better off in church.

"Sure you don't want a speck o' dis good ol' gin in nat stuff ya drinking?" Buster Jackson gave Wes a toothless grin.

Wes shook his head. "No, thanks. Coffee's about all I can handle right now."

"And don't look like you's takin' *that* too good," Buster observed wryly.

"Yeah, well, you could safely say this isn't one of my better days." And one he didn't want to talk about. Wes rose to his feet. "Think I'll go stretch my legs in one of these booths over here."

"Be my guest," Buster waved him on. "I's got work to do, anyway."

He lifted a pan of dirty glasses from under the bar and disappeared with them into the back room.

Wes sighed, relieved to see the old man go. He wasn't up to conversation, and wasn't, in fact, entirely certain what he was doing here in the first place. Last night, when he'd left the house, he had started out for the cabin, but had ended up just driving, oblivious to destination. Only this morning, when he'd realized he needed to stop for gas, did he come to his senses enough to recognize where he was.

So where the hell was he?

He was miserable. That's where he was. He'd been up all night driving around in circles, trying to convince himself that he'd done the best thing. He walked out on Rebecca instead of waiting for her to walk out on him.

Reaching in his shirt, Wes pulled out another cigarette and searched his pockets for a match, finding the book at the expense of his sore hand. Sometime during the night, he'd torn off the bandage and flung it out the truck window. He figured now it must have been about the time he was telling himself how proud he ought to be. He'd done what he'd set out to do from the very beginning, and played the scene to the hilt. Just the way he'd imagined it a thousand times in his head. But his head had a convenient way of making everything seem cut and dry. His head seldom considered his heart.

And his heart hurt.

His heart was killing him.

Wes brought the cigarette to his lips and took a long, slow pull. After all, he thought cynically, what good was life, if a man denied himself the things he wanted?

But that was Adam Dane's philosophy. Not his. His, on the other hand, subjected itself to a baser emotion—something that seemed a whole lot like fear.

It's not going to be easy, is it? He could almost hear the sanctimonious voice of prophesy, whispering with particular glee in his ears. *Letting her go without a struggle? Living without her for the rest of your life? And never telling her how you really feel?*

Wes snubbed out his cigarette and shoved the ashtray aside. Propping his elbows on the table, he splayed his hands against his head, which was pounding like a claw hammer, striking a ten penny nail. And with each ring his ears sang out: *Fool. Fool.*

"Wes?"

He hadn't heard the front door open, and he swung at the sound of his name.

"Alma? What in the—?" He started to his feet, but Alma put a hand on his shoulder.

"Keep your seat," she said, meeting his eyes with uncharacteristic steadiness. "This one you better take sitting down."

CHAPTER TWELVE

THE CONSTANT SUN, towering high in the summer-white sky, drove needles of fire through the French doors. Rebecca awoke feeling drained.

She had slept sitting up, her head against the hard oak headboard, and now as she tried to straighten, her whole body seemed to resist, aching both from her cramped position and the depleting aftermath of tears.

Tears. Futile tears. Why did it seem that new tears shed for the sake of old pain were the least cleansing kind?

Sucking in a deep breath, she dragged herself up and went into the bathroom to bathe her swollen eyes and face with cold water. It wouldn't do for Anna to see her in this condition. Heaven knew, she had upset her enough. And she didn't want Wes...

Wes. Wes.

"Oh, God! Don't start again!" she cried in anger at herself and desperation with her situation. She despised the tears, and the pain that was like a heinous hand inside her, wrenching her heart from its roots, flinging it away... still beating.

She turned from the mirror and, pressing a hand to her suddenly sick stomach, sagged against the marble vanity. Its coldness penetrated like a bitter truth. She was never going to see him again. No matter how hard she prayed. Or cried. Or wished that things could be different, she knew they never would. He didn't want her. In eight years, he had never wanted her for anything more than a quick tumble, and nothing had changed since then. Nothing except that she had proved herself only too willing to be used and hurt by him again.

Only, this time was worse. This time she had broken down and dragged someone else—Wes's housekeeper of all persons—into the middle.

Would the woman tell Wes about the baby? Yes, of course she would, Rebecca thought. The woman had been kind to her, but she was devoted to Wes. And the only real question now was how would he react? Maybe he wouldn't even care, after all this time, that she had gotten pregnant that day in the barn. Or maybe he wouldn't believe her.

And what did it matter now? He was gone and she was leaving. Still, Rebecca thought, if he had to hear the truth in some way, it should come directly from her, not channeled through someone else. Turning, she went downstairs to find Alma.

Minutes later, when Rebecca discovered the woman was not in the house, she felt her first pricklings of panic. Would she have taken it upon herself to find Wes and maybe even bring him back here?

No! Rebecca wanted to cry out. She didn't want him dragged back under those kinds of circumstances.

The sudden peal of the doorbell startled her, and she swung around almost guiltily toward the sound. Her heart hammered out several hard beats before she reasoned it wouldn't be Wes, or even Anna, who would have used their keys. Still, she couldn't think of anyone she expected or wanted to see and would have ignored the ringing entirely, if the caller hadn't proved so persistent.

Later Rebecca told herself that sheer persistence should have been her clue.

"Vicky Lynn!" One hand held the door as she stared at the dimpled brunette. The two women hadn't seen each other since the day of Rebecca's accident, that morning in Buck's café when everything had started falling to pieces. Oh, Lord, it seemed so very long ago. "What are you doing here?"

Rebecca's question sounded flat, and it probably wasn't the most polite thing to ask. But Vicky simply laughed mischievously and stepped inside.

"Well, I came to see you, of course!" she answered. "This is Sunday, isn't it? When we talked on the phone I told you I'd drop by."

Their conversation had completely slipped Rebecca's mind, so much had happened since then. And the last thing she needed now was company. "I'm sorry, Vicky. I guess I forgot. Maybe you'd like to make it some other time?"

"Oh, no. This is just fine," she replied, fanning her heat-flushed cheeks with her hand. "And if you have any compassion at all, for pregnant women or otherwise gaudy creatures, you'll offer me a chair and a glass of water before I faint!"

It took less than sixty seconds in the kitchen with Vicky Lynn for Rebecca to ascertain there weren't going to be any fainting spells. Not that she'd thought there would be; it hadn't been a literal threat. Nevertheless, how did one ask a heat-stricken pregnant woman to leave?

They were sitting at the kitchen table, Vicky talking nonstop, except when she paused to take a sip of her lemonade.

"...and then, you can't imagine how shocked I was when he pulled over to ask me for directions. A U.S. Senator, for heaven's sakes. And I said..."

She was talking about Adam, but Rebecca wasn't listening. Her eyes drifted to the wall clock behind the woman's head. Another ten minutes and I'm going to explode, she thought, her jaws clenched and aching, her hands gone numb from trying to hold them still in her lap.

Please go home, Vicky. Please go home and let me decide what I need to do.

She thought of her suitcases, half-packed, lying open on the bed upstairs. She thought of Anna, how concerned and sympathetic she had been, and wondered if she herself hadn't just been borrowing trouble, jumping to conclusions about the woman going to find Wes.

Her eyes shifted slowly back to Vicky. And yet...

"...even before that when Mable Davis, at the drugstore, told me about the car accident. I wanted to come over that very day, but Ted said..."

And yet, she couldn't shake the terrible feeling that if ever she'd entertained the slightest hope of staying on in Hurricane Bluff, of trying once more to win Wes's love, she might as well forget them now. He would never forgive her for this. And even if he chose not to believe it—he might decide she had made it all up—Rebecca knew he would go on hating her. Now, more than ever, if he thought she had lied.

"That, under the circumstances, I should give you both time to... well, you know, adjust."

For the first time since the two women had sat down together, Vicky Lynn actually paused for breath, and the sudden lapse in her chatter was like someone clicking off a blaring TV.

Rebecca blinked. She hadn't really been listening, but the sudden silence was distracting now, and Vicky was looking at her as if expecting some kind of comment or reply. "What?" She tried to look interested. "I'm sorry. What did you just say?"

Vicky laughed. She had grown accustomed to people sometimes tuning her out. "Oh, never mind." She waved her hand in dismissal. "It wasn't very important, anyhow."

She took another sip of her lemonade and sighed as if she had all the time in the world. And Rebecca wondered how anyone could be so oblivious to the body signals from another human being.

Another moment of silence passed between them, and all the while the second hand swept the clock Rebecca was thinking that if she simply remained uncommunicative, maybe Vicky would take the hint and leave.

She was wrong.

"All right, I admit it!" Vicky burst out. "Ted says I'm just nosy and he's right. But I can't stand the suspense any longer! So..." Wiggling forward, she grinned. "How are you getting along with your mother?"

It was a question so bizarre and unexpected, that it took a moment for the words to sink in. Yet even then, Rebecca was so completely dumbfounded, she had to wait for her powers of speech to return. "My *mother*! Vicky, are you serious?"

She thought, at first, that this must be some kind of joke, but Vicky didn't look as if she was joking. And strangely, something began to gnaw at the back of Rebecca's mind. Not thoughts exactly, but impressions: a look, a touch, a certain tilt of the head—vaguely teasing her memory.

She looked at Vicky and was surprised when she heard her own voice sounding so harsh. "I haven't seen my mother since I was eight years old, and you know it as well as I do. So, why don't you just tell me whatever it is you're up to? I don't feel like playing games anymore."

"Oh, my God," Vicky murmured, bringing both hands to cover her mouth, her eyes as big as saucers in her face. "They haven't told you. Oh, Lord, I don't see how but . . . you really don't know, do you?"

"Know what?" What was the matter? Why was her chest pounding, as though it wanted outside of her chest?

"She's here, Rebecca."

Three words. Three whispered words that she had somehow known were coming. "No," she groaned, squeezing her eyes shut.

"It's true, Rebecca. Oh, I'm so sorry I went and told you. What puzzles me is how they've kept it from you. But I swear, I wouldn't lie. Alma Whitney's been back a long time. She's living here with Wes, and has been ever since Mara died."

All the pieces fit so perfectly Rebecca wondered now why she hadn't been smart enough to figure it out on her own. The nagging air of familiarity about Anna that she had almost dismissed. The strange comment about her grandfather, which could only have come from someone who had known him well. The hair. The eyes. The thin, pale hands that never stilled, but were always busy, fidgeting as if in search of something to do. How they reminded her now of Mara's hands!

Anna was her mother. It didn't matter what she called herself, for the mere thought of Alma Whitney brought the sharp, metallic taste of bitterness to Rebecca's mouth. And in that moment she wanted nothing more than to stay and confront her, to fling that knowledge back in her face.

When Vicky finally left, Rebecca left her at the door, then turned and started slowly up the stairs, no longer feeling the same sense of urgency to go as she had before.

They had lied to her. The two of them, deliberately conspiring together to play some cruel trick on her. Rebecca could almost imagine how and why her mother would do it. But Wes? What part had he played? And for what purpose? What reason could he possibly have for helping Alma to conceal her true identity from the daughter she hadn't seen in eighteen years?

The air conditioner cut on with a mild rumble that was like a mini sonic boom. Rebecca was halfway up the flight, but she saw the door to Wes's studio open, and as if by rote, turned and went down to close it.

She had no sooner placed her hand on the knob, however, than she was gripped by an irrepressible impulse to step inside and look around. The door was normally kept locked, and since it wasn't, today, that in itself was intriguing. In all her time in this house, Rebecca had been inside this particular room only once: last night when she had come in to find Wes here alone. And then she hadn't been concerned with surroundings.

The room was, she noted now, rather small, but very well lit, with a row of tall windows covering the southeast wall, and giant, fluorescent panels in the ceiling. In one corner, the proverbial drawing board held a few loose sheets of heavy, blank paper. And next to it, a long worktable lay cluttered with an assortment of sable brushes, ceramic-tile palettes, turpentine, rags, and half-used tubes of paint.

For the first time, she noticed, too, the half a dozen or so canvasses leaned haphazardly against the wall and the legs of the table. Bending down, she picked one up. It was a beautifully detailed piece, a lone pair of wood ducks taking flight off a cypress-riddled bayou as the first weak rays of yellow, morning sunlight pierced the lingering mist.

When she was younger, Rebecca had heard of Wes's interest in painting, and knew that he had gone off to school somewhere for a couple of years, after he'd graduated from high school. But she was only in grade school back then and had never really seen any of his work. Even now her knowledge of art was limited to say the least. But this was the kind one didn't have to be inebriated, or otherwise unbalanced to understand.

Propping the ducks to the side, Rebecca had just started reaching for another canvas, which had been partially obscured behind the first. When she touched it, however, two others fell forward, and as she bent to catch them she felt her hip bump the edge of something else.

It, too, started to fall. She swung around to save it, but managed only to grasp one corner of the short, stiff cloth, which had been painstakingly draped over something on the easel. Wooden legs skidded, making a terrible racket on the slick mosaic floor. But in the end nothing fell. Nothing except the unveiling sheet that Rebecca was left holding in her hand.

She stared at the portrait, and for a moment she thought she must have been hallucinating; she couldn't believe her eyes. Cautiously, she moved closer, her shallow breath diminished to a vapor-lock in her chest.

What does this mean? a tremulous voice whispered from some forgotten outpost on the fringes of her mind.

"I don't know," Rebecca answered aloud, unaware that she had, and unaware that she was holding the paint-splattered cloth to her breast, while her other hand was reaching...

Oh, God! It was real. It was a portrait of her!

"Well, what do you think of the girl I couldn't forget?"

"Wes!" Rebecca swung around, dropping the cloth that had nearly tripped her in the process. She found him standing in the doorway, a brooding scowl on his face. She felt her own face flush guiltily. "I was just, uh..."

"Yes, I'll just bet you were. And how did you get in here? Break in?"

Rebecca glared at him. "Don't be absurd. The door was already open. If you'd wanted me to keep away, you should have said so."

He crossed the room to where she stood, glowered down at her for several long seconds and then, with a violent swing, snatched the drop cloth off the floor beside her feet.

Rebecca bit back a gasp, but it was all she could do to keep from flinching at the look he gave her as he straightened.

"I didn't think I had to worry about a locked door or Keep Out signs, since my understanding was that *you* were supposed to be clearing out."

"And mine was that you were staying out of my way, until I had the opportunity to do so."

Their eyes clashed, and behind his, Rebecca thought she could almost see the smoldering rage of a thousand flames, begging to be fanned.

He knows! she thought wildly, and knew that the panicked suspicion must have crossed her face, when she saw Wes smile. It was a strangely twisted expression that turned his mouth a sickly white, against the dark tan of his face.

"You could have told me, you know. I'm not an ogre. Don't you think I had a right to know?"

His husky voice was a desperate whisper, but there were no fires in his eyes now. The pupils had dilated, so large it was almost frightening, and they looked shockingly sightless and dead.

Rebecca's heart twisted. "I didn't want you to know," she said. "I didn't ever want you to know."

Without warning his control splintered, and he grabbed her upper arms, his fingers digging painfully into her flesh. "Why? Damn you, *why*? Were you ashamed? Afraid? For godsakes, Rebecca! Did you honestly believe I wouldn't *marry* you if you were in trouble?"

His expression was livid with anger and pain, and yet she had the craziest urge to throw back her head and laugh in his face. Instead she whispered savagely, "Interesting phrase, 'in trouble.' Would you have married me then, Wes? If you had known that I was in trouble—and you didn't already have a wife?"

His nostrils flared, and his fingers tightened convulsively on her arms, hurting her. She would have cried out, but he released her suddenly and, with a cry of rage and frustration, whirled away from her like a blind man. Driving his hands through his hair, he stumbled to the edge of the worktable and stood there, staring down at it.

Rebecca said acidly, "You wanted answers, didn't you? Is everything coming clear to you now?" Her heart begged her to stop, but she couldn't control the churning bitterness that had driven her for so long. "You wanted to know why I didn't come home when my only sister was dying. Well, believe me, it wasn't by choice. I stayed away to protect Mara...and yes, even you!" Her eyes narrowed and her voice dropped to a caustic, rasping whisper. "It would have been unforgivably *gauche* on my part, don't you think? To show up in my condition, wait around for my sister to die, just so I could lay claim to her husband... with the charge of paternity?"

"That's enough!" Wes shouted, slamming his fist down on the table as he swung around to face her.

"No, it's not," Rebecca screamed. "You want the truth? You want it over between us? Then, by God, let's hear, let's hear it *all*! Why did you do it, Wes? Why did you marry her?"

Shaking with anger and near hysteria, she had meant to fling the question in his face. But hot tears rushed to her eyes and to her horror, her words only sounded disgustingly wheedling and weak. "Oh, God, I know I never meant anything to you. But it didn't have to be *her*, did it? My own sister? It could have been somebody else. I mean... I think I could have handled it if it had been—" Despite her attempt at control, her voice broke off in a bitter, choking sob.

"No, Rebecca," Wes said then, and his own voice sounded so strange, drawn from the utter depths of him, that she forced her head up, staring at him through the blur of her tears.

"No," he said again. "It couldn't have been anyone else. Because no one else was your sister. Only Mara. Now, do you understand?"

No, Rebecca thought. She didn't understand. Was he saying he had done this thing to spite her? To hurt her deliberately? But why?

She never had the chance to ask. Or maybe she simply hadn't the heart or the courage any longer.

Wes straightened slowly. Moving away from the table, he went to stand in front of the portrait in something that was like a daze.

For long moments he just stood there, staring at it, his face bearing no expression at all, except for the almost alarming degree of pallor, undermining his tanned skin like a rubber mask, a sponge, draining it of color.

When he finally spoke, his tone was brittle, harsh for all that it was but a whisper. "You know, when I first started this, it was supposed to be a portrait of my wife. Every man should have something, right? Some little token of remembrance. But in my mind everything got confused." Wes shook his head now as if to clear it, as if he couldn't believe what had gone on inside his own brain.

And then, Rebecca saw the grim twist of his mouth, the bitter look of self-contempt, the same emotion that was in his voice. "In less than a week after Mara died, I couldn't even *remember* what she had looked like. Isn't that a hell of a note? You marry someone and you promise to..." He stopped himself, and drew in a breath. "Outside of everything else, I don't think I can ever forgive myself for that one."

Rebecca could feel her own eyes widen in confusion and disbelief. "Then why, Wes?" she heard herself whisper, needing to know, but afraid to hear. It was time she had clear answers. "Why did you marry Mara?"

He didn't look at her when he answered. He just kept staring straight ahead at the portrait. "I married Mara because she was dying. Because she was dying and she knew it.'' He said it flatly and without emotion.

Rebecca stared at him, in shock. ''No! No, you're lying,'' she cried, fighting to deny a truth that seemed too terrible, too unacceptable to even imagine.

Dull, black eyes flickered briefly to hers. ''Why should I lie, Rebecca? She's dead.''

A bubbling sickness rose up and clutched at Rebecca's throat. ''But I thought . . . They said it was . . .''

''No—it wasn't pneumonia. You didn't know that, did you? Although technically, I guess, that's what finished her at the last. The doctors said it was a rare kind of acute leukemia, that it didn't respond to treatment well. There really wasn't any hope.''

''But I don't understand! Why didn't she tell me?''

Wes's mouth tilted slightly, but his eyes looked flat and empty of all feeling. ''I guess she wanted to spare you. And I should have been trying to spare her. But at the time, I couldn't think of anyone . . . except myself. And you.''

Rebecca felt every ounce of blood ebb away from her face. ''What are you saying?''

His brows twitched in a kind of wince, as if some unseen hand had just given the last killing twist to a knife that had been buried inside him for a very long time. Glancing away, he answered slowly, his husky voice almost inaudible. ''I married Mara because of you, Rebecca. Because, to me, she was a small part of you. The only part I thought I'd ever have.''

His admission hit her with a force that seemed to numb every part of her body. She couldn't think. She couldn't move. She wasn't certain she even breathed. But she knew that she was feeling. And what she felt was the rending apart of her heart by contradictory emotions: fleeting hope for herself, remorse and pity for her sister, whom she had loved dearly...and hated a little, because of Wes.

Wes kept his eyes on the portrait, not venturing a glance at her, but went on talking in the same near-mesmerized tone as before. "I told myself, in the beginning of course, that I was being damned commendably charitable. Pity. Self-sacrifice. The whole bit. It was the least I could do, after all. It wasn't as if we were talking forever. And I could surely afford a few months out of my own life."

"But you never loved her?" Rebecca's voice trembled with the fear that he might say yes, and the guilty sense that she wanted so badly to hear him say no.

He gave a short, humorless laugh. "You know, the crazy thing is? I think, I really had started to love her a little. Or at least I'd like to believe that I had."

Rebecca felt his grief, his guilt, his pain as deeply as she felt her own, and her eyes filled with tears. How was it possible that so many lives, so many hearts had been affected, wounded and broken, all for the few hours they had spent loving each other in what seemed like another life?

"I'm sorry, Wes," she whispered, her heart aching for all the dreams that had slipped through their fingers. How she wished they could all go back and start over, knowing better this time!

"Funny," he murmured. "That's just what Mara said."

He turned his head, and this time when he looked at her and spoke again, Rebecca thought she had never seen such horrible anguish, or heard that kind of despair.

"She apologized, can you imagine? She was dying, so weak she could barely manage the strength to hold on to my hand. And yet, she was strong enough to look me straight in the eyes, and I swear to God she was smiling—that soft, kinda forgiving smile that always made her eyes look sad. 'I'm sorry, Wes,' she said, 'I'm sorry I couldn't be Rebecca for you.'"

The import of his last words struck her like a blow, a jolt, whirling through her head until she felt her whole body sway. "But why? Whatever would make her..." Her heart was pounding so that she could barely hear the sound of her voice above it.

Desperately, her eyes searched his for answers, but his features had gone rock hard, and his mouth curled cruelly up at one corner.

"What would make her say or even think such a thing, you're wondering?" He finished the question she couldn't, and went on. "I've asked myself that same thing, too, at least once a day—every day in fact—for the last seven years. But all I can say is maybe Mara thought she saw something in me. Something I couldn't see in myself. Or didn't want to."

"An...and what was that?" She forced the words out over lips that were suddenly dry and stiff with the fear of wanting something—someone—too badly.

Say it! Say it was me you really wanted! her heart cried out. While her soul prayed, *Mara, forgive me.*

But Wes remained mute to her silent pleadings. Coal-black eyes narrowed as he looked into hers. "It doesn't matter," he said bluntly. "Because whatever she thought—she was wrong."

The tenuous fiber of hope she had clung to was so shockingly severed from her grasp, Rebecca felt for a moment as if she'd been left to drown in a rushing flood of unrestrained desperation.

"You used me!" she screamed, hardly aware of what she was saying, knowing only that she had reached the limits of all control. "And then you used my sister! Like she was some kind of sacrificial lamb! Penance for your damned guilty conscience! You bastard! You dirty, unfeeling son of a—"

"Shut up!" Grabbing for her, Wes caught her shoulders, his hands rough. And yet his grip was curiously restrained, almost gentle. "You want me to admit it? All right, I was...I *am* everything you say. But what does that prove, Rebecca? Nothing."

His face was so close she could see his jaw muscles move as he fought for control, and the strange shadow that passed over his eyes. And for a split second, Rebecca thought, his expression was one of indecisiveness, as though he wasn't sure whether to hold her or let her go.

"Wes, listen to me. Please..."

She didn't want it to end like this, and lifting her hand she reached and tried to touch his face. But he dodged her with a twist of his head, stepping back, and letting his hands fall away from her shoulders.

"Go away, Rebecca," he said, and his tone was dull, as lifeless as the numbing sensation Rebecca felt seeping into her limbs, her heart. "Just go back to California, to your senator boyfriend and your pat little job. But, please, just go away and don't come back."

It was the finality in his voice that was most soul-destroying, and later Rebecca didn't know what more she might have done or said had Alma Whitney not come in just then.

"Is everything all right in here?" Her tremulous voice, filled with uncertainty and a hint of false gaiety, rang out more shrilly than was normal for even her.

"Yeah, I was just leaving." Wes started toward the door.

"But you can't go now! Look, what I've brought. Lemonade and fresh-baked cookies. I thought we could all—"

"Let it go, Alma!" Wes shouted. Having finally reached the end of his rope, he didn't realize he had called her by name until he heard her stricken cry.

Alma's eyes went to Rebecca's and time stopped for an immeasurable second. They stared at each other as mother and daughter, for the first time in eighteen years.

"You're on your own," Wes said to Alma. "This is one battle I can't fight—" his eyes touched Rebecca's "—for either of you."

And then, before she could find the strength or the words to call him back again, he was out the door and out of her life. This time, Rebecca knew, it was for good.

In retrospect, it seemed to her later that there was an ironically taunting sense of the anticlimactic, when she turned again to face her mother. She wanted to laugh and scream at the world, at the invisible puppeteer who pulled all the strings. She thought that this was transparent, predictable; no decent stage man in his right mind would shiver to create such a bold, theatrical stunt.

But in truth, the matter was no laughing one.

"Rebecca, I..."

"You don't have to say it." She held up her hand as a signal for her mother to stop. "I know who you are. Surprise, surprise. Vicky Lynn Hodge paid me a visit today, and guess what a wealth of knowledge she had to share?"

"Rebecca, baby, I never meant for you to find out that way." Alma's hands shook, rattling the ice cubes in the glasses that stood on the tray she held. "I was going to tell you, soon. I just wanted to make you see that we could be friends. We could be close. Almost like sisters . . ."

"I *had* a sister!" Rebecca snatched the tray from her mother's hand, sloshing lemonade and sailing cookies like tiny Frisbees over the art supplies on the table where she practically threw it. "I needed a mother. Not another sister. A mother, Alma! Do you know what that means? Do you even have the slightest idea?"

Monstrous-sized tears rose like floodwaters in Alma's doe-round eyes. "I know what it means. I had you. You and Mara, I carried you both under my breast, right next to my heart—"

"Oh, God! Is that what you think? That giving birth makes a woman a mother? Well, that's not it, Alma! That's not it at all. Being a mother means—"

She had promised herself that she wasn't going to cry anymore. Wasn't about to let this woman make her shed tears. But despite her vow, her throat choked up and she turned away, taking deep breaths, trying to maintain control.

"Being a mother means being there. And damned proud that you are the center of some little universe, where mommas fix everything, and even if they can't, there's never a doubt about who's in your corner, about caring . . . or love."

One trembling hand reached out, touching Rebecca's shoulder hesitantly. "But I always loved you, baby. You and your sister. And I love you now, can't you see?"

"No!" Rebecca cried, jerking away from Alma's hand. "I don't want your love now. It's too late. I don't need it."

"Oh, God, oh please don't say that, Rebecca."

"Why not? It's true." Her eyes flashed. "I needed you when I couldn't fasten the button on my Sunday shoe, because it was too small already and had been worn by three other pairs of feet before mine. I needed you—" her voice quivered with the anguish of remembering "—when Papa used to say I'd end up in trouble someday because I was trashy, just like my mother."

Rebecca saw the look of pain cross Alma's face, but she couldn't seem to halt the bitter flow of resentment spilling out with her words. And she wasn't sure she wanted to. "I needed you," she said, her voice low and filled with contempt, "when I was pregnant and unmarried with no place to go and no one who'd have me. Where was your love back then?"

Alma sobbed. "I made some mistakes. Oh, Rebecca, can't you see? I'm sorry now. Can't you forgive me? Don't you know that if I had it to do over—"

"But you don't," Rebecca cut her off sharply. "And neither do I." Silver eyes bore mercilessly into Alma Whitney's gaunt face.

"Can't you at least let me explain?" she pleaded, tears trailing in streaky lines down her cheeks.

"Explain what? What possible explanation could there be for a grown woman to abandon her two small children, without a word, without a call, without so much as a Christmas card every year or so?"

"I was going to. I meant to," Alma whimpered helplessly.

"Well, good intentions weren't enough, because we—" Rebecca's throat tightened. She had to swallow before she could go on. "For years we watched and waited for you to come home. Do you know what that's like for a child? Can you imagine what it was, to stand at that window, looking down that old road. Hoping and praying. 'Maybe tomorrow will be the day,' Mara used to say. But it never was tomorrow. And pretty soon, we just stopped looking down that road. Because, after a while, as you have so well proved, neither of us could remember what you even looked like."

Alma went to pieces. "Oh, Rebecca, I didn't dream— Please let me explain."

"Explain? *Explain?*" Rebecca repeated, her tone incredulous. "There are no explanations for something like that. No excuses good enough. And as for your love?" She laughed, a harsh sound that was only a sharp rush of air. "You keep it," she advised. "You couldn't give it to me when I needed it. And now I don't want it anymore."

CHAPTER THIRTEEN

SOMEWHERE REBECCA had read that the past is never dead, for it keeps on consuming the present, second by lonely second.

In truth, she wasn't certain if she had understood that statement before. But on that hot, sunlit, Sunday afternoon, when she turned away from the woman who had been no mother to her, and walked from Windspear, from Wes, for the last time, returning to her grandfather's house, Rebecca knew she understood it then.

She would never be free. With every moment, with every breath, with each new memory created, the past that she had come home to put to rest had endured despite her, and had grown ever larger, until now there seemed to be nothing left.

She had lost Wes. No, Rebecca corrected herself, numbly, without tears. That wasn't true. For in actuality, he had never been hers to win or lose. And if ever he might have been, she realized, that time was lost. It was too late now. Years too late.

For Wes.

For herself.

For her mother.

The night winds billowed the thin living room curtains that were yellowed with age. And, restless with her thoughts, Rebecca wandered to the window. The moon had disappeared behind a drifting cloud, but the lime-dust road, she knew by heart, shone even in the darkness. It was the road her mother had traveled when she had gone away and left her daughters far behind, those years ago. The same road Rebecca herself had taken when she was eighteen and had followed back again, only to realize that life in the outside world wasn't so different from the one she'd known here. Loneliness wasn't a place. And isolation held the same chill in silk as in hand-me-down shoes.

Tears blurred her eyes, and Rebecca turned away from the window, letting the curtain fall back into place. The room was warm and the cloth-shaded lamp lent just the right amount of light, so that the faded magenta sofa looked homey and comfortable, instead of only dusty.

In a sense, she supposed, it was poetic justice. The old farmhouse she'd always hated and had considered a prison of sorts, had now become her sole refuge. She had no other place to go. No job. No fiancé. No future life to hurry back to.

And yet, what did she have here that she couldn't carry wherever she went? Bittersweet memories in one hand. A fistful of regrets in the other. And a heart burdened to breaking with the knowledge that some love comes only after it is too late, and some comes not at all.

LONG INTO THE DARKEST HOURS of that same endless night, Alma Whitney stood at the window, looking down the graveled drive that led away from Windspear in the direction of her father's house.

"She's never coming back, Wes. Is she?" She didn't turn around as she spoke, but Wes thought her voice sounded old, almost feeble in the wake of her tears.

He closed his eyes. "No, Alma. I don't think so. She'll have her car back tomorrow. She'll go to the bank, probably sign a few papers. And then..." Wes sucked in a breath in an effort to relieve the aching tightness in his chest. "And then, I guess that'll be it."

Alma turned from the window, her eyes pleading. "But aren't you even going to try to do something?"

"Like what?" Wes swung away from the mantel, where he had been staring into the empty fireplace, as if he longed for warmth. "What can I do to stop her if she wants to go? I've done everything I know..."

"You could go and ask her to stay."

Dark eyes, circled with fatigue, leveled with Alma's. "No." Wes shook his head. "I can't do that."

"But why not?" Alma whined pathetically. "I think she would. If only you would..." She glanced away from him, her voice lowering. "If you told her you wanted her to stay. If you said that...you loved her."

Wes felt a blade of color rising to his face. "Yeah," he said gruffly. "I noticed how well that routine worked for you. No thanks." He turned back to the fireplace. "I think I'll just pass on the love business."

Alma dropped the curtain back into place and began to pace up and down in front of the window. "Oh, why do we have to lose someone for good before we can forgive them? Before we can admit how we really feel. You can't forgive her. She can't forgive me." She halted abruptly, staring off into nothingness. "And I didn't start forgiving my daddy until the day they laid him in his grave."

There was a tinge of bitterness in Alma's tone, and Wes glanced up, his eyes narrowed slightly. "This is different," he insisted. "He was your father. Rebecca and I..."

"Are what, Wes?" Alma swung on him quickly. "Two people who love each other and can't admit it? Or who wished it wasn't so, but it is?"

"That's enough, Alma," Wes warned. He felt rotten and he didn't need her adding to the weight of his mood.

But still she persisted. "No, it's not." She bucked him in a rare show of defiance. "You love her, Wes. I know it. Mara knew it. Why can't you admit it, before it's too late?"

Pushing away from the mantel, Wes stood to face her squarely, his jaw set and his eyes hard. His first thought was to deny all she'd said. His second thought was, what good would it do? If he was that transparent, why appear more foolish by arguing the point now?

"It's already too late," he said finally, and in his heart he felt it was true. "She's made her life without us. We don't belong. And I'm not certain I ever did."

"But don't you see what you're doing?" Alma cried in desperation. "You're not even giving her a chance. You're shutting her out. You're forcing her hand just like Papa did to me."

Wes frowned, failing to see what earthly relevance Will Daniels had to do with any of this. But sensing that Alma was in a mood to tell him, he let her talk, glad he didn't have to.

"My mother died when I was born," she murmured absently, pacing slowly up and down. "Truth is, I think she was the only person my father ever loved. And in his eyes, I never quite measured up to the daughter he thought was worthy of her. It was Mara who helped me see that. Mara and you, I guess. Because Mara never measured up, either, not for you. Isn't that right, Wes?" Her eyes drifted to his, and once again Wes felt the clutches of guilt laying hold of his conscience.

"Is that what she told you?" he asked.

Alma shrugged, a gesture that was more like a spasmodic shiver. "Maybe not in those words. But I know that's what she thought."

Wes inhaled a ragged breath. "I never wanted to hurt her, Alma. You know that. I cared for Mara."

"I know." She smiled tenderly. "But you see, I never meant to hurt her, either. Or Rebecca." Alma bit her lip, hesitating for just an instant, before she went on.

"When Luke left me, I was alone and afraid. I'd never made it even through high school, and the only life I knew was the farm and traveling with the carnival. That's how I first met Luke." She glanced up and smiled a little. "Papa had let me stay all night at Rosie Canfield's house and we hitched a ride across the river to Vicksburg. Luke ran a pitch on the rope pulls and sometimes he worked the ring toss pit. Anyway he said I was pretty and he told me that he was lonely. And after that I sneaked away to meet him every night. He wasn't as old as Pa, but he had seen a lot of things and been a lot of places, and I wanted to go there, too. And so, when the carnival left town, I left with Luke. And we got married that same night." Alma beamed as if, even now, that memory was still sweet in her mind.

"But he left you," Wes pointed out. "Don't you hold any bitterness against him for that?"

She shrugged. "Oh, I guess I did at first. But I had known when I met him that Luke wasn't the kind of man to be tied for long. And when we were together, he showed me the best times I ever had."

"But when it was over, you came back home."

"Yes," Alma admitted. "But only for a short while. Papa and I couldn't get along, as usual. Only this time, when I told him I was leaving, we had a terrible fight. He said that if I left, I couldn't ever come back again. And that he would go to the welfare people and have my babies taken away from me." Hot tears brimmed Alma's eyes. "He said I wasn't fit to raise them."

"Alma." Wes's voice filled with compassion. "You never told me that."

She shook her head and swallowed. "I've never told anyone. Except Mara, and only then because..." They looked at each other, both knowing the reason why. Alma glanced away first, lacing her fingers together, twisting, bending them. "And, I think, maybe because I was afraid he was right."

Wes watched Alma carefully. Maybe the old man had been right, but it was his educated guess that he'd been wrong. Somehow the three would have made it. Why do people do the things they do to each other? he wondered.

"Why are you telling me this, now?" Wes asked, suddenly feeling a strange sense of obligation, maybe even protection for this woman, who had been such an irritant to him in the past.

"I don't know," she confessed. "I guess because in my heart I know one of us has got to stop Rebecca. One of us has to make her see running away never solved anything. If I had stayed, if I had tried to understand my father better, then maybe I wouldn't be where I am today, and maybe my children wouldn't have had to suffer for the pride and the bitterness that had nothing to do with them."

The tears that had been standing in Alma's eyes for several minutes slid forlornly down her cheeks, and

Wes looked at her with a newfound respect. Underneath all the self-consciousness, the nervous twitchings and the grating voice, he saw a woman who had been beaten down by life and by her own mistakes. But she was still fighting back, facing her fears and her own inadequacies as best she knew how.

And what about him? Wes wondered. Was he still fighting back?

The grandfather clock struck 2:00 a.m. "Go on to bed, Alma," Wes said. "There's nothing either of us can do until daylight."

"All right, but are you going to see her? I know I've got to try. But what about you, Wes?"

"I'll think about it," he said. And seconds later he was alone, staring out the same window where Alma had stood minutes ago.

Looking out into the void of endless black night, Wes felt suddenly as if he were looking into the prospects of his own future, at his life without Rebecca; an empty, narrow, suffocating tunnel from which there was no escape, no light at either end. Past and future sealed.

Could he stand that? Could he bear knowing he would never see her again? Never know the deep serenity that came with waking up beside her? The sweetness of his lips against her skin, the scent of her hair, the sight of it stretched out in sleep tangles against his pillow? And her eyes, luminous, filled with emotion, shining like quicksilver in the night . . . when she looked at him . . .

Make love to me as if you really loved me. As if this were our first time ever.

His bloodshot eyes began to sting, and Wes reached up a forefinger and thumb, massaging at the graininess shuttered behind the tired lids. When he pulled his hand away, his fingers were wet and a salty dampness clung to his dark lashes. And for the first time in his life Wes thought he understood the kind of pain that could bring a grown man to his knees.

"I'M SORRY ABOUT all this. The delay and all, I mean," J. P. "Son" Deaton said around a fat cigar pouched in the already generous swell of his jowl.

Dabbing his thick, fleshy face with an ever-present white handkerchief, he nervously adjusted the nameplate on his desk.

"Don't worry about it. It's over now." Rebecca shoved the papers she had just finished signing toward him. "If I had known she was here in the beginning, though, it might have saved us a lot of trouble."

"Yes, well..." Son blotted the standing beads of sweat from the goiterous bulge of his white-collared neck. "It wasn't my idea, I can assure you."

Clearing his throat, he gathered up the succession documents and tramped them once on the desk, to straighten them before setting them aside. "Alma wanted to keep her father's farm. I guess, she was afraid if you knew who she was you would force a sale, out of spite."

"I wouldn't have done that," Rebecca said honestly. "I never wanted the place. She could have had it all for what I care." A trace of bitterness lingered in her tone.

"Well, now she does." Son mopped his palm, then extended it to Rebecca, who stood to accept his handshake. "Thank you again for coming in. I'm sure your mother will be pleased that you've so graciously transferred all rights and shares exclusively to her."

"Yes," she murmured. And then, as an afterthought, "Are you sure the taxes and interest will be paid?"

Son smiled and withdrew the cigar, spitting a little and wiping his mouth. "Wes has assured me he would see to it. And he is as good as his word."

"Yes, of course," Rebecca nodded. Wes would take care of it all. Why hadn't she thought of that? She said goodbye and left the bank.

It was a dismal day to coincide with the dismal mood she was in. Sometime during the hours between Sunday night and Monday morning, sullen gray clouds had banded together to form a sagging tarp that hung in suffocating dreariness over the sky...and Rebecca's heart.

Her suitcases were in the trunk. Wes had taken care of it all, from having her car delivered that morning—the bill had been marked Paid in Full—to seeing that every last reminder of her was neatly cleared from his sight, swept and tucked like dust under a rug. Forgotten.

Rebecca swallowed and tapped the brake, slowing her car to make the curve that led to Cemetery Road. She wasn't going to let herself cry anymore. Tears never cleaned a plow, her grandfather used to say, and she was inclined to agree with him. If tears could bring her sister back, or change the way things stood between herself and Wes, then after last night, Rebecca thought, the world might have been a brighter place.

As it was, it only looked desolate and bleak.

She pulled her car off on the soft shoulder of the road and stared through the windshield at the stormy, black clouds. A fitting backdrop for the fenced-off hill that everyone called, for reasons unknown, Dan Miller's Mound.

The wind whipped her jersey skirt and tore at her hair with wicked glee, as Rebecca got out of the car and climbed the hill.

It took her a moment to locate the twin headstones that marked the grave sites of Will Daniels and his granddaughter Mara Whitney Garrett. But once she'd found them and stood, staring down at those two lifeless pieces of stone, she couldn't remember why she had come.

To pay your last respects, a voice prompted in the back of her head. But Rebecca's heart knew it was much more than that.

"I'm sorry, Mara," she whispered, and the words had no sooner left her lips than the tears she had been holding at bay with a flimsy leash, broke all restraints then ran, unchecked, down her cheeks. "I love you very much. I wish I could tell you that. I wish I'd taken the time to tell you more often when we were together."

She sniffed back a sob and cuffed at her nose, then gave a hiccupping little laugh when she realized what she had done: wiped her nose on her sleeve like a child.

She laughed again, and then more seriously she glanced at the other stone. "How do you like lying right next to him for all eternity, Mar? I guess, that's the worst of it, huh? A person dies and everyone assumes she wants to park beside some grim relation she couldn't abide with in real life. But I s'pose all and all Papa wasn't such an awful guy."

The wind snagged her hair, and Rebecca anchored a feathery tendril behind her left ear. "You know, I think if I could've just got him to like me a little more..." Tears clogged her throat, and she let the words trail away.

It hadn't started to rain yet, but the air was damp and heavy with the scent of it. Something waggled in the breeze, and Rebecca saw the pink heads of briar roses nodding along the fence. On impulse she picked one, and then another. She turned her head toward the heavens, and for several long minutes she stood in silent vigil over her sister's grave, letting her heart say all the things words couldn't.

"I always loved you, my sister," she whispered as she bent and carefully placed one tiny rose on the stone. Turning then, she looked down at her grandfather's resting place.

A thousand images went through her mind, and she thought of all the times she had been angry with him and all the times he'd been angry with her. And suddenly, like pictures whirling on a projection screen, everything stopped, and in a flash, she remembered something she had kept hidden in her memory for years.

"She's not coming back, is she, Papa?"

A hard, callused thumb scraped roughly across her cheek.

"Hell, no, and it ain't no use in bawlin' about it, neither. Now, wipe them tears and git in the house."

"But what about you, Papa? Who's gonna wipe your tears?"

With trembling hand, Rebecca laid the second rose in place and made her silent peace to the man who had raised her, the gruff, old-fashioned farmer who never changed his ways, and whose pain and fear of loving she had never understood until now.

It was still afternoon, but the skies had grown so dark Rebecca didn't notice the battered blue pickup pull over in front of her parked car, until she was at the foot of the hill. Even then, she might not have paid any attention to it at all, if she hadn't heard the door creak open and glanced over just in time to recognize the woman sliding out from the passenger's side.

"Rebecca?" Alma's trembling voice carried on a gust of wind as her eyes met those of her daughter's. "Can I talk to you for a minute?"

Rebecca stiffened instinctively in cold resentment at the sight of her mother. "No," she answered flatly, proceeding toward her car. "We don't have anything to say to each other."

She wasn't listening but she overheard Alma thank Wes's foreman for the ride, and seconds later the man pulled away, short a passenger.

Alma turned back to her daughter. "Please, Rebecca. You've got to give me a chance to explain."

"I don't want to hear it," she said, holding up her hand as she skirted the fender of her car and opened the door. "There's no excuse for what you did. You left us! And I won't listen to any pathetic *explanations*!"

She slid into the car and slammed the door, reaching for the ignition. Alma stooped and began to knock frantically on the window.

"But where are you going?" she cried, her voice sounding muffled from where her daughter sat inside the car.

"Away!" Rebecca flipped the key, cranking the engine.

She had jammed the car in gear and started backing out, when the lightning crackled and a great boom of thunder shook the very earth. The rain broke loose in a hellish downpour. Through the blur that was her windshield, Rebecca glanced up to see her mother, huddled and shaking like a frightened hound in the storm.

"Dammit!" She slammed on the brake and cracked the window. "All right, get in!" she shouted. "I'll take you to the cutoff road. It's a short walk from there. But that's as far as it goes. Do you understand me?"

Alma nodded—or shuddered—and swiped hastily at the runnels of rain, blackened with mascara and streaming down her cheeks.

"All right, then. Come on." Rebecca switched up the window while Alma dashed around to clamber in on the other side.

Once she was situated, soaking wet but secure inside, Rebecca yanked the gearshift into drive and pressed down on the accelerator. Mud and rocks flew, battering the car's undercarriage with a deafening racket, but the tires only whined and spun in place.

"Oh, that's just great," she muttered. "I'm stuck!"

To prove it, Rebecca tried again, this time stomping the gas nearly to the floor. The car eked forward a meager inch, before the hood began to smoke. "Wonderful. *Terrific!* Now the engine's overheating. I thought that stupid garage was supposed to fix the body, not destroy the motor."

With no other alternative left to her, Rebecca let up on the accelerator. The engine promptly died and the car rolled back with a klunk, a nasty sound that she decided couldn't have offered a more befitting accompaniment for the state of her mood had she requested it in advance.

"I probably should have warned you," Alma said, her teeth clattering together. "They've been grading up the shoulder to widen this road. You shouldn't have pulled off in that loose dirt."

"Well, it's not dirt now, is it?" Rebecca retorted, glaring out at the rain. "It's mud. And what I'd like to know is how we're supposed to get out of it."

Alma looked at her blankly. "I don't know. Do you? Maybe we could just sit here till the rain stops."

"And do what? Chat?" Rebecca snapped bitterly, feeling as if she had finally been pushed to the breaking point and beyond. "And what shall we talk about, Mother? Abandonment! Deceit? Or how about rejection? That's a good one to kick around a while. So tell me, how does it feel to be on the receiving end for a change?"

Alma's gaze leveled with her daughter's and her own eyes filled with tears. "It's not so different for me. I've been on that end before."

She tried to smile—a rueful, it-doesn't-matter twist of unevenly painted lips. But the smile sat so poorly with the sadness in her eyes, Rebecca felt a sharp pang of guilt.

And that guilt made her angry. She had nothing to feel guilty about! None of this was her doing. And she wasn't going to let this woman get to her with a ploy for sympathy!

It was more for the sake of diversion than for any hope of cranking her car that Rebecca turned the key and tried the smoking engine again. The starter churned several sick, grinding revolutions that disintegrated rapidly to an impotent *click-click*.

"Lovely," Rebecca muttered facetiously. "Now the battery's dead. I expect the hood ornament will be struck by lightning any moment now. And then all our troubles will be over."

Under other circumstances both women might have laughed, seeing the ridiculousness in their predicament. But instead they sat tensely, silently, listening to the deafening roar of the pounding rain on the roof of the Mercedes, intensely aware of each other in the small confines of the car's interior.

"I went to the bank today," Rebecca announced, when she could no longer stand the unrelieved drumming sound of the rain. "The farm is yours. And just for the record, you didn't have to deceive me to get it. It's yours by right. I wouldn't have tried to keep you from having it. I'm not that kind of person."

Alma shifted uncomfortably in her seat, tugging the clinging wet hem of her Hawaiian print dress over the protruding caps of her knees. "I never thought you were. I was just afraid of what you might think, when you found out who I really was."

"And so you deceived me. You and . . ." She had to stop and draw a fortifying breath before she could say his name. "Wes," she whispered, and paused again, biting down on the inside of her cheeks, warding off another, deeper pain. "You know, I can almost understand why you would do that. But why? Why would he go along? What did he have to gain?"

Alma's restless hands stilled for one clutching second. "Time," she answered simply. "He wanted time with you."

Rebecca's hands gripped the steering wheel as she stared straight ahead at the windshield, grown foggy with the contained heat of their breaths. "And why do you suppose he wanted time with me, or why did he feel he had to trick me to have it?"

"Because he loves you, Rebecca. Don't you know that by now?"

"Why do you keep telling that when I know—I know!—it isn't true. Are you trying to soft-soap me, is that it? Do you think by telling me more lies, things you think I want to hear that you'll be endearing yourself to me? That then we can all forgive and forget? Just like that?'' Rebecca snapped her fingers. ''Well, you're wrong. I don't need you, and I don't need your lies. I can make it by myself. And I will. I—'' She cupped her hand to her mouth, choking off a sob.

''You're afraid,'' Alma stated factually as she stared at her daughter in shocked realization. ''All this time I thought that I was the only one, but now I see...'' An image of Wes came to Alma's mind. ''You're afraid of forgiving, of risking too much because then you might lose, and I know that hurts. But what happens if we never risk caring, loving someone? Then, don't you see, we've lost already. You have to try, Rebecca. Everyone has to try.''

''Like you? Like you tried to love and care for Mara and me? Who are you to lecture me on love and forgiveness? To accuse me of being afraid to give of myself? Look at you. Look at yourself. You're wasted. You're empty. And I hate you, do you hear? I despise you and I wish... I wish...'' She couldn't bring herself to say the angry, hurtful words that trembled on her tongue.

''You wish I were dead. Is that it? Well, that's okay, because that's kinda what Papa said, too. The night I left you and Mara. He said... he said I was no good and that if he'd had a choice when I was born, it would have been me who'd died, instead of my mother.''

Alma's small face crumpled, and in that moment as she sat huddled close against the door, her hair slick-wet, thin bones poking through her sodden garments like sticks, Rebecca couldn't help feeling sorry for her. She remembered the night she had asked the woman she'd thought of then as Anna—a friend—if it had seemed possible that Wes could blame her somehow, because she lived and Mara had died. She recalled the strange way the woman had reacted. And now, looking at this same woman as her mother, Rebecca felt years of bitterness ebbing away. Alma Whitney was nothing like the ruthlessly selfish individual Rebecca had always pictured. Instead, she was only a weak and broken woman, an object of pity. And, after all the years of resentment and hate, Rebecca was astounded that she could feel nothing but pity for her.

"I'm sorry," Rebecca apologized, trying to comfort her. "I didn't mean those things I said. Please, don't cry...Mama." She forced herself to say the word, and reached across the seat—forcing herself again—to take her mother's hand in her own.

Alma lifted her head, and the look she gave her daughter was like that of a small child, hopelessly lost, finding a light in the darkness at last.

Rebecca smiled and patted her clinging hand. "We'll talk about it, okay? Somehow, we'll get things worked out. But right now, I've got to figure out how we're going to get out of here."

Once more Rebecca glanced up, trying to see out through the driving rain and the moisture that had collected on the windows.

"Are there any houses around here?" she asked, using her fist to clear a small circle on the fogged windshield above the steering wheel.

"Windspear's the closest," Alma offered.

Rebecca's hand froze. "I don't want to go there."

"Rebecca—"

"Please. Please don't push it. I just can't handle it right now."

"Then, I guess you could try the Coopers. But you still have to cut through Windspear land."

Rebecca drew a breath and leaned back in the seat.

Yes, she remembered the old Cooper place. An eyesore if there ever was one. All she'd have to do would be to cut across the road to a speck of woods that thinned to a pasture she must have crossed a thousand times in the past. The only problem was that the Coopers' house lay on the other side of that pasture, and she would have to pass within fifty yards of the place where it all began.

"I wonder if that old barn's still standing," she mused aloud, then shook her head and shrugged. "No matter. We can't keep sitting here. You stay put." She reached down to pull the door handle. "I'll be back in a jiffy. . . I hope."

Alma protested, but despite her contention that rain might cease, before dark, even yet. Rebecca didn't see any indications of its slacking, and she had no penchant for spending the night in her car.

Minutes later, however, the prospect didn't seem as unacceptable as before.

Ducking her head against the wind and the rain that whipped her face in a stinging fury, she darted around palmetto bushes and skirted clumps of brambles, which made a mockery of her panty hose and legs.

Her shoes, though the heels were short, gripped the ground like spikes, making hungry, little mud holes that sucked like miniwhirlpools at her feet. A couple of times she almost fell, and rain was coming down so hard she lost all sense of direction. Later she thought that it had been through sheer accident she'd stumbled upon the old barn.

If she'd had any qualms about reentering it, any old feelings of déjà vu, Rebecca didn't stop to reflect upon them. All she could think of was getting in out of the rain.

"Lord," she murmured. Once inside, she wrung her skirt and lifted the tail to wipe her eyes. "Enough is enough. I'm soaked to the bone."

"Didn't anybody tell you, little girl? You get all wet when you go walkin' in the rain."

The voice came to her, sounding husky-soft and seductive, like a dreamy memory on a hot, sultry night. She caught her breath. "Somebody told me," she whispered. "But I wouldn't listen. I thought it was only a dream."

"Ah, but it wasn't. It was a lifetime in a moment. Do you believe it could ever happen again?"

Rebecca watched, her heart pounding, as a piece of shadow swayed and pulled itself away from the rest of the darkness. She straightened slowly and tried to swallow. He was as wet as she was. His shirt was undone, and soaked Levi's clung with a shameless ardor to his long, lean hips.

"I don't know," she answered. "What do you think?"

He didn't come toward her, but stood in the darkness with only the rain muting the sound of his heart. "I think I wish it had been different for us," he murmured softly.

"So do I," Rebecca said with all her heart.

The old barn was still warm and musty, with the scent of hay, soft earth and scorching suns. But for one moment, as she and Wes faced each other, Rebecca thought it smelled faintly of two lives coming together in bittersweet longing, before moving on in the scheme of time.

And her heart ached. Oh, God, she thought, it wasn't fair. She shouldn't have to live through this moment a second time. She didn't know if she could bear it.

Take a chance, her heart whispered. But she said, "I'd better go."

She had already started for the door, when Wes's voice stopped her, sounding curiously unsteady and far away. "But it's raining. Can't you wait a little?" *Or forever?* "Until it stops?"

Blinking back tears and struggling with a hoarseness in her own voice, Rebecca shrugged self-consciously. "I, uh . . . I left Alma in the car. We got stuck on the cemetery road. And I—" she cleared her throat "—I promised I'd be back with . . . help." *Help me. Help me tell you I love you. I need you. Please ask me to stay.*

Wes took a step toward her, then hesitated, shoving his palm down the length of his thigh in a gesture that seemed to imply some inner uncertainty, as if his thoughts weren't related to the words he spoke. "Alma will be okay," he told her. "I sent Hank back to get her."

"Hank?" Rebecca recalled the man in the blue pickup truck, who had dropped Alma off earlier. "But how did you know . . . ?"

"I knew she had gone to look for you. And when Hank came back and said he'd left her there with you, I told him to give her an hour. Then to go back and make sure she had a way home."

Rebecca strained to see his expression in the steamy half-light, drifting down from a crack in the roof. "You thought I would leave her there? Stranded?"

"I wasn't sure what you'd do," he answered honestly. "I was too busy trying to figure out what I was going to do." *Without you.*

The rain was beginning to subside, falling softly now, like music almost, on the roof above their heads. Outside Rebecca could hear the last grumbling complaints from the thunderclouds, moving like ill-tempered fat men on down the line.

And suddenly she knew with every breath of life inside her she couldn't let this moment pass unimpeded. She had to try. She had to take the risk she should have taken long ago, in another storm but with the same man.

"Wes . . ." It was a whisper. It was a yearning plea. It was a breath of hope that Alma had been right, that maybe he did care. And that even if he didn't, she was never going to settle for loss by default again.

It was Rebecca who took that first step up, offering her heart in her hand. But it was Wes who closed the distance, quickly, desperately.

"Oh, God, Rebecca. Don't go. Don't leave me."

There were tears in his eyes and in his husky voice as Wes pulled her to him, hugging her, kissing her. Her lips. Her face. Her cool, wet hair. "I love you." Pride was forgotten as he confessed, "I love you." His knees gave beneath him. "I love you." His heart swelled with the greatest joy he had ever known, when he opened his eyes and saw that she was kneeling with him.

"Oh, Wes. Wes. My love, my life. Promise me you'll never want me to go."

Outside, warm rays of yellow sunlight caressed all things washed clean and new. Inside, Wes's arms enclosed Rebecca and in his low, mesmerizing voice, Wes whispered to her words of love and gentle longing, of hope and commitment. And Rebecca pledged her heart and her trust and all her tomorrows through coldest winter or sweet summer heat.

* * * * *